THE
STAY-AT-HOME
MOTHER

BOOKS BY NICOLE TROPE

My Daughter's Secret
The Boy in the Photo
The Nowhere Girl
The Life She Left Behind
The Girl Who Never Came Home
Bring Him Home
The Family Across the Street
The Mother's Fault
The Stepchild
His Other Wife
The Foster Family

THE
STAY-AT-HOME
MOTHER

NICOLE TROPE

Bookouture

Published by Bookouture in 2023

An imprint of Storyfire Ltd.
Carmelite House
50 Victoria Embankment
London EC4Y 0DZ

www.bookouture.com

ISBN: 978-1-80314-961-5
eBook ISBN: 978-1-80314-910-3

For David, who says, 'I bet that's going to be a book,' anytime anything remotely interesting happens. You're right.

PROLOGUE

'Hi, this is Andrea. I can't take your call right now. Leave a message and I'll get back to you.'

'Hello, hello... Look, I am assuming that this is the Andrea Gately who is listed as a contact on the Missing Children of the World website. I know your post said to only contact the police with information, but I found you on Facebook – where you have your phone number. I have no idea why you would have your phone number on your Facebook page, but that's not what this call is about. I know you're in Australia and I am in the USA, so I'm not sure about the time difference, but I really don't care. I'm calling to let you know I've given your number and contact details to the police over here and they have assured me they are going to look into this immediately.

'Why are you using a picture of my son on a missing children's website, Andrea Gately? Why are you using it and where did you get it?'

ONE

ANDREA

NOW

She is standing at her front door, her keys in her hand, when the car screeches into the street, squealing to a stop in front of her house, filling the air with noise and the smell of burnt rubber. The streetlight flickers as if disturbed and she squeezes her keys in her hand, her heart racing.

The wind whips around the house, scattering soggy brown leaves as the car idles in front of her house, the engine growling with menace in the dark. Andrea's pulse pounds in her throat, making it hard to swallow.

The back passenger door opens and she squints, trying to see inside, frozen where she is standing, her muscles tense.

Terry emerges from the back seat, his body falling onto the street in a heap. With the door still open, the car roars off into the night, leaving behind the tortured tyre smell and her husband crumpled on the ground.

She cannot move, cannot even think what to do, but inside her the baby kicks frantically.

Terry doesn't move and the words 'he's dead' fill her mind. She starts towards him, holding the keys so tightly in her hand they are cutting into her skin. As she gets to where he is, he groans and uncurls, looking up at her, both eyes swollen and puffy, blue-black bruises visible in the yellow glow from the streetlight.

She looks around her, relieved that no one else is on the street, relieved they are alone as she struggles for something to say, something to do.

Their gazes meet and he stands, slowly, painfully limping towards her. She takes a step back.

'I've messed up,' he says, his throat hoarse. 'I've messed up really badly.'

TWO
GABBY
NOW

Even as she feels it buzzing in her hand continuously as she walks, trying to keep her steps slow enough and yet move quickly enough, she knows that she should not look at it, should not allow the messages to be read. She doesn't want to know what they say, but, as if a magnet is pulling at her, she cannot resist, cannot stop herself from glancing down, from seeing the words.

Are you crazy? Why are you doing this? You have to stop. You have to turn back. I'm begging you.

Her heart is in in her throat, her skin is perspiring, but she cannot turn back now.

'No,' she says aloud. 'No.' People turn and stare at her, but she cannot stop. She has to do this now. She has to change everything now.

THREE
ANDREA
FIVE WEEKS AGO

Andrea surveys the room, trying not to let the heaviness of despair stop her from doing what she needs to do. Which is everything.

They moved into this house three days ago, and for three days she has been doing little except cleaning and unpacking. This morning it looks as though she hasn't even begun the mammoth task. Over in one corner of the living room is a stack of boxes as tall as she is, leaning slightly and crumpling with the weight of all they contain. They are labelled GARAGE and GARDEN and TERRY, because they are the boxes that Terry assured her he would unpack this weekend. They are stacked against a window, blocking out most of the meagre daylight coming in. The heavy grey sky offers little enough light as it is, so, despite the time of day, she switches the lights on and discovers that two light bulbs in the room need to be replaced. Light bulbs are broken all over the house, including in Jack's room. She really should check on what Jack is doing. The thought slips from her mind as she glances around the room again. 'Baby brain,' her mother said with a laugh when she told her she couldn't seem to hold on to a thought for even a few

seconds, but Andrea knows it's more than that. Her mind is on a
constant loop of fear and worry, the overwhelming emotions
crowding her brain.

Things are only made worse by the fact that the house – this
draughty house on what is, granted, a very good street – is in
such bad repair. The carpets are clean and the paint on the
walls is new, but everywhere she looks she can see decay, from
the pitted timber window frames to the cracks running along
the ceiling. They must have reappeared only days after the
painters finished. The house creaks and groans all night long as
though complaining about being inhabited. The last owner died
in her bed, having lived here for fifty years, so perhaps the house
misses her and doesn't want a new family to occupy it.

'I don't exactly love you either,' Andrea mutters, and then
laughs at herself for talking to an inanimate object.

'There will always be cracks,' Terry said to her last night as
he tackled assembling their bed. 'The house is on clay and so
whenever it rains or whenever there's a drought or...'

'Or a slight breeze,' Andrea had added.

Terry had laughed but it wasn't funny.

Andrea sniffs. The musty, thick smell of mould is everywhere, but then it is everywhere in Sydney these days. Autumn
rain turned into spring rain, which turned into summer rain,
and now they are at the beginning of April and autumn rain
again. The gaps under the doors and at the side of the windows
allow sneaky slices of cold air in, making her shiver. She was
running the heater but then she thought about the price of electricity and turned it off again. If she just keeps working, she can
stay warm enough.

Andrea's despair is well suited to the weather. It would be
wrong for the sun to shine now, when all she wants to do is cry.

'At least my home isn't flooded,' she says aloud, reminding
herself to count her blessings, as her grandmother always told

her to do. *There is always someone whose struggles are greater than yours. Gratitude is the way to get through every day.*

Her sister, Brianna, lives in a small country town close to the Queensland border where her husband is the local doctor. Brianna's home has been inundated with water twice in the last six months as the rain comes down day after day and week after week. 'It feels like this will never end,' she told Andrea only yesterday, as she sent through the latest batch of photos – one of which was of her brand-new leather sofa floating out of the living room double doors. 'I didn't want the kids to eat on it so they wouldn't drop any food or drink on the lovely leather and now it's gone the same way the last sofa did, out the door and into the rubbish,' she said with a sad laugh.

'I wish I could come and help you clean up,' Andrea said.

'You have a three-year-old child and you're nearly nine months pregnant,' Brianna replied. 'And you've just moved. You have more than enough problems of your own.'

'I sure do,' mutters Andrea aloud now as her gaze sweeps the room.

She leans over the box marked TOWELS and, using the box cutter in her hand, slices it open, sighing as she confronts a selection of towels that would better suit the garbage bin than her bathroom. They are all slightly threadbare because they are the ones Terry bought when he moved out of home ten years ago. New towels were on her Christmas wish list before... before everything. She takes the blue set to the family bathroom and hangs the green set in the small, old-fashioned en suite, where the walls are tiled in a pink and black mosaic that might almost manage to be chic in a retro way if it weren't for all the cracks and the fact that whole patches are missing in some places.

'I'll go through the garage and see if I can find some spare ones. The old owners must have left some – they always do,'

Terry promised her, but she has little hope of that actually happening.

The small cupboard she has chosen to put linen in is already full of sheets and tablecloths, all neatly stacked, leaving no space for anything else.

'No storage space and no light,' she mutters. 'Right.' Andrea roughly shoves a bunch of mismatched brown and cream towels into the cupboard. She needs a cup of tea and some chocolate.

'We have more than most people do,' Terry said last night and she wanted to agree with him because everything will be easier if she can just convince herself of this. But she is struggling, especially when she looks at the grocery bill after a big shop or reads about electricity prices going up or glances around the house she now lives in.

'You're stuck here, so stop whining,' she says aloud, trying to jolt herself out of her mood, as she shoves the last of the towels into the now messy cupboard.

She has a child and another on the way, and Terry is the breadwinner in the family. She couldn't leave even if she wanted to. *I don't want to leave. I love Terry. I love or loved the life we created together.* Terry is a charmer. A man with the widest smile and the loudest laugh. He's funny and sweet and no one can make her laugh like he can.

This morning, before he left for work, he kissed her gently on the forehead. 'Things will get better, I know they will,' he whispered. She had closed her eyes and sent a plea up to the heavens that they would get better.

In an ideal world, Terry should be making more than enough from his job in a large electronics store, where all the salespeople work on commission and the sales are very large. But this is not an ideal world. It's not like she can go out and get a job right now, so there is little she can do about the situation. She is tied to Terry and Terry's problems.

As she flicks on the kettle, Gemma, as the baby is already

called, kicks her mightily from the inside. Both she and Terry wanted to know the gender of the baby and they quickly agreed on the name Gemma. It goes nicely with Jack. Terry is surprisingly good with babies, able to soothe them out of crying fits and never averse to changing a nappy. He has a level of patience with Jack that Andrea sometimes lacks and can happily spend hours playing with him, both of them loving the toy cars and the large plastic garage filled with ramps her parents sent Jack for his birthday.

Andrea pushes away the thought that Gemma is a mistake. She had wanted to wait before falling pregnant again.

'Jack needs a sibling and it's only a year ahead of your schedule,' Terry said, shrugging and smiling, when she told him she was pregnant, and Andrea had decided to be grateful for another healthy pregnancy, even though she questioned how on earth they would manage financially.

As the kettle clicks off, a tiny prick of alarm runs through her as she realises she hasn't heard from Jack for at least five minutes, which means he is doing something he shouldn't be doing.

'Jack,' she calls. 'Where are you, bubs?'

There is no answer, so she leaves the kitchen and goes in search of her son. She knows he is bored and lonely and has had enough of his grouchy mum. She doesn't blame him. She's had enough of herself.

He is in his bedroom, chatting to himself, an entire packet of sliced cheese spread across the carpet, most of it crushed into the grey fibres. The slices are not individually wrapped, so Andrea can see that the whole packet will have to be thrown away. Seven dollars in the bin.

'Oh, Jack,' she says, unable to stop some tears escaping as she crouches down to begin picking up enough cheese for at least two weeks' worth of sandwiches. The ripe smell turns her stomach and she swallows quickly. This pregnancy has been plagued by nausea morning, noon and night.

'Sometimes stress makes it worse,' Brianna said when they discussed how sick Andrea was feeling.

'I'm in trouble then,' Andrea replied and Brianna had sighed, knowing exactly what Andrea was stressed about.

'Why would you do this, Jack?' Andrea asks as she sniffs.

'I was hungry,' he says, his big, deep blue eyes the picture of innocence. He has perfected the same 'who me?' look his father gives her. He shares Terry's light blue eyes and chestnut brown hair, so different to her own plain brown eyes and dead-straight mousey brown hair. In the bar where she met him, at a birthday celebration for one of the women she worked with at the online homewares company, she had turned to look at him only because so many of the other women in her group were looking. Terry is really handsome, and when he smiles and the dimple in his cheek appears, Andrea has a hard time staying angry at him.

Jack looks just like his father, right down to the dimple on his cheek, but he has a more serious nature. He's sensitive to her moods and will try to help her instead of jollying her out of them with a joke. He stands up now and comes over to her, wrapping his arms around her. 'Don't cry, Mum. I make you a sandwich.'

If she had the energy, if she had even a single ounce of energy left, she would yell at her small son, who knows better than to take all the cheese out of the packet, but she doesn't. She leans forward and continues picking up the pieces, hating the cold waxy feel of them.

'I help,' says Jack and he picks up a whole lot and then takes a bite of what he has in his hand.

'Jack, no,' she says. 'It's dirty.' She grabs the cheese from him and throws everything in his bedroom bin, picking it up to take outside and empty, as he begins to howl in despair. Andrea feels the prickle at her scalp of a headache coming on and then she walks out of Jack's bedroom and into hers, closing the door behind her, placing her hand over her heart and taking three deep breaths.

Jack should have been at pre-school today but he had a slight temperature this morning, so she couldn't send him. Whatever he had is obviously over already – in the way that these things usually go with children – but she still has him here the whole day and that means she will get little done. She thinks longingly for a moment of her small house on Robertson Street, forty minutes away from here, of how neat and tidy and clean it was, despite it being small. This house is bigger but it's so far from feeling like a home it makes her want to sit and weep. She doesn't want to cry in front of Jack, who hates her tears and has seen too many of them lately. What she would like to do is to call her husband and tell him exactly how much she hates him right now. This is all his doing.

She takes another deep breath, hearing Jack call for her and at the same time the front doorbell ringing – a strange jangly noise that reminds Andrea that here is yet another thing that needs fixing.

'What now?' she mutters, opening the bedroom door and lifting her chin. *What now?*

FOUR

GABBY

Gabby glances up from the computer, focusing her gaze on the large window in the kitchen that looks out onto the garden, with its manicured stretch of bright green grass. The rain is still going, see-sawing between a heavy downpour and a light drizzle. She would love to see some sun, but she is happy enough tucked away in her little alcove at the side of the kitchen with her slimline desk and computer as she works on a new Facebook post. Looking back down at her screen, she cannot help the smile that plays on her lips as she scrolls through pictures of Flynn at one and two and three years old. She doesn't have many of them, certainly not as many as she would like to have. He was such a beautiful baby, with his big brown eyes and thick copper-coloured curls. His hair is a darker brown now and of course he's cut off all the curls, something that she was against, but you can't tell a sixteen-year-old boy what to do. She sighs. Next to her tall strapping son she always feels small and plain. 'Ghost girl' they used to call her at school because she was so pale. 'What's wrong with you? Are you sick?' they asked. Children are cruel. Adults are cruel too, but in more subtle ways.

'Aren't you clever to stay out of the sun entirely,' a shop

assistant had said once, as she observed Gabby trying on a blue one-piece bathing suit, her white skin on glaring display. Gabby had smiled and nodded but she hadn't bought the swimsuit.

'Smile. You're making me want to kill myself with that face,' her mother said often enough for Gabby to struggle with the idea of smiling at anything. In the mirror she will practise moving her lips around her teeth, hoping that it looks natural, but when she talks to people and someone says something that makes her laugh, she always feels like she's faking it.

She's tried self-tanning creams and real tanning by exposing herself to harsh summer sun and all that happens is she turns orange or burns bright red, so she's had to accept her skin. And she's tried forcing herself to show her teeth for photographs, but she always feels like she looks ridiculous. 'You're beautiful. Don't worry about what other people say,' Richard tells her – or he used to tell her.

Flynn is lucky with his skin tone, still fair but tending towards olive. He tans beautifully in the summer, even with the lashings of sunscreen she makes him use. He looks like his father, of course, like Richard, and he never has a problem smiling – but then, why would he? His whole life is perfect and both she and Richard do everything they can to keep him happy. She adds a hashtag to the post she is working on: #just-likedad. It's a Facebook post but she likes to add hashtags. She still needs a picture for it, but the gist of the post is there – how interesting it is to be a mother to a teenager, especially an uncommunicative teenage boy – though she has made sure to say that she and Flynn get along really well. A close reader will be able to see what she's really saying, but she doesn't want to be too obvious. Raising a teenage boy is more difficult than interesting, but she's not yet ready to share that truth so blatantly.

She keeps scrolling through her photos, watching her son age through the years, and then she selects one from only a week ago: Flynn with his hockey team, a trophy held aloft. She blurs out the name of the team on their jumpers, knowing that she needs to protect the privacy of all involved, and posts it to her Facebook page with *#proudmum* added to the post under the caption: *There are some days that are really hard, but I always know that the baby I loved and the little boy who held my hand is still there. As mothers, we need to find joy in the small things and remind ourselves that just because our children are no longer sharing every thought and feeling with us doesn't mean we are any less involved in their lives. Flynn is such an interesting human being now and I am loving watching him mature.*

She's careful about who is allowed to see her Facebook page, making sure that only other Australian mums can view it. You can never be too careful about scammers and nefarious people on the internet. It's not necessary for her page to go all over the world. She's happy with her many thousands of friends who all read her posts and ask for her advice. When she receives a friend request, she is careful to look at the profile to make sure it's the right kind of person she wants to be sharing things with. The advice she gives is always practical. She hates those gurus who say things like 'love them into being better people,' and then don't explain exactly how to do that. *How exactly does that help anyone?* She gives practical tips to any mother who asks for help, along with her positive posts about her child, and she is gratified to know that her advice works well. A lot of women look to her for guidance. Not that she would call herself a guru. Only last week a woman had written that she was going crazy trying to get her teenage daughter to clean her room, and instead of telling her to 'leave your daughter to do what she needs to do with her own space,' as many people said, she suggested multicoloured storage boxes and cool labels. The woman was overjoyed, messaging her that it worked, as she and her daughter had a fun day sorting everything into its own special place. That's what mothers need: good common-sense advice. Gabby believes routine and firm parenting is the way to go with teenagers.

Flynn would say she is overbearing and smothering, not that she would tell anyone that. He wants her to back off and let him make his own mistakes, but as far as she's concerned, she gave birth to him and she's not stepping back until he turns eighteen.

Yesterday he told her to 'stay out of my bloody room,' and she quickly and firmly replied, 'Don't use that language with me, young man, and if the room is tidy, I will stay out of it. The choice is yours.'

She smiles as she remembers this exchange because Flynn laughed then.

'Fine, Mum,' he'd said. 'What's for dinner?'

He's always hungry after hockey practice. Flynn is not the captain of the team, only vice-captain, but she's sure that next year he will be in the lead role.

She jots down a note on the pad of paper next to her slim black laptop. *Post about accepting when your child is not in the top spot?* She will have to do some research. The mothers of Australia are avid readers of her page and as she watches the likes and comments pile up on her new post, she smiles.

You're so right – we need to remember the little children they were, a woman named Kathy writes.

I needed this reminder today, so tired of fighting with my daughter, Debbie posts. The likes click over one hundred and Gabby sighs with satisfaction.

There are so many women out there who are happy to engage, and she knows that if anything goes wrong, they will be there to support her because that's what Facebook is like. Lots of people ask which team Flynn plays for but she is ready with a reminder that she is protecting her son's privacy and that of his team-mates. The last thing she needs is one of the other mothers of kids in the team giving her a lecture. She is not Facebook friends with any of the other hockey team mothers. She doesn't need any comments from them on her page. Jealousy rears its ugly head when you have a good-looking, talented son. It's easy enough to stand separately from them during games. She closes her eyes and envisions herself with a large cup of takeaway coffee in her hand, standing away from a group of gossiping mothers, her eyes on her son and the game, because it's all she cares about. Perhaps the other mothers would call her aloof or cold, but that's not her concern.

As if anyone would want to be friends with you, her mother's ever-present voice whispers, and Gabby is suddenly surrounded by the sickly-sweet smell of her lavender perfume. Lifting her own wrist to her nose, she inhales the rich musk of her own perfume, banishing her mother.

Maybe when Flynn is captain, she will befriend all the mothers, because that feels like something the mother of the captain should do. But not yet.

She's so proud of Flynn, of everything he does, even though things are getting a bit tricky now. She picks up her pen again, writes another post idea. *Post about navigating a relationship with your more mature son – some tips?* She likes to put something up every day, which she has done since she started this page three months ago. Starting the page was an outlet, a way to cope, a way to connect with other people, because sometimes in the silence of an empty house, her mind replays every mistake she has ever made and her stomach churns and inevitably her mother's voice appears, filled with criticism and contempt. A young child takes up so much more time and space than an older one who is mostly at school or playing sport or out with friends.

Initially she thought about reaching out for help with everything she was dealing with, but then she realised that she was as qualified as anyone to dish out advice, and when people ask her for tips on dealing with their difficult children, it makes her feel less alone. Lots of mothers of teenagers question exactly what they have done with their lives, if they don't work. Plenty of mothers find it difficult to really like their teenage children. Motherhood can be a fraught and desperate experience when children are young, but Gabby is painfully aware that the sudden relegation to 'unnecessary' hurts when a child becomes independent. Each time another mother on the page says something negative about her child or children, Gabby is comforted. She is not alone in this situation.

She sits back in the office chair she is using, thinking about some carefully chosen words for another post. *Flynn used to be such a willing model for all my shots but lately he seems to be against my posting the pictures I take of him. At first he didn't mind me using all the photographs I have of him on my new page, but over the last few weeks he has become critical of what I'm doing. He wants to separate himself from me, but I am finding it hard. Sometimes I wonder if I am treading too fine a line between sharing my joy at raising my son and the advice that I know I can give other mums, and making sure that Flynn stays happy.*

Reaching up, she smooths her fine hair behind her ears as she dismisses the words. It's not really the time to be that open, that vulnerable. That's a post for another time. Her phone pings, and she looks down to see a text from Richard. *I see you've posted another picture of Flynn.* Right on time, as usual, but he doesn't say whether he liked the picture or not.

Gabby clicks her tongue, irritated. Richard is watching her Facebook like some stalker. He's in the US on business, and he needs to leave her to do her thing. She knows what she's doing. *Is your spouse a help or a hindrance as you raise your teenage child?* she writes on her pastel blue notepad. That's a good idea for another post.

She shouldn't get irritated at Richard. He is only trying to protect her, as he has always done. She smiles as an image of Richard at seventeen comes to her – his chest puffed out as he argued with a store owner who accused her of taking a lipstick. The man was far bigger than Richard, but he was no match for an angry seventeen-year-old protecting someone he loved. But she's not fifteen anymore and she doesn't need his protection like she used to. 'You have no proof,' Richard had yelled at the man. The store had no security camera, so it was his word against Gabby's, and she had stood quietly while Richard argued with the hugely overweight security guard. The man finally backed down and Richard had taken her for a milkshake to celebrate. The lipstick was in her shoe and it was an ugly colour on her, so the whole thing could have been avoided, but Gabby loved watching her knight in shining armour protect her. He's less happy to jump into the fray for her these days, more apt to tell her she's done something wrong. *Because you are always doing something wrong.* Gabby physically shakes off the presence of her mother. The woman is more persistent these days, appearing regardless of how hard Gabby tries to make sure she stays away.

She gets up from her chair as she mulls over what she will write about next. Picking up her empty coffee cup, she walks into the kitchen, where she puts the kettle on to boil again. A quick glance tells her there is nothing to clean in the perfectly neat kitchen, so while she waits she walks to the front of her small home and out the door to go and check the mail. It usually arrives around mid-morning and it's mostly junk, but if she doesn't collect it, it spills out of the mailbox and onto the path in the front garden. The rain has settled into a slight drizzle, which is better than the sheeting downpour from this morning. She picks up a few stray brown leaves and crushes them in her hand to throw away, hating the way they mar the perfect beauty of the white stone path that leads to the front door.

Her mailbox is empty but her eye is drawn to the house across the street – or 'the eyesore across the street' as she likes to think of it. Wattle Street is lined with mostly well-tended houses. She prefers to live in a nice space, and she has no idea how someone can stand to live in a house like number seventeen. There were painters in there last week and she also saw a new carpet being brought in. That the speckled grey carpet was cheap and utilitarian was obvious to her, although she knew it may not have been to someone who didn't have an interest in these things.

When the house sold a few months ago, she assumed it would be torn down. But instead, a family have moved in. They must have a fair amount of money because she knows that the house went for a good sum, so perhaps they are waiting for plans to be drawn up before renovating.

She caught a glimpse of the heavily pregnant woman on the first day they arrived. She's pretty, with thick straight brown hair and olive skin. Gabby knows there's a child because of all the toys that were being taken into the house by the movers, but she's not sure how old that child is or if it's a boy or girl. A young couple is a nice addition to a neighbourhood and hopefully they have plenty of money and soon the ugly house will be a beautiful new house. She really hopes that the young couple will begin renovating the home soon, but given how pregnant the woman is, Gabby can't see how she could manage it. A new baby throws everything into chaos.

She studies the house for a moment and then, on impulse, she opens the black latticework metal gate at the front of her property and crosses the road to ring the bell, undeterred by the light rain. She might as well say hello and welcome. But halfway across the street she stops and turns back. She can't turn up empty-handed. In her pantry is a lovely box of chocolates she bought to enjoy as a treat, but it will make a fine 'welcome to the neighbourhood' gift. She goes in to get it, and then heads back out, imagining Richard laughing at her. *You don't talk to the neighbours*, she hears him say, and she has no idea why she is doing this today.

When she's standing outside the weathered front door where cream paint is peeling and she can see that most of the surrounding bricks are cracked, she thinks that she should really have baked a cake or some biscuits instead. The chocolates are Godiva, very expensive, and will probably not be appreciated by the young woman.

'Too late now,' she sighs and she pushes the bell, listening to the odd jangling tone bouncing through the house.

The sound of a car in the street makes her turn and look and she shakes her head, seeing a battered old red sedan. They must be lost. The car moves slowly, too slowly, and she experiences a twinge of alarm. Is the driver watching her? She turns around again, her back straight and her head up, listening for the sound of the car driving off. But she can hear it idling behind her. She wishes she had taken a closer look. She may need to tell Richard and he will want a proper description. But she doesn't want to turn around again and let the driver of the car know he's worried her. Is it a man or a woman? She really should have paid more attention. *You never pay attention when you should,* her mother berates her.

She can't hear any movement inside the house and has turned to go when the door is opened by the woman, a little boy of around three years old standing next to her, big blue eyes wide with interest, his arms wrapped around the woman's thigh. Behind her, she hears the car roar off and she relaxes, fixing a smile on her face.

'Hello, I'm Gabby,' she says, noting that the woman's eyes are slightly red, as though she's just woken from sleep or she's been crying. The woman sniffs and Gabby has her answer. 'I live across the street. I wanted to come over and say hello and welcome to the neighbourhood.' She holds out the box of chocolates in their beautiful gold box, regretting giving them away. If the woman doesn't know what they are, a box of only nine chocolates could seem almost insulting.

The woman nods and tries to smile, really tries, but instead she cannot help the tears that fall and Gabby's heart instantly goes out to her. She recognises someone who is overwhelmed when she sees them.

'I'm Andrea,' says the woman as she tries desperately to wipe the tears away with the sleeve of her slightly grubby hooded sweatshirt. 'I'm sorry, they look lovely. I love Godiva... It's just...' She tries to take a deep breath, but it catches in her throat and Gabby wishes she could touch her arm to comfort her.

'I understand completely,' says Gabby. 'Some days are hard and you've only just moved in. Why don't you come across the road for a cup of tea and a bit of a rest? Your son can play with some of my son's old toys.' She can feel her mind filling with ideas on how she and this young woman can build a friendship. It's been a long time since she's had a friend IRL, as the teenagers say. All through her life people described her as cold, but she's not, she's just unsure, and she knows she'll make a mistake by saying or doing the wrong thing. *You're impossible to get along with and so horribly bossy,* she hears her mother say. She releases the words as she hears them, not letting them land their emotional punch. She's quite capable of being a good friend. This young woman needs help and Gabby is here for that. Helping this young woman, Andrea, may be a good use of her time and it may lead to other things. She doesn't know what, but Richard has recently been telling her she should be looking ahead to the future. 'Flynn is nearly an adult, Gabby. You cannot post about him once he gets to eighteen. No one will want to read about him then.'

The woman opens her mouth to refuse the offer of tea and Gabby jumps in. 'I'm just across the street and it can't hurt to take a break from the unpacking. Come on – it's okay to have a few minutes off.' She makes sure to keep her tone encouraging. The woman looks like she could really use a break.

The woman finally nods. 'Let me just get my keys,' she says.

'No need for that.' Gabby smiles. 'We never lock our doors. I know times have changed but this is such a safe street. Come on then,' she says to the little boy, holding out her hand. 'I bet you'd like a chocolate chip cookie.'

The little boy looks up at his mother, who nods quickly, and then turns away for a moment to put the chocolates inside the house. The child slips his small soft hand into Gabby's and her heart swells at the feeling, the wonderful complete trust he has in her. She makes sure to conspicuously look both ways before crossing the empty street as Andrea follows behind her.

She will tell Richard about this young woman when she speaks to him tonight. He may not be happy that she's brought someone into her life, but he can't expect her to just wait around for him to get back from another one of his endless business trips. Flynn is sixteen and pushing at boundaries and she has nothing else to focus on. Helping someone like Andrea is an ideal use of her time.

FIVE

ANDREA

Andrea is not sure about what she's doing but she follows the woman holding Jack's hand across the street anyway, moving quickly through the light rain. The truth is that she would love a cup of tea. She would love to sit down and drink it while it's hot, and she would love to have someone else pay attention to Jack for just five little minutes.

She looks at her son, with her neighbour, so trusting. He probably understands she needs a break from his antics this morning. When she left the bedroom to come and check who was at the front door, she found Jack on top of the unsecured bookcase in the living room. He loves to climb and she had to reach up and grab him off before he fell. A nightmarish image of her small son under the huge bookcase made her shiver, and she shouted, 'No, Jack, that's naughty,' as she headed for the door with him in her arms, putting him down to open it.

The hours ahead of her until Terry comes home seem to stretch for days. At least here is something different to do for a few minutes. No one tells mothers-to-be how long the days can be. 'Some days last an entire year,' Brianna laughed when Andrea confided in her how she feels about this. She is grateful to have her sister to speak to so they can compare notes, even though Brianna's children are already at the mostly easy ages of ten and twelve. She would never share some of her thoughts with her friends. Mothers can be very judgemental of each other. If she needs to find some help, she goes to her sister or Facebook, eagerly reading other people's problems in the hope of seeing her own experiences reflected there.

The woman opens a tall black metal gate and Andrea follows her up a perfect stone path to a beautiful frosted-glass front door. Inside, the house is not as big as some of the other homes on the street, but it is completely perfect – from the wide marble tiles and timber floors to the pristine white walls. Andrea looks around in awe. A parquetry timber dining table is surrounded by white fabric chairs with not a single stain anywhere to be seen. On the walls are real framed paintings of two landscapes with the sea in the foreground and mountains behind, peace in every brushstroke. At home, she is hoping Terry will eventually get around to hanging their reproduction prints of famous paintings by Picasso and Dalí, but now that she's seen Gabby's walls the prints feel cheap and tacky. Framed silver photographs are on a timber console and a coffee table and side tables in the living room. Andrea can see they are of a boy, but she doesn't get time to examine them as she walks through, following Gabby.

A beeping sound makes Gabby sigh. 'The laundry is done. I always think I can have a day off, but I never can with Flynn,' she says as she walks.

Andrea follows Gabby to the white marble kitchen and looks around at all the shiny stainless-steel appliances, everything matching and sparkling. A feeling of calm orderliness is everywhere.

'We redid the kitchen two years ago and they did a fabulous job. I can give you the name of the company if you'd like,' says Gabby.

Andrea nods her head a little as she tries to calculate the cost of the kitchen and then gives up. It wouldn't matter if it cost ten thousand dollars or a hundred thousand dollars – even a hundred dollars would be too much. *It will happen, babe, I promise you. We'll get back on our feet and it will all be good again*, she hears Terry say, but even in her head he sounds unsure. Where is Terry now and what is he doing? She knows where he is supposed to be, and she even has an app to track his movements on her phone, but he often has the location permission off and then seems mystified as to how that happened when she confronts him about it. *He's at work. You know he's at work. Believe he's at work.*

'Now what can I get you?' Gabby asks as she lifts a padded, built-in striped blue and white bench seat and picks up a box with some effort, putting it on the floor. 'What's your name, young man?' she asks, and Jack studies the box and answers, 'Jack.'

'Well, Jack,' she says. 'Over here I have a box of toys that I'm saving for' – she laughs lightly – 'I don't know what, since my son is only sixteen and grandchildren are probably a decade or two away, but I've kept them anyway.' She glances up at Andrea, who smiles weakly. She cannot imagine Jack at primary school, let alone nearly done with high school and independent.

The box is filled with toys, some a little advanced for Jack, like tiny Lego bricks, but some perfect for his age, like the large collection of dinosaurs and plastic mountains and trees to create a world with. Jack is fond of imaginative play, and Andrea feels a real smile as she watches his excitement.

'Wow,' says Jack as Gabby pulls out the plastic bag filled with the toys. 'That must be all the dinosaurs in the whole, big world.'

Andrea and Gabby share a glance and a laugh as Gabby

opens the bag and hands it to Jack, steering him to a corner of the kitchen. 'This is a good spot for dinosaur world,' she says.

Jack immediately sits down and starts to set up the dinosaurs on the white tiled floor, chatting away to himself. 'And you can go here, Mr Tyrannosaurus, and you can also go *roar.*'

'Thank you,' says Andrea.

Gabby waves her hand. 'It's nothing. I remember what it was like to be the mother of a young child. It can be absolutely exhausting, and you've just moved into a new home and you're pregnant. Really, I have no idea how you're coping at all.'

Andrea lowers herself onto a chair and feels enormously comforted by the older woman's words, by her tidy and clean house, by the fact that Jack is now playing quietly and by the fact that she is now off her swollen feet and resting. She pulls at the red hooded top she is wearing. It belongs to Terry and she knows that there is a small stain on the back that she hasn't been able to get out. She feels like a slob, but the top is comfortable, and she hadn't anticipated seeing anyone today or she would have at least put a dash of make-up on. She can't even remember if she's washed her face this morning.

Gabby is dressed in light blue jeans and a beautiful striped top that looks soft and expensive. She is thin and Andrea can see from the way she moves that she is strong and confident in her own skin. Right now, Andrea feels like her body belongs to someone else and her mind is always exhausted and struggling to focus.

'You have such lovely skin,' Gabby says, as if reading Andrea's thoughts and the comparisons she is making. Andrea flushes, pleased with the compliment. It's been a long time since anyone told her she had lovely anything.

'I'm sorry,' she says, as her eyes fill, 'about the silly tears.'

'Nonsense,' says Gabby. 'When Flynn was small, I probably cried twice a day on a normal day, let alone a day when I had so much to do. Now what kind of tea can I get you? Camomile or peppermint or... I know – how about peach? It smells lovely.' She has opened a wooden box and Andrea can see at least ten different kinds of tea, all separated into little squares. In her kitchen, Andrea has stuffed three open boxes of tea at the back of a cupboard, one of which she is sure she's had for over a year. Sitting in Gabby's kitchen, she feels like a chaotic child instead of a mother with one child and another on the way. Will she ever have her life, her house, her world as under control as this?

'Thanks, that would be great,' she says to Gabby's offer, even though what she really wants is a giant cup of coffee. Gabby doesn't seem like the kind of woman who would have indulged in caffeine when she was pregnant, but sometimes the only thing getting Andrea through the day is her treat of one single coffee. She hasn't had hers today yet.

'And is watered-down apple juice okay for this young man?'

Andrea nods, thinking guiltily of the juice box she gave Jack this morning with breakfast. He should be drinking only water, but he had wanted the juice and she could see a tantrum coming when she said no, so she just let him have it. She shouldn't give in to her son's demands as much as she does. She should be firm and patient and make sure that Jack has good routines and rules to live by. But everything she should do has gone out the window in the last few months. She used to be much better at being Jack's mother. Rubbing a hand across her eyes, she lets go of this thought. Tomorrow is another day to try and do better.

Gabby busies herself with making the tea and putting it in front of Andrea in a mug covered in a design of intricate pink swirls, along with a plate of cookies. She puts apple juice mixed with water in a sturdy blue plastic cup and hands that, along with a matching plastic plate with two chocolate chip cookies to Jack, who says, 'Thank you very, very much,' in his most polite voice. He eats while he plays, absolutely absorbed by the dinosaurs.

Andrea takes a cookie from the white plate in front of her and bites down, enjoying the chewy dough and the large chocolate chips. 'This is delicious,' she says. 'Did you make them yourself?'

'Once a week,' Gabby says smiling. 'Flynn eats five at a time.' She laughs lightly. 'Just wait – you'll see when this young man is a teenager. They eat non-stop. I go shopping and fill up the fridge and then go upstairs to do something and come down to find it empty again.'

'I can't imagine him as a teenager,' says Andrea, finishing the cookie and then taking another one.

'My grandmother used to say that the days are long but the years are short,' says Gabby, sitting down with her own cup of tea. She doesn't take a cookie. 'I've only ever had one child, which according to him makes me overprotective and nosy. I would have loved another. You're very lucky.'

Andrea cannot miss the wistful tone in Gabby's voice and she reminds herself, once again, to count her blessings. 'This one's a girl,' she says to Gabby, patting her bump and laughing as she gets a kick in reply.

'May I?' asks Gabby, reaching out a slim hand, her nails perfect and polished in a light pink.

Andrea nods. 'Sure.'

Gabby's hands are cold, even through the hoodie Andrea is wearing, but Gemma obligingly kicks so that Gabby can feel her presence.

'What a strong kick,' she says, spreading her hand wide over Andrea's belly, holding it there until Andrea shifts a little.

'She's keeping me up at night, that's for sure.'

'When are you due?' Gabby sits back and takes a sip of her tea, scrunching her face at how hot it is.

'Five weeks,' says Andrea. 'I was on time with Jack, so I think I will be again.'

'Lucky you. I was three weeks early with Flynn and he had to be in the NICU. It was a bit of a worry, but he's grown up clever and sporty, so I have nothing to worry about. But now tell me more about you. Where did you move from?' Gabby picks up a cookie and breaks it in half, putting a minuscule piece in her mouth and leaving the rest on the plate in front of her.

'About forty minutes away – Pembroke,' says Andrea, her hand reaching for another cookie before she pulls it back.

Gabby sees and slides the plate closer to her. 'Go on,' she encourages, and Andrea takes a cookie.

'Have you lived here long?' she asks.

'Oh... long enough,' says Gabby and she sips her tea.

It's a strangely vague answer, which Andrea finds odd, but even as she thinks about it, Gabby says, 'Two decades at least – I stopped counting' with a slight shake of her head.

Andrea nods her understanding and sips her tea, which smells nice but tastes mostly like hot water. After a moment of silence she asks, 'Have you got a picture of Flynn?'

Gabby's face lights up and she grabs her phone in its slim black case from the table. 'Yes, I actually post a lot of photos of him on my Facebook page. He doesn't love me doing it, not anymore, but I'm his mother. I should get some joy out of raising a teenage boy.' Gabby laughs but Andrea hears a slight under-current of tension.

'Kids at any age are hard work,' she says. When Jack was born, she had posted pictures of him nearly every day, knowing that only friends and family could see her Facebook page. Her mother and sister loved seeing the photos. Lately she's stopped posting so much and she's sure that one day she will regret that.

'Don't I know it,' agrees Gabby, closing her eyes for a second and then taking a deep breath. Then she opens her eyes and turns her phone to show Andrea a picture. 'Look, that's my boy,' she says. 'Do you have Facebook? I'll find you and send you a friend request.'

'I do. It's Andrea Gately,' says Andrea, leaning forward a little to look at the photo of a tall broad-shouldered teenage boy with a wide smile, dark hair and big brown eyes.

'He looks like his dad,' says Gabby. 'He has Richard's hair and eyes.'

'Jack looks like his dad too, although I think our face shapes are the same. He's a good-looking boy.'

'He is,' sighs Gabby. She takes the phone back and quickly swipes on the screen for a moment. 'Found you and I've sent you the request. I suppose you have a lot to do.'

'I do,' agrees Andrea, a little shocked at the abrupt end to the visit but knowing that it's time to leave. She wouldn't want to overstay her welcome. She struggles to her feet and says, 'Come on, Jack. Let's tidy away the dinosaurs.'

'Oh, don't worry, I can tidy up,' says Gabby, standing up as well.

'But I want to play,' says Jack, his voice rising. 'I want to play with the dinosaurs. I'm making... a big giant forest and the mountains and the...'

'Jack, please,' says Andrea. She cannot bear a tantrum right now. Gabby is so nice. In Pembroke she got along well with the neighbours on either side of her and she would like to feel she has a neighbour she can call on here as well. If Jack throws one of his spectacular tantrums right now, then Gabby may not be inclined to invite them back.

'Now, Jack,' says Gabby, 'if you behave nicely and go with Mum, I promise you that you can come over any time and play dinosaurs and have cookies. But if you shout and cry, then I will have to take all the dinosaurs and give them to another little boy.'

Andrea doesn't love the threat, but Jack immediately stands up. 'Okay,' he says. 'Can I come tomorrow?'

'Your mum and I will talk about that,' says Gabby firmly as she leads them both to the front door. Jack runs out to the gate. There is a break in the rain, the sun struggling to come out from behind the clouds.

'Thank you so much for having us over,' says Andrea, 'and for the lovely chocolates.' She reminds herself to hide them from Terry, who won't appreciate them and will eat half the box without thinking. If she unpacks two more boxes, then she'll allow herself just one of the expensive chocolates. The thought of something to look forward to cheers her.

'My pleasure,' says Gabby as she lifts her face to the sky. 'Wow, it looks like the sun may struggle out today. Richard is in San Diego and he says it's almost too hot there right now.'

'Lucky him,' says Andrea. 'I'm so tired of this awful weather.'

'I know, but today I've met you, so I'm going to declare that a good sign. You need to know that I am always home and you can call on me anytime at all. I'm an excellent babysitter.'

'That's so good to know,' says Andrea. 'Do you work from home?'

'Oh no,' says Gabby, adding a trilling laugh. 'I don't work. I'm an old-fashioned stay-at-home mother. Richard would never have tolerated it. Flynn is older now, but he still needs to be looked after. I'm a taxi driver and a chef and a cleaner all rolled into one – and sometimes a psychologist.'

Andrea flushes. 'Sorry, I didn't... I mean, I'm not working either right now.'

'But of course you are,' says Gabby. 'Even though we're not paid, I still think it should be counted as work. This is the hardest job there is and I will be so happy to help you any way I can. It's lovely to have a neighbour I can talk to. The people on either side of me are much older and not very friendly.'

'Oh,' says Andrea, a little crestfallen. Knocking on the doors of all the houses around her and introducing herself was something she had planned to do on the weekend, but now she's not so sure if it's a good idea. 'I like to meet my neighbours,' she says, glancing around at the other houses in the street with high walls and closed front gates.

'Oh, you don't want to bother with them. Believe me, I tried,' says Gabby. 'But I'm here, so no need to worry about a thing. I have a feeling we're going to be good friends. You seem like my kind of person.'

'How wonderful,' says Andrea. This is exactly what she hoped to find in her new neighbourhood. She feels a physical lifting of her spirit and knows that getting through the afternoon will be much easier because of this small break. 'Come on, Jack,' she says, reaching out her hand for her son. She waves to Gabby as they cross the street.

When she gets to her own house, she opens the door to let Jack inside. He runs off to find his own toys and she turns to wave at Gabby again, but the woman has gone inside. The street is silent and empty. As she watches, an old sedan cruises slowly by the house. It's red and covered in dents. Andrea feels her breath catch in her throat and she quickly steps inside the house, locking the front door with both locks.

No, no, no, she thinks. *Not again.*

SIX
GABBY

Once Andrea and her son Jack have left, she cleans up, packing away the dinosaurs. Then she goes upstairs to Flynn's room, although she's already cleaned in here today so everything is neat and tidy. As usual, he left things in complete chaos: laundry everywhere, a wet towel on the floor and a collection of plates near the bed. She asks him to clean it himself, but in truth, she doesn't mind doing it. He has plenty of storage but seems to prefer things messy. Having to tidy up his room means she gets to be in here, and sometimes she will just sit on his bed for a bit and think about how things used to be when he was little. She has such a clear picture in her mind of Flynn at the same age Jack is. He also loved dinosaurs and playing make-believe, and he always included her in his games. Sometimes she questions herself, wondering if he did include her, but then she will remember building forts with him under the dining room table and pretending they were camping in the forest surrounded by bears. All of that seems so long ago it is as though it never happened, and she has to remind herself of the baby she had because it's hard to see that needy creature in the strapping young man her son has become.

Glancing around the room, she takes in the bookcase that holds all Flynn's hockey trophies from the age of five, along with his books, including the ubiquitous collection of the Harry Potter series and other novels from the fantasy genre. He won't play hockey beyond high school because that's not what she wants for him. He's good but not good enough to become a professional player. Flynn will go to university and study science, which is his other passion. She can imagine him in a white lab coat – saving the world from cancer or some other disease. She can see him up onstage accepting an award for his work and thanking her for pushing him to be the best man he can be. It's a comforting daydream, especially when he's as difficult as he was this morning.

'Back off and stay out of my life,' he had spat as he climbed out of the car to lope into school.

She remembers a time when he had shouted, 'Love you, Mum,' before running off to join his school friends. She thinks of another post idea: *When your child stops saying, 'I love you.'*

He hasn't exactly said that he wants to study science, but Gabby is determined that it is the path he takes. She posted about it already when she talked about encouraging your child to find their passion. He just needs a little shove in the right direction. His current recalcitrance will surely not extend to his career. 'I'm only steering you in the best direction for you,' she says aloud, practising the words. She may post them on her Facebook page as inspiration for other mums.

She sits down on his double bed, neatly made with a blue and green duvet. Blue and green are his favourite colours. She stands up and takes a quick picture of his room from a good angle and then posts it with the words *When mum tidies for you* and a smiley face emoji. It's a lovely room, just perfect for a teenage boy. She quickly takes some books off the bookcase and positions them on the desk – old textbooks, but no one needs to know that – and snaps another picture. She'll post it later with *My boy hard at work* as the caption.

Staring at her phone, she waits for likes and comments on the picture of Flynn's room. It doesn't take long for likes to come in but there are no comments. She gets more reaction when she writes something heartfelt, rather than just posting a photo with a caption. If she wants everyone to stay engaged, she needs to stick to proper posts.

Because she is looking at her page she sees instantly as Andrea accepts her friend request.

'Yes,' she says aloud.

Andrea looks like someone who is drowning, and Gabby is here to help. There is a whole lot more to her story, Gabby is sure, and it won't take her long to find out and to make herself indispensable to the young woman. *Careful*, she hears Richard say, but she brushes his concerns away. He hates it when she does something impulsive, but he's not here and she is, and she is quite capable of making some decisions herself. 'Before you do something, give me a call if I'm not around. I'm here for you day or night,' he has told her and she loves knowing that. He wouldn't want her to be friends with Andrea, wouldn't want her to be in a situation where she could let some things slip, but she likes Andrea and she really likes Jack. Jack reminds her so much of Flynn at the same age, so very much. She will keep her inter-actions with Andrea to herself for now because she knows what happens when Richard gets angry with her, when he tells her she's pushed him too far. Smoothing her hair down, Gabby lets go of any thoughts about Richard's unhappiness with her. He'll be fine, everything will be fine as soon as he gets back from the US.

After another quick glance around the room, she decides that the walls could use a repaint, although she will stick with the light blue they have been since Flynn was a baby. Her most cherished memories are of him in the early years. His big brown eyes, his smile, the dimpled hands. Everything is different now, but her son still loves her. Andrea is lucky that she will have another child in her family, lucky that her love can be stretched between two children. Gabby would have loved another baby, but it wasn't meant to be. She had never imagined, growing up, that having a child could be so difficult.

Her mother appears before her, thin lipped and accusing. *You just think you can have whatever you want, don't you, Gabrielle.*

'No one wants to hear from you,' hisses Gabby, as she leaves Flynn's room. She's over forty and she wishes that she could get her mother's voice out of her head once and for all, but the woman is stuck there, judging everything Gabby does. She grew up with nothing but rules and disapproval, ugliness and pain. If she were still in touch with her mother now and the woman knew the truth about her life, she would be horrified at the way Gabby lives, at the things that are important to her and at what she has done to make sure she always has the best of everything. Smoothing a hand along the sleeve of her blouse, she revels in the feel of the soft silk. It cost nearly three hundred dollars, but Gabby hadn't hesitated to get it for herself. *Wasteful and silly*, her mother spits. Gabby pushes her shoulders back, lifts her chin and marches away from the voice. She doesn't care what her mother thinks and in fact she doesn't care what anyone else thinks either. The only person she cares about is Richard – and Flynn, of course. She loves her beautiful son, who brings her joy every day.

She goes downstairs to the kitchen to get her laptop. She wants to find out everything she can about Andrea Gately. She would like to know how much they bought the house for and what her husband does. Andrea is so sweet and so tired, and Jack is so lovely. It will be nice to have them in her life for however long she knows them.

Before she looks into Andrea, she scrolls through Flynn's

Instagram page. Most sixteen-year-old boys wouldn't allow their mothers to see their Instagram, but Flynn thinks she is a fifteen-year-old boy named Max. Max liked a lot of Flynn's posts and then followed him and luckily Flynn followed him back. Max has issues, a lot of issues. He hates his parents and fights with them all the time and Flynn, lovely Flynn, is always there to comfort him and talk through his problems. A lot is said about this generation being selfish and lacking a moral compass, but Gabby has found that Flynn and his friends try their best to be genuinely inclusive and to help someone in need. Before she put together a profile for Max, Gabby contemplated being a girl, but that felt wrong – Flynn was her son and she didn't want him saying things to her that she shouldn't be hearing. She settled on troubled Max, who posts just enough to keep Flynn's attention and sympathy and allows Gabby access to Flynn's page.

She thinks for a moment and then writes, *Tough day today – can't take this negativity in the house.* It only takes her a moment to find the perfect image to accompany the comment. It's a silhouette of a boy in a hooded jumper with a dark sky heavy with storm clouds behind him. It could be Max or it could be anyone at all. That's the beauty of the internet.

Max has quite a few friends on Instagram and there are immediately comments telling him that they are there for him to turn to. She loves this alter ego, always getting a twinge of excited joy whenever people respond to him. Somehow, comments directed at Max feel different to comments on her posts on her Facebook page. On the page she has to open herself up to people, bare her soul a little, so that they respond. It's lovely to be someone else, to be a boy who no one expects anything from. Whenever Gabby is feeling a little low, she can always post as Max and receive the affirmation she needs to improve her mood. *Selfish liar,* her mother mutters and Gabby has to look away from the screen as her eyes blur with tears. Every single day of her life as a child was filled with criticism and abuse. She knew that her mother hated her whenever she looked at her, could see the contempt in the woman's eyes.

Her alter ego, Max, also believes his parents hate him, but in this different time he can post about these feelings and be rewarded with comments from friends about nothing being his fault. Max has never put up a picture of himself where his face is visible, preferring to use pictures of the ocean and silhouettes. On good days he puts up a picture of a beach in full sun, people on the sand and children laughing. On bad days, he puts up pictures of the ocean in a storm, the sky above dark and threatening. Taking a deep breath and blinking away her tears, she searches through images until she finds one that she likes to add for a second post. Two in a row keep Max's followers on his side and paying attention. The image is of the ocean as a storm is ending with the sun just starting to peek through heavy grey clouds. She adds a caption: *#thanks #friends #support*. The likes stream in and Gabby smiles, feeling much better. It's so easy to manipulate teenagers who think they know everything. It's so easy to manipulate everyone, actually. Most people don't expect you to be hiding much about your life. Maybe you say you're fine when actually things are a bit difficult, but no one expects you to be telling complete lies. Her mother always hated it when she lied as a child. 'I can see the devil on your tongue, Gabrielle,' she would spit, her thick hands reaching for her daughter to hit the devil out of her. Gabby would never use physical violence on a child, at least she hopes she wouldn't. She's never had reason to so far.

Once she's liked all the comments Max has received, she scrolls through Flynn's page. He has posted a selfie with a young girl she has never seen before. She's pretty enough but nothing special. Underneath Flynn has captioned it *#newfriends #herdadisacop #careful* and then a whole lot of laughing emojis. Gabby shakes her head and picks up her phone. She had no idea Flynn was dating the daughter of a policeman.

We may have a problem, she texts Richard.

Would a policeman look into the boy his daughter was dating? Probably. Will Richard just think that this is her being overprotective and snooping in Flynn's life? Definitely. But why hasn't she seen this girl before? Whatever she is hiding from Flynn, she hates the idea that he is hiding anything from her. She's his mother and a mother should know everything about her child. Every single thing.

SEVEN
ANDREA

In her car, Andrea is concentrating on counting her blessings as she waits for the traffic light to change. Ten days after moving in, she feels like she is finally getting the house in order, although the creeping mould from all the wet weather is really starting to bother her. She hasn't met any of her neighbours apart from Gabby although she waved to the man who lives next door when she saw him in his front yard. He waved back but didn't seem keen for a chat. In her old neighbourhood she had gone around and introduced herself when they moved in but she is mindful of Gabby's words about the people in the street and has resolved to leave introducing herself for now. The light turns green and she pulls off, thinking about Jack's eagerness to get into school this morning as he ran off with a quick wave. Things definitely feel a little easier. She has found a local supermarket that she likes, and Jack is happy at his new pre-school now that he's attended for a few days in a row.

'He'll adjust. He's three,' Terry said, when she complained about Jack having to leave his friends at his old pre-school.

Terry has been proved right about Jack adapting but it has still caused Andrea some long nights of worry. Jack had only just settled into his pre-school near their old house and they were uprooting him. She had considered driving over there every day, but it would mean at least forty minutes in traffic every morning and every afternoon. His new pre-school is five minutes away and has a lovely feeling about it, from the cheery yellow and blue walls to the teachers, who always have a smile for every child.

At least when Jack's at school she gets a lot done with her day. She is aware of the passing of time and of the birth of her second child creeping closer and closer. She remembers not being able to wait for Jack to be born, but she is happy to stay pregnant with Gemma for as long as possible so she can get herself into a new routine. Having done her usual Monday shop today is a step in the right direction. Things feels like they are back on track, and she's not even bothered by the permanently grey sky.

She pulls into her driveway, unable to stop her face scrunching at the sight of the house. If the sun did come out, it would probably make everything look a lot better. There is not a single piece of wall where the paint isn't peeling, and the front garden is just a mass of waterlogged weeds and a wonky brick path, where more water collects.

Count your blessings, she reminds herself, putting the car into park and turning off the engine. It takes longer than she would like to get out of the car, her belly heavy and cumbersome. She's much bigger than she was with Jack, but she is pretty sure all the comfort eating has contributed to that. It feels impossible to imagine not carting around a baby inside her – being able to move the way she wants and to eat and drink what she likes. Breastfeeding is still restrictive in terms of things she can eat, especially the spicy foods that she loves, but she is looking forward to bending down without thinking about it.

As she is getting the last load of groceries from the car, she sees it again – the old red sedan with the one unmatched door cruising past the house. This is the fourth time she's seen it since they moved in. She is not imagining this. The car moves slowly, so slowly it could be someone looking to pull over, as the engine puffs white smoke into the air. In the driver's seat is a thin man with a short black beard. One arm is resting on the door where the window is wide open despite the cold. His whole arm is covered in a sleeve of tattoos, red and blue and yellow, blending together into something she can't make out. Holding one bag of groceries, she finds herself frozen, staring at the slowly moving car, aware of her rapid heart rate.

It's something to do with Terry, she knows it is. It cannot be a coincidence. Each time she has seen the car, pinpricks of anxiety have itched at her scalp, but she has dismissed it, not wanting to have to confront what she thinks it means. The car is going so slowly now it's barely moving, and Andrea is a statue stuck in place – though her mind whirls.

He could be a tradesman, she supposes, working on a house in the area. But why go past her house so slowly? The man turns his head to look right at her and his small dark eyes break the spell. Andrea moves as quickly as she can. She takes the bag into the house, opening the door with one hand and shutting it behind her with a loud slam. She stills herself as she tries to listen for the car, knowing that she has left her boot open. The baby kicks her bladder and she realises she desperately needs to use the bathroom. Dumping the bag in the kitchen, she goes to use the toilet. When she returns to the front door, she doesn't want to open it. She peers out of the small grime-encrusted peephole, trying to see if the car is still there, but she cannot make anything out through the wonky glass. She needs to get her groceries inside and so, taking a deep breath, she wrenches open the door and stamps outside, fear shooting through her veins.

The old sedan is parked opposite her home, in front of Gabby's house. Andrea stops, her resolve dissolving. And as she watches, her heart in her throat, the door opens and the man climbs out of the driver's seat and then he shuts the door and leans against the car, staring at her, oblivious to the lightly falling rain. He wipes a hand across his face and grins at her, and then he folds his arms across his long skinny body and leans even further back against the car, as if to indicate that he is able to stand there all day. He turns his head to glance at Gabby's house and then turns back and nods at her. Who is he and what does he want? Is he watching Gabby? Is he watching her?

Andrea wishes she had the gumption to confront him – to walk across the road and ask him what he wants – or that Gabby would come out of her house right now, because Gabby wouldn't hesitate to talk to the man. In the few interactions she's had with her neighbour, Andrea has only seen Gabby ooze confidence.

'I don't accept bad service from my gardener. If they say they will work for two hours, I make sure that's exactly how long they work for,' she informed Andrea when they were discussing the weather and what all the rain was doing to the gardens in the street.

'Next door had their television on so loud last night that I just marched over there and told them to turn it down. Flynn was studying and it wasn't fair and it's not our fault the old woman is deaf,' she said when she came across the road to ask Andrea how she was settling in.

'I'm not going to get roped into participating in this silent auction at school until I know exactly where the money will be spent,' she stated when she saw Andrea holding a box of chocolates she had bought from Jack's school, which led to a discussion about school charity events. Gabby seems to have a firm opinion on everything, and she is never shy about telling Andrea exactly what she thinks.

Every night before bed, Andrea scrolls through Facebook and always finds herself on Gabby's page, looking for new posts and sometimes rereading old posts where Gabby gives advice to other mothers. Her page is filled with everything from practical advice about healthy lunches and establishing routines, to more emotional sharing about the difficulties of being a woman in today's world and of choosing to stay home and raise your child or children. Andrea finds it reassuring to know that someone like Gabby lives across the road from her and it's soothing to read comments from other women who also have their bad days.

Thanks, I really needed to hear this today. I always feel judged by everyone for wanting to be with my kids.

Wow, what a great idea for using leftovers!

It's so wonderful to have you to turn to, Gabby. You make my day. I wish more people understood how difficult our days as mothers can be.

I was really struggling today. Thanks for reminding me that I'm doing my best and tomorrow can always be better.

Gabby always replies to anyone who posts, making sure that everyone feels seen and heard.

Her neighbour is so sure of herself. Andrea wants to be that way, but her confidence has disappeared along with everything else she has lost in the last few months. There is no way she has the composure or the energy to confront the man. She is too fearful of what he might say and what he might do. It's not like she hasn't experienced this before. Even in the cool April weather, she feels her cheeks heat up. She drops her gaze as she walks to her open boot and looks down at her parcels. She has to get the food inside. She can feel his eyes burning into her back, feel her own vulnerability because she is so pregnant. If he came for her, she would not be able to get away. She hurriedly grabs the rest of the parcels and then closes the boot of her car, making sure to lock it. The plastic handles of the bags, heavy with her weekly shop, cut into her arms. She is carrying too many at once because she needs to get inside and lock the door. She feels her breath coming fast as she walks the few steps towards the front door.

'Can I help you there?' she hears from across the street, and she speeds up, not responding, not turning to look. *No, no, no.*

Inside, she dumps the bags in the entrance and turns to close the door. The man is still leaning against the car. He lifts a hand and gives her a lazy wave, sending her heart into overdrive. Sweating in the cool air, Andrea slams the door shut and then locks it, grateful that Jack is at school. Sinking to the floor, she tries to calm down.

She needs to call Terry, but she doesn't want to. She needs to know what the man wants but she doesn't want to know. Her leg begins to cramp and the baby kicks, squashed because of the way she is sitting, so she gets up and then turns to look out of the peephole in the door. She thinks he's still there, but she can't see properly. She moves to the side of the door where there is a small thin pane of glass covered with a white net curtain and she pushes it aside, trying to see without being seen. He's still there, smoking a cigarette now as he studies the house. He sends a plume of smoke into the air and scratches at his beard. In her head she sees herself wrenching open the front door and screaming, *What are you doing? Get out of here!* But she would never have the courage to do something like that. Wishing for the heavy rain to return and send him back into his car, she turns away.

She paces back and forth in the small living room, her nose twitching at the mould smell that she cannot seem to get rid of. It must be in the pale green and white striped fabric sofa, and once mould gets into fabric it is near impossible to get it out. Andrea feels a sob rise inside her throat and she goes back to the door and the window at the side. He is still there, but now he's on his phone. He turns to look at Gabby's house and nods before turning around again as he continues speaking. After a final nod, he shoves his phone into the pocket of his jeans, which are torn over one knee, and then he climbs back into the car and drives off. Andrea slaps her hand across her mouth, the ever-present nausea making itself felt – sending her running to the bathroom, where she hangs over the toilet, retching.

Afterwards, sweating and shaking slightly, she makes herself a warm drink and consumes half a packet of chocolate digestives as she unpacks the groceries. Eating is the only thing that keeps the nausea at bay, but she also eats so that she can concentrate on taste and texture and nothing else for a few minutes. She's gained a lot more weight with this pregnancy and her obstetrician has started to encourage her to get her eating under control.

'Your sugar levels are at the high range of normal and we need to watch you carefully.'

She knows she should have chosen a healthy snack instead, but it wouldn't have the comfort of the biscuits, and right now she needs some comfort. All her optimism from this morning has disappeared and she is once again confronted with the stark reality of her awful situation. She thinks of Jack and the baby inside her. They need to be protected from whatever their father has done and is probably still doing. That's the trouble. He is probably still doing it. This thought stuns her and she stands in the middle of the kitchen with a bag of carrots in her hand. He is probably still doing it. *No, he's not. He promised and he's at work.* She shoves the carrots in the fridge and takes another biscuit.

When everything is put away and she is slightly calmer, she sits down on the sofa, steeling herself for a conversation with Terry. As she lifts her finger to hit his name, her phone rings, playing the annoying baby shark song that Jack begged her to put on as her ringtone for a couple of weeks. It's Terry.

'Hey, sweetheart, how are you feeling?' he asks, his joviality irritating her.

'The nausea is bad today. Listen, Terry—' she begins.

'Sorry, love, this is going to make you unhappy but I'm calling to let you know I've got a staff dinner after work. We're going on sale and Baz wants to make sure we're all up to speed with discounts we're allowed to give. He's taking us to dinner, only pizza, but I wanted to let you know that I'm going to be late.'

The baby kicks her hard, and Andrea imagines her responding to the surging fury that nearly overwhelms her. She bites down on her lip so that it hurts, and she takes a deep breath. If she yells, Terry will cite work and put down the phone. If she screams, then she is being ridiculous and irrational. She knows her husband, and she needs to hold her temper.

'Really?' she says, the word dripping with bitterness.

'Yeah, we're going to that place around the corner from the shop,' says Terry, his voice slightly less upbeat.

'Are you?' she asks, making no attempt to disguise her disbelief. There is a spot of something on the sofa, chocolate probably, and she scrapes at it with her nail.

'Andrea,' he says, frustrated, 'we're having a staff dinner. Everyone is going. We have to be there to discuss the sale. Do you want me to go and get Baz to tell you that we're going? Is that what you want?' His voice has taken on an indignant childish tone meant to make her back off.

If this were seven months ago, Andrea would have said, 'Of course not,' but then if this were seven months ago, she wouldn't have even questioned such an innocuous call from Terry. But this is not all those months ago. Because then she was sitting in her lovely home, completely ignorant of the fact that her life was slowly and quietly falling apart.

Instead of telling him to go and get his manager, she says, 'Someone's watching the house, Terry.'

'No, they're not,' he scoffs, but she hears it – hears the tiny spark of uncertainty. He knows it's possible, which means he is, once again, hiding something from her. A tightness in her throat makes her swallow hard.

Her free hand curls into a fist and she looks down at her bitten fingernails. 'Yes... they are. It's an old car and I've seen it a few times already. Today it parked across the street and a man got out and he looked at me.'

'And then what?' her husband asks, and she wishes he were here because she would like to grab him and shake that sarcastic tone out of him.

'Then he left,' she says, and she can feel that she's going to cry, so she takes a deep breath. Holding on to her anger at her husband is better than falling apart.

'Listen, Andy. Listen to me, love... you have to just listen. It was probably some guy on his way to another house.' The words roll off his tongue, smooth and convincing, as Terry the salesman appears.

'This bloke can sell ice to Antarctica,' she remembers Baz telling her the first time they met, at a staff Christmas party. Baz had his arm drunkenly wrapped around Terry's shoulders and her husband had flushed with pleasure. He was a very good salesman and he earned a fair amount in commission. They should be fine financially.

'Then why have I seen him more than once?' She now knows the truth behind her husband's public persona. And no matter how much she loves him and how good his intentions are, she can't let him lie to her ever again.

He sighs. 'Maybe you're exhausted and feeling sick and you

think you've seen him more than once. I know you're dealing with a lot, love. It's been a hard move.'

'It's a red sedan, old with one off-colour door, as though it's been replaced and doesn't match. I know what I'm seeing, Terry.' She speaks slowly, enunciating her words carefully as she sits forward on the sofa.

'Maybe he's a tradesman working on one of the houses in the street and he's just taking a break. People have the right to get out of their cars, Andy. Imagine if you called the police and told them that some guy looked at you. They would think you were insane.' This is what Terry is so good at – turning things around on her, forcing her to question things she has seen and heard. But she's not giving in so easily this time.

'The police don't know what you did, Terry.' She rubs a hand over her stomach, calming the baby, who is twisting and turning, making her more nauseous.

'You're never going to let this go, are you?' hisses Terry, lowering his voice because he is obviously near someone in the large store. 'I am so sick of apologising. I screwed up, I know I did, but I'm making it right. I can't talk to you when you're like this. I have to go. My break is over. I won't be home for dinner.'

Andrea holds the phone to her ear for a moment even though she knows that he's gone. Lately, whenever she confronts him or reminds him of his past misdeeds, he finds a way to get out of the conversation. He leaves the room in a huff or hangs up on her. He's done exactly what she thought he was going to do, and she wants to call him back and tell him that she hates him, scream that she hates him and he ruined her life, but he simply won't answer the phone. It's so easy for him to be out in the world, working in the store and constantly distracted by customers. He can put aside everything he has done, pretend it never happened and just be Terry the charming salesman. But she is at home and mostly alone or with only a three-year-old for company. The things that have happened go around in her mind on a constant loop, as she tries to adjust to the new house and a new way of living. All the women she was friends with from Jack's baby group live forty minutes away – more in traffic – and that's a lot of time in a car for her at this stage of her pregnancy. And she can't stand the shame of selling her house and not having something newer and shinier to show off to indicate that she was moving up in the world. She has not invited anyone over and she knows that she is probably the subject of some gossip. On the Facebook page they all belong to she was asked for pictures of the new house many times, but she always found a reason not to post any and so everyone has simply stopped asking. But they know she's hiding something – they must.

Stop this now. it doesn't do you any good, she thinks, rubbing her stomach as Gemma settles down.

It's getting close to pickup time anyway. She needs to get Jack from pre-school. She sighs and heaves herself off the sofa, making her way to the bathroom for another visit before she goes out to the car again.

She thinks longingly of her mother and sister, who are both so far away. They know what she went through; they would listen to her fears and not dismiss them. But she also knows that her mother especially would say, 'Come here. Bring Jack and come and live with us until he gets himself together. We'll take care of you.' But Andrea is not ready to leave Terry and she knows Jack would miss his father every day, so she swallows down her fears and her worry and gets herself into the car to go and fetch her little boy. As she drives, her eyes wander to her rear-view mirror, wishing she could stop her heart racing as she keeps expecting to see the red car.

EIGHT
GABBY

She is walking past the window in the living room with an empty teacup in her hand when she glances out to the front yard and the street beyond. The red sedan is in her street again. She feels her heart beat faster with alarm. Moving closer to the window, she is thankful for the special blinds that allow her to see out but prevent anyone seeing in.

The car moves slowly along the street and Gabby sees that Andrea has returned from wherever she went. Her boot is open and she is holding a bag of groceries and staring at the car as it pulls over. Gabby goes closer to the window, hoping to glimpse the registration, the cup clutched so tightly in her hand her fingers begin to cramp.

Andrea turns quickly and goes inside, leaving her boot open. Gabby hears her front door slam. And then she watches as a man climbs out of the car, a tall man with a black beard, a sleeve of tattoos exposed by his T-shirt, worn despite the cool weather. *Who is he and what does he want?*

Placing her teacup on a nearby small round table, where she has placed a beautiful yellow orchid in a terracotta pot, she steps closer to the window but she doesn't raise the blinds. *Is he here for her? Is he someone looking for something?*

Her heart races and the muscles in her neck immediately tense up hard enough to cause a shooting pain in her head.

Do you imagine that you can keep taking what is not yours and get away with it, Gabrielle? her mother whispers in her ear. She is fifteen again, a shopkeeper has his beefy hand wrapped around her thin arm, holding her tight as they wait for her mother to arrive. On the counter in front of him he had placed the bottle of vodka Gabby had secreted in her oversized coat. She didn't even like the drink, but the bottle was a beautiful shade of blue.

Her mother arrived, her face pale without any make-up, her hair pulled back severely as she usually wore it when she got ready for bed at 7 p.m. In silence she paid the exorbitant amount of money for the vodka and then she said, 'Do you want to have her arrested?' A slight lifting of the sides of her mouth indicated some delight at the possibility of her daughter being carted away by police.

The man's grip on her arm released slightly with shock. 'I just, I mean… she's only a kid and… ya know… I think she's learned her lesson. You paid, so we're good. I just don't want her in here no more.'

'She never learns her lesson,' her mother sneered quietly. 'She gets up every morning and makes me sorry I ever gave birth to her.' Without looking at her daughter, she left the store and went home, leaving Gabby to walk home alone. The man let go of her arm, and the worst thing about the whole situation, the very worst thing, was the sympathy she saw in his grey eyes. She had stolen from him, or tried to, and he felt sorry for her. He gave her the bottle to take and she dropped it in the bin outside the store.

A craving for vodka flows through her body. In the freezer is a bottle of Belvedere Midnight Sabre vodka, its high price obvious in its luxurious black and blue bottle. She doesn't even like vodka that much, but she is never without it. It's too early for a drink, too early to lose control, especially now, with this man in the street.

If he is here to watch her, here to confront her, it would not be the first time – but he doesn't look like some low-level detective. They usually come in cars that blend in with the grey of the roads and they are dressed in cheap suits, resignation at how boring her stealing is written on their faces. This man looks like something different.

Her body will not move away from the window. How worried does she need to be? As she watches, Andrea emerges again and looks at the man, quickly turning away and grabbing the rest of her bags from the boot of her car. She is carrying too many, straining with the weight as she moves as fast as her pregnant body will allow her to. 'Can I help you there?' Gabby hears the man call and Andrea moves faster. She seems scared. Why would she be scared?

'Everyone is hiding something,' Richard used to tell her. 'It's just that some people are better at it than others.' The man answers a call on his phone and then gets into his car and drives off. Gabby's muscles loosen, her heart slows as she pulls up the blind and gets a glimpse of the number plate, repeating it to herself as she goes to write it down. She needs to look into this. *Who is the man here for and what does he want?*

NINE

ANDREA

The few minutes' drive to Jack's pre-school seems to take forever as she finds herself behind a slow- moving bus and is then stopped by a construction worker with a pink hard hat who holds up a sign, making Andrea wait as the woman furiously chews her gum. Andrea has to watch as a giant cement mixer backs out of a house and turns to drive off down the road. Without thinking, she pushes her sister's number on her dash and listens to the phone ring thinking, *If she answers, I'll tell her. If she answers, I'll ask her what she thinks.*

'Andy,' says Brianna, picking up on the third ring.

'Hey,' she says, trying to inject some enthusiasm into her voice.

'You sound depressed,' Brianna says, and Andrea almost wants to laugh at the uncanny ability her sister, older by only two years, has to read her moods. But she also instantly realises that she will not confess anything to her sister. She's not ready to discuss her fears – as though discussing them will make the situation real. Maybe she is imagining it. Maybe the red sedan and the man have absolutely nothing to do with Terry. He was parked outside Gabby's house, so maybe it's something to do with her or her son or maybe he's a man looking for a place to take a break and nothing more.

'No, I'm fine, just tired of being pregnant. You sound okay for someone who is living in a motel again,' she replies.

'Nothing I can do but start again. At least we have insurance to start over. A lot of people don't have that. And we were only renting. Now that we're ready to buy, we'll buy up on top of a hill and build up higher than that. A tsunami won't get us.'

Andrea tries for a laugh, but she can't quite manage it. All her worries over what Terry will really be doing this evening stop her from feeling anything except the terrible heavy stress she has been living with for over six months. It comes out as a sob instead.

'Oh, Andy Pandy, what's wrong?' Brianna says. 'You can tell me.'

'Nothing, it's just the end of pregnancy,' she says quickly, forcing herself to regain her composure. Her sister has so much on her plate right now, she doesn't need one more thing to be concerned about. 'Anyway, Bri, I'm at the school and I have to go and get Jack. I'll speak soon. Good luck with getting everything sorted.' She hangs up on her sister's surprised 'Bye, love you.' She's still a block away from the school.

Andrea keeps checking behind her, but no one is following, and by the time she parks at the pre-school she has managed to shove aside her fears so that she can greet her little boy without bursting into tears. She walks into the school, greeting with a smile the few mothers she has met and answers the question 'When are you due?' from a mother she hasn't been introduced to. 'Around three weeks,' she says, making sure to smile widely.

'Won't you be busy,' says the woman, who has a baby on her hip and is holding the hand of her daughter, who is in Jack's class.

'Aren't we all,' says Andrea, dredging up a light laugh, and the other mother joins her. *Are you lying too? Are you staying*

awake all night wondering what's happened to your life? If I told
you what's really going on with my life, would you understand?

'Mum, Mum!' shouts Jack, beyond excited to see her, his red
jumper bearing a black mark and his face smudged with dirt.
She reaches down to lift him for a hug, inhaling the scent of the
cut-up strawberries she gave him for lunch. She wishes she
could just enjoy him, enjoy this time, but she is moving through
mud, thick with worry.

'Eddie in my class has got a new baby sister,' he says, 'and I
said I am also getting a new baby sister.'

'You are,' says Andrea as she puts him down, taking his
hand for the walk to the car.

'Eddie said his granny came to stay with him when his mum
wented to the hospital, but I said that cousin Patty is coming to
stay with me,' he says and she can hear the slight question in his
voice as he looks for reassurance that he will be taken care of.

'That's right. Cousin Patty is going to come and take care of
you and you're going to have a lot of fun because she likes to
draw and paint and make things,' says Andrea, silently thanking
God for Terry's cousin who lives forty minutes away but is just
waiting for the call to come and take care of Jack when Andrea
goes into labour.

'Last Christmas, she made me a paper aeroplane and it flew
high up in the air,' says Jack as he climbs into the car.

'I remember,' says Andrea.

'My friend Kenneth has a million billion dinosaurs and he
said I can come and play with them,' says Jack as they make
their way home.

'That's nice,' says Andrea, her eyes straying to the rear-view
mirror. There is a blue Porsche behind her, its shiny metallic
body squat and expensive-looking.

'And I said that I also had a million billion dinosaurs too,'
says Jack.

'But you don't,' says Andrea. 'You only have three

dinosaurs.' She glances at her son in the mirror. He is walking his fingers along the window as he speaks, one errant brown curl over his forehead, his cheeks slightly red from the cool air. Her heart lurches at the sight of him and she is reminded once again of how easy it is to love someone more than your own life. But however much she loves him, she has to help him become a good man one day, and that includes not accepting things that she shouldn't. 'Why did you lie about how many dinosaurs you have, Jack?' she asks him, keeping her voice firm.

He shrugs. 'It's just a tiny lie,' he says, sounding exactly like his father, in fact using words she heard Terry use when he told his boss he wasn't feeling well the day of the move so that he could stay home and still get paid, since he'd used up all his paid days of holiday leave already. He hadn't used them on a holiday with his family, as Andrea well knew, and as she listened to him lie to his boss, she couldn't help the sting of anger inside her at what he had used his holiday days on. Terry hadn't known she was listening to him and she hadn't known that Jack was listening as well. When she confronted him, he said, 'Stop being ridiculous. It's only a tiny lie. People do it all the time.'

Hearing the words come out of her son's mouth makes her despair of the lessons he has already learned from his father.

'You shouldn't lie,' she says sternly now, her heart heavy.

'Okay,' says Jack mildly, sounding unconvinced. Andrea glances in the mirror again, her body heavy with exhaustion. She is too tired to give her three-year-old son a lecture. The blue Porsche turns off, and behind it, the old red sedan speeds up a little so it is just behind her.

Bile rushes into her throat and she opens a window so she doesn't throw up, her foot pushing down harder on the accelerator. She is stopped from speeding up too much by the line of cars in front of her and she wants to scream with frustrated fear. Each kilometre is agony as her eyes constantly stray to the rearview mirror. The man in the red car is unconcerned, his thumbs drumming on his steering wheel in time to whatever music he is listening to as he mouths the words. Andrea glances around her, panicked as she looks for a side street to turn into, but she is trapped on the road, only able to go straight until the next traffic light. *Calm down, breathe. Jack is in the car. Calm down and concentrate.*

Finally, they are at the traffic light and she watches as the car turns right when she turns left. She travels the last few minutes in silent heart-pumping terror. But he's gone.

Gone as though he were never there at all.

TEN

GABBY

As usual, she is out the front of her house when Andrea returns from fetching Jack. High school ends forty minutes later than Jack's pre-school, so whenever Andrea is returning from fetching Jack, Gabby is on her way to get Flynn.

'I can take the bus, you know,' he says every now and again, but she likes picking him up, likes to have a beginning and end to her day. What are women with older children supposed to do all day if they don't work? There is only so much cleaning and tidying and baking she can do. Her Facebook page takes up a lot of time as well, but there are still empty hours and she loathes empty hours. *The devil will find those hands something to do*, her mother said if she ever saw her simply sitting and reading a book. Her mother equated busy with good and, try as she might, Gabby finds it hard to just relax. Also, when it's just her and Flynn in the car he will sometimes talk to her, mention something going on at school – without looking up from his phone, so he doesn't have to actually look at her when he tells her he did badly on a test or something like that. It's a way for her to keep tabs on his life. She has advised other mothers on her Facebook page about the wonders of a car ride with a teenager, although the effect is a little muted now that they are all on their devices all the time.

Instead of getting straight into her car now, Gabby waits so she can say hello. She has come to enjoy her exchanges with Andrea, and once or twice she has even received a text from Flynn saying that he wants to stay later to do some work at the library, so she can invite Andrea and her son in for a cup of tea. She has admonished Flynn over and again about letting her know his plans ahead of time, but all he does is roll his eyes and say, 'Okay, okay. Oh my God, why do you have to repeat yourself so much?' Gabby doesn't tell Flynn the words sting, that his disdain for her hurts. She knows that there is no point appealing to a teenage boy's better nature. It's a while away from kicking in. She never mentions any of this on her Facebook posts, preferring to project a normal and loving relationship, but sometimes she wonders if letting other mothers out there know that she is also struggling may be a good thing. It may be time to start letting out some truths, otherwise those who rely on her for advice will start to question the things she says. No one's life is perfect, after all, and only showing perfection leads people to assume you are concealing something. Gabby knows that she is like everyone else, in that she has her secrets.

If she never tells anyone she is having a hard time with Flynn, what will happen if she ever needs help? They won't believe her or they'll just be smug and filled with judgement.

The rain has blessedly stopped for a few minutes and the sun struggles out as Gabby lifts her face to the touch of warmth as she waits to speak to Andrea. She'll only be a few minutes late for Flynn and, as Richard points out, 'the boy won't melt if you're five minutes late. In fact, it will be good for him to not have you turning up exactly when and where he wants you to.'

'Hello,' she calls as Andrea climbs out of her car, and she can immediately see that Andrea is not happy.

'Hello,' shouts Jack, jumping up and down. 'We learned

about dinosaurs in class today and my teacher said I knew so, so much stuff and my friend Kenneth has a million dinosaurs and he wants me to come over and play with them and I said...'

'Enough, Jack. Please go, move away from the door so I can close it,' Andrea snaps. The woman's face is pale and Gabby can see that she is wearing Ugg boots that look more like slippers than boots, along with baggy tracksuit pants and the same hoodie she always seems to be in. Her feet are probably swollen in this late stage of pregnancy. Her belly sticks out in front of her, the reason for her exhaustion there for everyone to see.

Gabby debates for a moment about saying anything, but they're neighbours and she wants to help. 'Bad day?' she asks.

Andrea slumps against the car, with Jack's Hot Wheels backpack in her hand. 'I'm not feeling so good,' she admits.

Gabby quickly crosses the street and comes to stand next to her. 'You poor thing, you do look a bit pale. Is it the nausea?' Gabby knows from their chats that the nausea that was supposed to disappear after three months has not done so for Andrea.

Andrea nods, dropping her gaze, and Gabby has a feeling that there is more to the story, but she doesn't need to pry. The red sedan may have something to do with Andrea's despair, and Gabby experiences an unwelcome feeling of relief. She should feel bad for her friend, not better for herself. The question about the man and the car are almost in the air before she stops herself. She and Andrea have become friends and Andrea will tell her if she wants to.

Her phone pings, and she looks down and then shakes her head. 'I really wish that boy would give me just a little more notice,' she sighs. Gabby has tried to not see the curt texts telling her to fetch him later as him avoiding spending time with her. She would like to tell him 'no' and that he needs to come home, but there is no point in arguing with him over text, and he certainly won't answer if she calls his phone.

Andrea nods her head. Gabby has shared Flynn's tendency to change plans with her before with a roll of her eyes and a laugh, so Andrea cannot know how irritating Gabby finds it.

'He says that he and a couple of friends are going to study and grab an early dinner. It's not that I mind, but I just wish he would have told me so I could have planned my day around it. I wanted to go and look at some new furniture for the living room, but the store is an hour away and I didn't want to be back late for him.' She doesn't want Andrea to think she has nothing else to do with her day.

'Ah well,' sighs Andrea. 'At least you get the afternoon to yourself. Jack is full of beans because he had a nap at school, and I just want to sleep the whole afternoon away.'

'Oh, you poor love,' says Gabby. 'I remember what that was like. But you're in luck today because I suddenly have a free afternoon and now I can babysit young Jack.'

'Oh,' says Andrea. 'I absolutely couldn't ask you to do that. He gets so cranky around four and...' She stops speaking and waves her hand. Gabby can see that Andrea is desperate to be convinced, desperate to have an afternoon of sleep instead of an afternoon wrangling a pre-schooler, and Gabby is here to help. She is more than happy to. Gabby knows that Andrea's mother and sister are far away and even her friends are a long drive from here. Andrea is, essentially, all alone and that makes her vulnerable.

'Nonsense,' she says. 'I live across the street and you know me and Jack knows me, and he will only be playing with the dinosaurs while I do some life admin. It's no trouble at all and you can come over and get him at five when it's time for dinner.'

'Yay, dinosaurs!' shouts Jack. 'Please, Mum, please can I go and play at Gabby's house, please?' He starts jumping up and down, and with each jump, Gabby can see Andrea's slight resistance wearing down.

'Please, please, please, please,' sings Jack and finally Andrea says, 'Okay, okay. Gabby, are you absolutely sure?'

'I'm positive. Richard never liked the toddler stage, but I've always loved it. And he's in New York, so I am free to indulge my love of babysitting,' says Gabby, unable to stop smiling. 'It's been such a long time since I spent real time with a little one. I'll really enjoy it.' A whole lot of new possibilities fly through her mind. She is looking forward to spending time with the little boy. She would have offered to take care of him every day since the day they met, but Andrea would have found that strange behaviour. No one wants to constantly take care of other people's children unless they are paid for it.

'You're a lifesaver,' says Andrea and she leans forward, offering Gabby an impulsive hug. 'Jack, you behave for Gabby or you won't be allowed to play there again, do you understand?' she says sternly.

'Hold my hand, Jack. Let's get you an after-school snack,' says Gabby and the little boy places his hand trustingly in hers.

'Didn't you say Richard was in San Diego?' Andrea asks suddenly and Gabby grits her teeth. 'He was... but he's travelling all around the place... busy, busy, you know. Now you go and rest, Momma. Jack and I are going to have some fun.'

Andrea laughs. 'Your American accent is perfect,' she says and Gabby feels her breath catch.

'I should have been an actress in New York,' she says with a smile, hamming it up, and Andrea nods and sighs, touching Jack briefly on the head. 'Be good,' she repeats.

Once she and Jack have crossed the street, Gabby turns and they both wave at Andrea, who waves back and goes into her house. Gabby wants to shout with glee.

Inside, she sets Jack up with the dinosaurs and gives him a snack, cutting up an apple and adding some cookies, so she's covered healthy and unhealthy. Jack eats as he sets up the dinosaur world, and for a few minutes Gabby just watches him, loving the way his mind works as he makes the dinosaurs talk to each other. 'Excuse me, Mr Allosaurus, would you like some tea?'

'No... I will bite you, chomp, chomp.' He giggles and Gabby giggles with him.

Her phone is sitting on the kitchen table and she sees a text come in from Richard. *Flynn looked a bit upset in the photo you posted today.* Flynn did look upset but not for reasons Richard believes. She had actually taken the photo from Instagram, where Flynn had captioned it with a question: *Who will I be ten years from now?* The picture is of him looking out over the ocean, his face more pensive than sullen, but she can see how it might be interpreted that way. She posted that picture for a very particular reason. It went well with her post about seeing your child as the age he is rather than the little boy he will always somehow be in your mind. It's laying the groundwork for future posts where she becomes slightly more candid about her difficulties with Flynn.

Gabby wants to ignore the text and concentrate on Jack, but Richard gets angsty if she doesn't reply. If he is so worried about Flynn, he should come home and be here instead of overseas. You can't have any kind of relationship when you are thousands of miles apart. *He's getting tired of being photographed. He's getting more and more difficult. Last night he told me he wishes he didn't live here.* She sends the text and waits for his reply.

So, you're really upsetting him.

You're not here, Richard. I know what I'm doing. Just leave me alone. Right now, I'm babysitting the little boy from across the street.

What? Why? Why would you get involved like that?

I know what I'm doing.

Gabby switches the phone to silent, knowing that Richard will keep texting her and then he will start calling. She can call him back later tonight and explain everything, but until then he's just got to trust that she knows what she's doing.

She lets Jack play for an hour until he grows bored with the game. She spends the time on the computer, writing out future posts and planning when to put them up on her page.

'The dinosaurs want to sleep,' says Jack and she knows that he's had enough. It is only twenty minutes until Andrea will want him to come home. She could easily find a show for the boy to watch but that's not what she's going to do.

'Let's put them back in their bag so they can have a nice rest,' she says, getting onto the floor next to him and gathering up the plastic toys. Jack helps, but not very well. When Flynn was little they used to sing the tidy-up song and he was always very enthusiastic. She remembers writing about that in one of her first posts about how to cope with the messy room of a teenager. Her son is a long way from the tidy-up song now.

'Jack,' she says, as the little boy finishes putting all the dinosaurs back into their plastic bag, 'I have the best idea. What about a wonderful treat?'

'Yay,' he says, jumping up from his position on the floor.

Young children are so easy to please, so easy to keep happy. Flynn is so very different from this little boy and she wishes she had a child like Jack, a child Jack's age. That would make everything much, much better. It would be like starting again from almost the beginning without the bothersome baby years, where sleep deprivation dogs every footstep and everything feels completely out of control. Gabby prefers the age when a child can at least speak and understand, even if it's a small amount. Jack is the perfect age.

ELEVEN

ANDREA

As soon as she sees Gabby close her front door, Andrea makes for her bedroom, dropping her bag and Jack's backpack by the front door.

She sinks onto her unmade bed, feeling the heavy weight of her body and of all the worries she is carrying on her shoulders. *Where is Terry going tonight and what is he really doing?* She'll check later that he's where he says he will be, but now he is still at the shop, still working. She thinks – she hopes. She could get her phone from her bag and check, but she doesn't have the energy to stand up right now. The nausea roils inside her, forcing her to swallow. She's already thrown up four times today and she hates the terrible feeling it leaves her with. The back of her mouth still tastes of bile despite the fact that she brushed her teeth.

She has almost two hours. Another woman, a better woman than her, would use the time to rush around the house cleaning and tidying and getting dinner ready, but Andrea cannot find the strength for any of that. She remembers the final weeks of her pregnancy with Jack, remembers the way she whirled around the house cleaning everything she could touch. The energy inside her bubbled over and even the smallest tasks gave her joy.

'You're going to hurt yourself,' Terry told her one night when he came home from work and found her on top of a ladder, cleaning the ceiling fan in their bedroom. But she knew she wouldn't.

'I need to use this last week productively,' she said. 'When the baby's here, all I'll want to do is sleep.' She had never imagined she could feel so filled with happiness as she had the day she put away all the newly washed tiny blue rompers and bright white singlets in the chest of drawers in Jack's soon-to-be room. It was already decorated with cream walls and an animal frieze running along the top. A giant stuffed lion with a friendly face waited in the corner and a cream-painted rocking chair with a comfortable yellow pillow was ready for her to use when she fed her baby. Now the stuffed lion is in storage, probably impregnated with mould after all the wet weather, and Gemma's room has a cot and a chest of drawers filled with Jack's old baby clothes, but nothing new for her.

She moves the pillows around on the bed, putting one between her knees and one under her heavy belly, and she lets her eyes drift closed as she tries not to think about the night nine months ago when her whole life changed. But the images return and she gives in and lets them come, along with her tears. It rushes back at her, the night that had begun so well. She was coming back from her Pilates class and she had been in a good mood because that hour on a Tuesday night, away from her lively two-year-old son, always put her in a good mood and allowed her to feel ready to deal with the next few days. There had been a slight problem at the beginning of the class when Marcia had let her know that her credit card had been declined and she needed to try and send through payment for the term again, but Andrea was confident that Terry just needed to transfer some money to cover the last credit card bill. Pulling into her garage, she had been humming as she thought about the snack she would reward herself with and the new novel she wanted to start. Terry would have put Jack to bed already, so the couple of hours before bedtime stretched luxuriously before her. She was counting her blessings, grateful that she had a husband who was so happy to give her some time off during the week, even though he left early for work and spent a long day on his feet on the shop floor.

She climbed out of her car and raised her hand to push the button to close the garage door, but before she could do that there was movement, a rush of air, a presence in the garage.

She didn't even register it was a man until he had his hands around her throat, squeezing tight before she could even scream. He was large and smelled thickly of cigarette smoke, but she couldn't see him properly because the light in the garage had gone out and Terry had not replaced it. A garbled sound emerged from her throat as the hands, rough with broken nails that scratched, tightened.

Sheer panic overwhelmed her and fear stopped her thinking straight. Odd sounds continued to emerge from her mouth as his hands clamped tighter around her neck and she clawed at him to get him to let go.

'You tell Terry,' his voice rasped in her ear, 'this is not a joke. We want our money.'

And then he was gone, leaving her coughing and choking and crying as she called for her husband. Afterwards, as she sipped sweet tea and tried to explain to Terry what had happened, she wanted desperately to be able to dismiss it as a mistake, as her being in the wrong place at the wrong time. But she couldn't. The man had used her husband's name.

Terry refused to call the police, refused to let her call the police. He told her she had imagined what the man said, had not heard correctly. He said it was a mistake and the man was probably after someone else and it was best to leave it alone and pretend it never happened. Terry was good at pretending. Until he couldn't pretend anymore. Nine months ago, she had forced herself to dismiss the attack, but she could not dismiss everything that came in the months after that, everything that led to her being here in this house.

And now there is a man watching her, watching the house, and once again Terry is acting like she is being irrational.

Six months after the incident in the garage, she finally realised the extent of the trouble they were in.

Terry came home with a broken finger.

'It was a work accident,' he said as she fussed over the splinted wrapped finger, concerned about how swollen his hand was. 'We were moving a television and it fell.'

'I hope workers' compensation will cover it and I assume Baz has said he'll cover all the medical bills until then?' she said, angry at how his safety was being compromised at work.

'No, that's not going to happen. It's fine, Andy, just leave it. I don't want to make a fuss.'

He went to the fridge and pulled out a beer, struggling to open it until she took it from him and helped him. He took a long swallow, a man desperately thirsty, or desperate to let the alcohol help him forget. His face was pale, his blue eyes dulled with pain.

She remembers watching him gulp the beer, fast, and without savouring it as he usually did. When he reached for another, everything came rushing at her as pieces of a puzzle fell into place. The incident in the garage, phone calls to Terry's phone at 1 a.m., a black car that seemed to be always in their street but belonged to no one, her credit card getting declined at the checkout of the grocery store just that week. *Must have been a mistake, you're imagining that, you're seeing things, it was a wrong number.* Terry had an explanation for everything, but the broken finger was something different.

'I can help you, Terry,' she told him, growing dread twisting inside her. 'But you need to tell me the truth.' She knew, by then, what it was – knew and wanted it to not be the truth. It amazes her now how she'd managed to fool herself into dismissing so many things until then, but that was human nature, she supposed. She just didn't want to know. After his finger was broken, neither of them had the luxury of choosing ignorance anymore.

And finally, Terry started to talk and, with each word that fell out of his mouth, a chunk of Andrea's world crumbled into dust.

And now she is pregnant and they have moved house and Terry keeps painting it as a new beginning, but she can't see it that way. This pregnancy is so very different, and not just because of the nausea. Gemma hasn't arrived yet and already all she wants to do is sleep but she knows that a lot of that comes from the weight of her worries. She has no idea how things are ever going to get better, especially when she is beginning to suspect that they are actually getting worse.

She stretches a little on the bed, her back muscles loosening, grateful to be able to relax with the bed taking the weight of her nearly grown baby.

The night Terry confessed everything hovers over her, a grey cloud of despair. Jack was sleeping and she remembers that she was wearing a pair of jeans that had a red spot on the front. She and Jack had gone to a community art class and he had touched her with paint on his hands. 'Tell me the truth,' she had said again, trying not to look at her husband's swelling bandaged finger as he finished his second beer and took his time putting it in the recycling.

'You don't... I can't,' he began, leaving the kitchen and forcing her to follow him into the living room.

'Tell me,' she commanded and then she looked away from him, unable to bear the stricken look in his eyes. Instead, she stared down at the red dot, which she knew would easily wash out, knowing that what her husband was about to say would not so easily be dealt with. She remembers him pouring himself a whisky before he began to speak, filling the glass up – shocking her, since he rarely drank more than a beer and he had already had two beers. He gulped back the drink, his eyes watering as the liquid went down his throat. Then he sank down onto the sofa and she watched him, her mind churning as she waited for him to speak.

'I bet on a football game in the US,' he said. 'I bet a lot of money and my team lost.'

'Football? In the USA?' she asked, incredulous. 'But what do you even know about that? Why would you bet on that? How much did you lose?'

'Thousands,' Terry mumbled, shaking his head in dismay.

'What?' she yelled – sure she had misheard him.

'Thousands,' he shouted back, standing up from the sofa and beginning to pace around the room. 'It's not just that... I've been... It was so easy at first. You know that necklace you wear?'

She had put her hand up to the beautiful white gold and small scattered-diamond necklace that he had given her a month before, telling her it was to celebrate their sixth wedding anniversary. She had been overwhelmed since they didn't usually give each other gifts. 'What about it?' she asked.

'That cost five thousand dollars. I bought it after I won on another football game.' Andrea touched her skin where the necklace lay, moving the suddenly hot chain away from her throat. 'It's so easy to do and there's so much information about the players and I can listen to it or watch it on my breaks at work, and I was doing so well but then I wasn't.' He hung his head and she could see his shame. 'I'm just grateful that Baz never caught me. At least I still have my job and I'm working hard to get the money back, I am...' He rubbed his eyes and she knew he was rubbing away tears. 'I'm so sorry, Andy. I've let you down and I've stuffed up our lives and I wouldn't blame you if you just took our son and walked out that front door.'

'Is that what you want me to do?' she asked, the shock of what he was saying making her feel like she was going crazy. She rubbed at the dot on her jeans, scraped at the red with her nails, needing to get the colour off.

'No,' he said hoarsely, coming over and dropping down onto his knees in front of her. 'I love you and Jack more than anything, but something happens to me... I don't know why I started – maybe it was the job or us being a family and suddenly everything felt so... It was quick and fun and we don't have a lot of fun anymore.'

'Don't you dare – *dare* – blame me or our son for this,' she said between clenched teeth, her nails working harder at the spot.

'I'm not.' He shook his head. 'I'm sorry, I'm not. It's me... all me. I'm a screw-up and I need help. I really need help.'

'How long have you been doing it?'

Terry hesitated, moved away from her and sat on a recliner. Dropping his head into his hands, he stared down at his expensive black sneakers. 'A long time. We'll have to sell the house. I need to pay back the guys I borrowed from or they'll do worse than break my finger,' he told her, and her stomach twisted as she imagined what 'worse' might be.

Suddenly she was running for the bathroom, where she threw up until there was nothing left inside her. She was only just pregnant with Gemma, but she didn't know that yet. She only knew that her life as she knew it was over. She had never imagined such a thing was possible. Her father bet on the Melbourne Cup horse race once a year along with most of Australia, but he never bet more than fifty dollars and he was able to shrug and smile if he lost.

'Gambling...' she had murmured, unable to take it in. It felt impossible. It wasn't something she had ever expected. There had been moments over her years of being with Terry when she had watched him speak to other women at parties or when they were out and felt a tiny stab of jealous watchfulness. He was very good-looking and his smile lit up his face, so she was always aware that she needed to pay attention. She never wanted to be one of those women who said, 'I never suspected a thing,' but he had never given her cause to question him on anything like that. Gambling of any sort, gambling that meant everything was lost, had never even crossed her mind as a possibility until the incident in the garage. An incident she had forced herself to dismiss. Gambling on American football was so out of her scope of understanding it felt like a joke. It had never even occurred to her to worry about something like that. Her legs felt heavy as she left the bathroom and returned to the living room, where her husband sat with his head in his hands. She sank into a pale green armchair, wrapping her arms around herself.

'I'm so sorry, Andy. I will make this up to you – I promise.' He looked up at her and leaned forward, meeting her gaze, and she could see he needed her understanding but she couldn't get her head around it. They would have to sell the house they had worked so hard to buy. *How was that possible?*

And now they are here in this horrible house only because of the largesse of one of her father's friends, and she is keeping that a secret from everyone, including Gabby, who is so kindly babysitting Jack.

The night Terry confessed, the discussion went round and round, as they tried to figure out what to do, and eventually she had insisted on calling her father so they could get some advice. Bert was a man who had always believed in a hard day's work. He owned a business that imported and sold carpets and he had worked hard, sometimes seven days a week, until he had built it up to be a good-sized company. Andrea's parents were not rich, but they were very comfortable.

'Please don't call him,' Terry begged. 'I can't take the shame of it.' But Andrea insisted.

'Daddy,' she said when he answered his phone, his voice alarmed at being woken up, and then she embarrassed herself by bursting into noisy tears as Terry stood watching her, his face a mask of humiliation. Once she had calmed down, she explained and her father asked to speak to Terry, who took the phone and walked away. 'Yes, Bert, I know, I know, I know,' she heard him say and she knew that her father would berate her husband, but he would also listen and find a way to help. Terry's father had never been around for him, and his mother had worked her whole life to raise Terry and his brother, Nick.

When Terry gave the phone back to her, her father said that he agreed that they would have to sell the house to settle the debts. 'I know you are going to suffer for this, my darling, and I would like to just pay off these men and let you stay in the house. But this is more than I can afford, and I fear that he will not stop what he's doing and then he may end up losing his whole life over it. The big shock of losing the house is terrible but maybe it will stop him from continuing with his behaviour.'

'Oh, Daddy,' she had cried, not wanting to ask what the full amount was. Terry had obviously confided in her father, out of earshot. 'How can we lose the house? What will we do? Where will we live?'

'Andy Pandy,' he said softly, using her childhood nickname, 'your husband needs help. You can stay with him and help him struggle through this – and I can tell from speaking to him that he wants to beat this – or you can come home to me and Mum. It's up to you. We have a friend who's just bought a house in Sydney and he is going to tear it down but it will stand empty for a while as his plans need to go through. He takes ownership in a couple of months. I can call and ask him to let you live there while Terry gets some money together so you can rent something else. I'll tell him that I can pay him some rent.'

Andrea had felt her face flame up with mortification. 'Oh,' she said, because she couldn't find words to express the horror of her father's friend knowing that her husband had gambled away their house, but she knew she had to accept the offer. The only other choice was for her to leave Terry and take Jack to live with her parents in Queensland, and even though her anger at him was starting to bubble up through the fear she held for his life, she still loved him. She wasn't ready to throw in the towel on her marriage.

They couldn't afford a big campaign to sell the house, so they sold it quietly and it took months. Terry went to work and came home. He agreed to the tracking app and gave her access to the credit cards and the bank account. He started going to Gamblers Anonymous meetings, coming back from each Monday night group unusually quiet, as though his whole personality had been muted in the hour-long gathering with others going through the same thing.

When the real estate agent called with an offer on the house, her first instinct was to say no, but she knew she had no choice. As she packed up her house, she cried more tears than she imagined possible.

She breathed easier when they were free of the debt he had accrued, but she was devastated at how little was left. How was it possible to lose so much money?

And since they moved here, Terry has been staying later at work, turning off his tracking app locater, and now she knows there is someone watching her, watching the house. She doesn't even have the energy to cry as she feels herself stepping back, shutting down.

The nausea comes in waves as she tries to lie still, a passenger on a rocking boat.

She doesn't want to think about it anymore. She will just close her eyes for ten minutes and then she will get up and really make use of her time.

As soon as she makes this decision, giving herself permission to rest, she floats into a deep dreamless sleep, everything washing away.

It feels like only a few minutes later when she is woken by Terry roughly shaking her. 'Andy, Andy, what's going on? What's happening? Are you okay?'

She moves away from him. 'Just a few more minutes,' she mumbles. She only needs another ten minutes and then she is definitely getting up. She'll make dinner and do at least two loads of laundry if she can just have a few more minutes.

'Andrea,' shouts Terry, 'what's going on? Where is Jack?'

Andrea's eyes snap open and she realises that it's dark. She sits up quickly, wiping her mouth and trying to make sense of what she's doing. 'I was... taking a nap,' she says to her husband, who is standing in front of her, illuminated in the light from the hallway coming into the bedroom. He is still dressed in his black pants and blue shirt with the logo of the store on the pocket. He usually changes when he comes home. He must have just come home – but he was going out to dinner, wasn't he?

'Why are you here?' she asks.

'I left the dinner early. I've been calling you and calling you. I must have called ten times and you didn't answer. You never do that, so I got worried.'

Some part of Andrea takes a small amount of pleasure in Terry's worry. She is always the one who worries about him. Gemma kicks her bladder and she stands up off the bed. 'I need to go to the bathroom.'

Terry grabs her shoulders, forcing her to stop and look right at him. 'Andrea, it's after seven. I don't know how long you've been asleep, but Jack isn't here. Do you understand me? Jack isn't here.'

Even though her mind is still thick with sleep, Terry's words finally penetrate the fog. 'Jack,' she yelps. 'He went to Gabby's house. He went to play there for a couple of hours. I was supposed to get him at five. She's babysitting him.'

'God,' says Terry, shaking his head. 'What that woman must think of us.'

'Don't you dare put this on me, Terry. I was exhausted and I just needed a rest,' she says, pushing her hair away from her face. 'If you had been coming home, I would never have agreed to her babysitting him, but you were off having pizza – or so you said.'

'So I said,' he yells, waving his hands in her face. 'I was at an important dinner and I had to leave in the middle of Baz telling us about the sale to come home and check on you, and now our son is being cared for by someone else. It's not like you had anything else to do today.'

Andrea wants to slap Terry. She actually wants to reach up and slap him, but instead she curls her hands into fists, digging her short nails into her palms so that she doesn't lash out.

'I need to use the bathroom,' she says slowly, enunciating each word. 'Go and get Jack. Apologise to Gabby. Just go.'

Terry has never come home and found her asleep before; even in the early stages of this pregnancy, when the nausea was even worse and the hormones ravaged her body and she was packing up their house and getting it ready to sell, she has never taken her eyes off Jack. Instead, she has allowed fear and anger and worry to keep her going, to keep her doing what she needed to until the house had sold and they were left with precious little to start again. And so, perhaps because he has never seen her like this, or perhaps because he can sense she is on the edge of an explosion, Terry turns and leaves the room. 'I'll take him for some hot chips for dinner,' he calls.

'Fine,' she spits and she hurries to the bathroom, slamming the door shut as her heart races and her anger flares. She is furious with Terry but she is also furious with herself. She should have set an alarm or had her phone next to her at least so she would have heard Terry calling. What if Gabby had needed her because something happened with Jack? What kind of a mother hands her child over to someone else and doesn't keep her phone next to her?

She uses the bathroom and splashes some cold water on her face. In the kitchen, she takes some dry pasta out of the cupboard. Jack won't want it after hot chips, but she needs to eat, the nausea will return if she gets hungry. As she's filling a pot with water, Terry comes back into the house and she turns, ready to greet her son. Maybe Jack wanted to see her before he went for chips.

But Jack is not with Terry.

'Where's Jack?' she asks.

'He's not there, Andy,' says Terry, real fear in his voice. 'The whole house is dark and they're not there.'

'But...' Andrea turns, looking for her phone, but it's not in the kitchen. 'Ring my phone,' she shouts, and Terry pulls his out of his pocket and does so. Andrea listens and finally hears the silly shark song playing, the sound coming from her bag by the front door. She pulls out her phone to see eleven missed calls from Terry but nothing from Gabby.

Hitting Gabby's name with trembling fingers, she waits as it rings a few times and then she gets her voicemail. 'Hello, you've reached Gabby. I really want to hear from you, so please leave a message.'

'Hi, Gabby, it's Andrea... I'm so sorry about oversleeping. I don't know what happened. Can you call me so we can come and get Jack?'

'Ring her again,' says Terry as she hangs up the phone, and Andrea does as he says. After five minutes of calling and leaving messages, Terry goes across the road again to knock on the door and ring the bell. When he returns, he is pale. 'Doesn't she have a son? Where is he?'

'Out with friends,' says Andrea.

'I don't get it. Jack must be feral by now, or at least asking for us. It's nearly his bedtime,' says Terry, looking at the time on his phone.

'Do you think she's reported us to the police or something?' asks Andrea in a small voice. 'Maybe she thinks I'm a bad mother.'

Terry shakes his head and Andrea is overwhelmed with dread. 'Oh God,' she says, feeling her nausea hit her again, 'what if she's called social services and told them I'm a bad mother?'

In the living room she sinks onto the striped sofa, her nose twitching at the mould smell.

Terry sits down next to her and puts an arm around her shoulders. 'You're not a bad mother, Andy. You fell asleep. I don't know why she didn't just knock or ring the bell.'

'But maybe she did,' says Andrea, hysteria making her voice high. 'Maybe she did, and I was so fast asleep I didn't hear her and she got angry and now she's gone to the police or something.'

'Okay, look,' says Terry, standing up. 'We need to think about this logically. She lives across the street, so it's not like she's going to disappear. She'll be home soon enough. I'll go and watch her house and hopefully she won't be long.'

'Should we call the police?' asks Andrea. 'I mean, is it possible that she's... taken Jack? Would she have taken Jack? Why would she do that?' Andrea cannot comprehend how something like that could happen. It's the stuff of movies, of nightmares.

Terry runs his hands through his hair. 'I think we wait on the police. I mean, we don't want to look like lunatics. Let's just wait another hour and if she's not back, we can call them. You keep ringing her and I'll go and watch the house.'

'Okay,' says Andrea, grateful to be told what to do. 'Okay.'

Holding her phone in her hand, she presses Gabby's name,

listens to it ring, leaves a message. Presses Gabby's name, listens to it ring, leaves a message. Presses Gabby's name, listens to it ring, leaves a message. She feels herself rocking back and forth on the sofa, swallowing compulsively to keep from throwing up, her little boy's face, his smile, his laugh, tormenting her.

TWELVE

GABBY

Jack is crying, the noise he is making drilling right into Gabby's head. 'I want my mum,' he keeps saying. 'I want my mum.' He has gone from a perfect little angel – wide blue eyes and a giant smile – to an absolute monster in the space of only half an hour. His nose is running and his voice is high pitched with stress. He pulls at his red and blue striped jumper in frustration and stamps his feet in their matching blue sneakers.

They are at an arcade, so at least no one can hear him over the ringing bells and buzzing games and the thumping bass of some strange song that keeps playing over and over again. There are very few small children left here. They've all gone home to bed, where small children should be, and only slouching teenagers are at the games, throwing bits of food at each other and laughing hysterically at everything. Is this the kind of place Flynn hangs out at when he's not at home? No, Flynn would never tolerate such asinine entertainment. He's a smart boy.

It is nearly 8 p.m. and Jack is obviously overtired. She crouches down next to him. 'Listen, Jack, if you stop crying, if you just keep quiet for a moment, I will buy you anything you want, anything at all.' She feels herself physically crossing her fingers that the ploy works, as multicoloured lights flash and a whistle blows at screaming pitch. Her headache is fierce and strong, the blood pounding in her head along with her mother's voice. *What kind of an idiot does something like this, Gabrielle? Any mother worth the title would know not to do such a thing. What a terrible mother you are.* She clenches her fists – the words 'shut up' repeating in her head as she tries to get the woman to quiet down: 'Shut up, shut up, shut up.'

Her own pale grey pants and cream-coloured top are grimy with sweat and stained from the milkshake he dropped on her while she was carrying him. This has all gone quite horribly wrong.

The little boy's eyes are red rimmed, his distress obvious. She has to get him out of here and go somewhere quiet so that he can sleep, but she hadn't planned for this and she knows that's why things have gone terribly awry. When she suggested a visit to the arcade in the middle of the large shopping centre, he was delighted. It was impulsive on her part, a momentary lapse in her usual constrained self. Even when she sometimes takes her little souvenirs from stores, even then she plans carefully, making sure to study everything before she makes her move. But this time she acted with her heart instead of her head, and she's paying for it.

She had wanted to see how long it would take, see how far she could go. *People are not toys you can play with, Gabrielle,* her mother's voice spits in her ear. *Everything, everything has consequences.* Gabby wants to cry with frustration. She had so wanted this to be a nice outing. As they were driving here, her head was crowded with images of Jack laughing and holding her hand, of other people smiling indulgently at the lovely mother-and-son duo as they shopped together and went to the arcade together, but that's not how things have turned out.

She had given him hot chips, a milkshake and a chocolate bar before they made their way into the arcade. He had gone from being a reasonably well-behaved little boy to something of a nightmare, but that was all the sugar, and she was fine with him running around the arcade, shouting and touching everything, starting a game and immediately losing interest. But now his sugar high has worn off and he is exhausted.

In her pocket, her phone buzzes continually. She knows it's Andrea calling her, but Andrea had not called her until after seven. What kind of a mother was she? She just handed Jack over and then forgot he existed. Gabby had expected a call at only a minute past five when Andrea came to collect Jack and found the house empty, and then she would have explained about the treat of taking him to the arcade. But that's not what happened and the longer her phone was silent the longer she kept the child out. Andrea has no idea how lucky she is, with her daughter on the way and her husband who comes home to her every night. She has no idea how grateful she should be. Resentful jealousy wriggles through Gabby's body at how easily Andrea has been able to have children and how quickly she has given her child over to a virtual stranger.

The other person who is contacting her is Richard. She should never have told him what she was doing, but she had been filled with joy as she watched the little boy run around the arcade, giggling and playing.

I've taken Jack out and he's having the best time, she texted Richard.

What? Why would you have done that? It's bad enough that you were babysitting him. Since when are you getting involved with the neighbours? Take the kid home and give him back to his mother.

No! He's having fun. I'm not doing any harm.

Gabby, please, this is going to get you into trouble. Go home
and maybe do another post about Flynn.

She stopped reading his texts after that. Flynn was sixteen
and more out of the house than in it, and she is sick of being
alone. Maybe Jack is a way to move forward. She wants to be
involved in his life, to be someone he turns to, knowing he can
trust her. He could come over to her house and they could have
sleepovers and then it would be like he was really hers. *Are you*
mad? Are you completely mad? her mother's incredulous voice
asks.

'I want the Hot Wheels, the Hot Wheels,' shouts Jack,
pointing to a few packaged cars for sale behind the counter in
the arcade. The man serving people has a large stomach and a
thick red beard. He raises his bushy eyebrows at Gabby as if to
criticise her parenting.

'I'll take those,' she says, pointing as she squares her shoulders and lifts her chin. Who is he to judge her?

The man grabs the package and hands it to her. 'Twenty
dollars,' he says, which to her seems a lot for just a few tiny cars,
but she pays him and hands the package to Jack.

'I want to open them,' he says.

'Not now,' she tells him through gritted teeth. 'Let's go.' She
takes his hand and pulls a little, getting him out of the arcade
and away from the man watching her.

'I want to open them now,' says Jack, stopping and stamping
his feet. 'Now, I want to open them now. I want to open them
now, now.'

Gabby stops walking and takes a deep breath, crouching
down, her face close to Jack's. 'If you say one more thing, I will
take them away and throw them in that garbage bin over there.'
She hates the way her voice sounds. Her mother's tone coming
through her mouth always upsets her. She has tried to be so
different from the woman who raised her, but she is inside

Gabby, lodged there forever, and nothing Gabby does can make her disappear. *Now you see,* she hears her mother say. *Now you see what happens. You always think everything will be so easy, Gabrielle, but life is hard, life is painful, and you don't get whatever you want.* She touches her silk top, reassuring herself that she and her mother are different people. She is not like the woman who narrowed her dull brown eyes at people who followed fashion, preferring to stick to her polyester pantsuits because they 'washed well'. Gabby has chosen to embrace all the beauty life has to offer instead of scoffing at it and hating anyone who wanted something different.

Jack opens his mouth but then glances at the round silver garbage bin only a few steps away from them and shuts it, holding the package of toys tighter. She takes his hand and he walks quietly next to her until they get to the car. He climbs obediently into his car seat and she straps him in. The seat had been stored in the garage because you never knew when you might need one. She would never have taken Jack out otherwise, knowing that would be illegal. She is a responsible mother, a responsible parent. She deserved a nice afternoon with the child. Why couldn't he have just behaved?

'I want my mum,' says Jack softly, and she can hear he's going to cry.

'Of course,' she says. 'We're going home right now.' She needs to take him home because she is completely unprepared for anything involving a child right now.

As she is pulling out of the car park, her phone buzzes again. Andrea is getting very worried. *Good. She should be.* She drives around for a bit, watching Jack in the rear-view mirror until he falls asleep as she knew he would, and then she pulls over to the side of the road and thinks about how to handle this. First, she listens to Andrea's increasingly desperate voicemails one after the other. On one voicemail she thinks she hears a man's voice in the background, which means Terry is home. But of course, he would be by now. She hadn't thought that through either. This is one of those times when she hasn't exactly been thinking straight. Moments like this have plagued her all her life. It feels like a rush of heat through her body. Her mind goes blank and suddenly she is doing something she shouldn't be doing. Like the time she set the fire alarm off at school, or the time she got on a train to another city without a ticket and had to hide, or the time she rammed her car into someone who had cut her off in traffic. Another Gabby takes over and then she has to figure out what she was trying to do. *There is something very, very wrong with you.*

'Shut up,' she murmurs, conscious of the sleeping child in the back. It all felt so natural, so easy, and almost like she was being given a sign. When Andrea wasn't frantically phoning her at 5 p.m. she knew that the woman didn't mind being without her son for longer and Gabby just wanted to see how much longer. But she hadn't factored in an overtired three-year-old. She should just have kept Jack at home until Andrea came to get him. This was quite a big mistake.

She is not quite sure what to do, how to play this. If she simply turns up now, she will never be allowed to see Jack again and Andrea will probably never speak to her again either. That's not what she wants. She contemplates asking Richard what she should do but he will just get angry. He hates it when she does something that jeopardises their lives. *You need to be careful, Gabby. You don't like it when you get negative attention. Not everyone will love you like I do. Just be Flynn's mother and things will be fine.* Sometimes she can see them side by side – her mother and Richard – one with nothing but hateful contempt and the other kind and loving but always trying to manage her. They are both controlling in their own ways and Gabby hates to feel controlled. She doesn't always want to do the right thing. The right thing eventually starts to gnaw at her, making her edgy.

Richard had been quite forgiving over the little incident of taking the necklace from the jewellery store last month, because it was the first time she had been caught. Or so he thought. It actually wasn't the first time she had been caught, but it was the first time she had not been able to talk her way out of things and had to call him to explain.

'Please, I'm begging you,' he said on the phone, 'just stay home and do what needs to be done.' When she had to call Richard so that he could call the police from the US, she let him assume that she had been caught on her first try at shoplifting this year. He knows she's done it before, but she had promised to stop. *You risk everything we are working for when you do something like this, Gabby*, he lectured as they spoke over text after she got home. He had explained to the police about her high levels of stress after her mother's death. The policewoman had been very understanding, saying, 'I lost my mother only a month ago as well.'

Gabby had managed a few tears and then she had used her credit card to pay for the necklace. 'I won't do anything like that again,' she assured him. And she hasn't. She has been good for a whole month, but she can feel herself getting restless. There is nothing quite like the rush of taking something that doesn't belong to you. It doesn't have to be anything big because it's not about the item, it's about the thrill. It can take her a whole afternoon to plan a theft sometimes. She will watch the store for a few hours, seeing how many people go in and out, and then she will go in and browse and maybe buy something small and then she will keep browsing, watching the security guard or the shop assistants until finally she will pocket something and leave slowly, her heart racing and her mouth dry with each step to the door. And once she's out in the fresh air and she knows she's gotten away with it, she experiences a rush of pure exhilaration.

She is not even completely certain why she took Jack out. She only knows that she wanted to, needed to. *It's all about you, isn't it, Gabrielle,* she hears her mother hiss. *You never think of the consequences. You just waltz through life acting as if you won't get caught, but every time you* are *caught.* How she hated the word 'consequences', and everything it stood for. Gabby can remember the hot tears she shed over those words because her mother had been right. It had been a small thing, hardly even worth anyone getting upset over, but her mother hated to feel ashamed of her child. Gabby had been twelve years old and was caught cheating on a maths test, which she'd only done because her mother had told her that anything less than perfect was unacceptable. She conjures her mother now, standing in front of her, the ever-present cane in her hand because of her damaged leg that had never healed after a childhood accident. That cane wasn't just used for support. Her mother was the same age Gabby is now, but she looked so much older, with her severe grey bob and shapeless pantsuits. Gabby grew up knowing that she needed to be better than anyone else to prevent the shame that came from only having a mother. Her father was someone she was never allowed to ask about. He was never discussed, only mentioned when Gabby did something wrong, and her mother repeated the words she had heard so many times they were ingrained in Gabby's psyche: *Do you want them to know you are like the dirt on their shoes? You have no father. No one to protect you because he did not think you were worth staying for. He took one look at you and then he was gone, running away so fast I couldn't believe it.* It took Gabby a long time to realise that the person her father was running from was her mother, and not her, but by then she was already an adult and her mother's damaging words about her worthlessness were lodged inside her.

Her mother worked hard to keep them fed and housed. Her days were spent cleaning offices and her nights were spent cleaning their tiny, ugly apartment in case dirt dared to settle anywhere. Gabby had inherited her need for cleanliness, but she grew up longing for beautiful things and beautiful clothes, for soft hands and beautifully styled hair. She has all of that, but her mother's voice will not be banished from her head.

Time is ticking away and she needs to figure out what to do. She looks down at her phone and inspiration strikes. Typing quickly, she sends four separate texts to Andrea's phone.

Hi Andrea. It's just after four and Jack's getting a bit restless, so I'm going to take him to the shops for a treat. I have a car seat, so don't worry at all. Hope that's okay. xx

Hi Andrea. I haven't heard from you, so I assume you're asleep. Jack and I are at the shops and I may stay a bit longer. Let me know if that's a problem. xx

I'm a bit worried that I haven't heard from you, but I just wanted to let you know that Jack is fine and has had something to eat. I will probably be home with him around eight. I am more than happy to keep him since you looked so tired this afternoon. You rest. We are getting on fine xx

It's nearly eight – sorry we're a bit late getting back but we'll be there soon. Jack's had an amazing afternoon. I really hope everything's okay? I'm worried that we haven't heard from you. xx

It's really mystifying to her that these texts did not arrive when she sent them. She practises shaking her head. 'I don't understand,' she murmurs.

If Andrea asks why she didn't call her phone, she can say she didn't think of it. A few swipes of the screen turns the phone to silent mode. *I didn't want to concentrate on anything but Jack, and by the time I switched it back on, we were already on the way home and I thought it best to just get here*, she hears herself say. So many people communicate by text these days, and maybe Andrea won't swallow the lies but maybe she will.

She puts down her phone and pulls back into the traffic and she is soon turning into their street. When she gets to her house she can see Terry hovering worriedly outside, his head swinging left and right looking for her car. She's only met Terry twice but there's something odd about the nice-looking man, something just a little fake in his demeanour, and Gabby should know. She can spot a fake miles away. Andrea is hiding all sorts of information about their lives, but everyone is hiding things about themselves. The world would be in chaos if everyone just went around telling the truth. She stops the car in the driveway and isn't even out of her seat before Terry is upon her.

'Where've you been?' he yells. 'Where the hell have you been? Where's my son? Jack, Jack,' he shouts. Jack wakes up in his seat and yells back, 'Dad, Dad, I got Hot Wheels, look, look.' Jack is only three and he can't hear his father's outraged panic. He's had a nap and now he's ready to play again, his meltdown in the arcade forgotten.

Gabby sighs with relief as she steps away from her car and Terry's fury. 'Why are you yelling at me?' she asks, making sure her confusion is obvious. 'I don't understand why you're yelling at me.' She allows her voice to drop, indicating distress.

Terry wrenches open the back passenger door and fumbles with the catches on the car seat.

Gabby goes to stand behind him. 'Let me,' she says, but he doesn't move and finally he gets Jack out of the seat and, holding him in his arms, he snarls, 'Who do you think you are? You can't just take someone's child. You should be ashamed of yourself. Andrea is pregnant. How could you?'

Before she can muster a reply, the front door to Andrea's house opens, light spilling into the neglected front garden. Andrea comes out, moving as fast as she can with her huge bump in front of her. 'Stop, Terry,' she says. 'Stop, she texted... Gabby texted.'

Jack starts crying again, upset by all the shouting and the confusion that seems to be going on around him. Andrea gets to where they are standing, brandishing her phone, showing it to Terry. 'She texted all along. She's been texting me but they've only just come through. They've only just come through.'

Gabby bites down on her lip, biting hard enough to cause herself some pain so that her eyes fill with tears. 'Of course I texted,' she says, her voice thick with indignation. 'Why wouldn't I have texted? Didn't you get them? Andrea, please tell me you got my texts. I thought you were... Oh my God, I am so terribly sorry,' she sniffs.

'I didn't, not until now, not until now,' and Gabby can hear the relief in the woman's voice.

'You must have been so worried,' she says, stepping forward to offer Andrea a hug, but the woman steps back, still wary and unsure.

Terry is shocked into silence. He peers at his wife and Gabby can see his disbelief. But he can argue all he wants, no one can prove that she didn't send those texts when she says she did, unless they take her phone, and neither Andrea nor Terry would have the audacity to do that.

'You should have just brought him home at five. I mean I was...' She stops speaking.

Gabby catches a quick glance between Terry and Andrea, a flash of guilt, and she takes a chance. 'I did actually come across just before we left and I knocked but no one answered. I thought you were either asleep or you'd gone for a walk and since you didn't answer my text, I assumed you were asleep. I'm so sorry if you were worried. I was just listening to your messages and I had no idea. We were in the arcade and my phone was on silent and I only realised as we left the parking lot that it was still on silent. Of course, I drove straight home after that. You weren't terribly worried, were you? He was with me and you know me,' she laughs lightly.

Andrea offers her a weak smile as Jack's shrieking intensifies and he wriggles in his father's arms. Terry moves off, away from both of them and across the road to their house.

'Is everything okay, Andrea?' Gabby asks and the young woman nods but even her nod is not completely convincing. Not to Gabby.

'Best you get that little man to bed. I'm afraid he was having so much fun I didn't want to pull him away. I hope we can do it again soon.' Her phone buzzes in her hand and she looks down. 'Oh, and there is my big man wanting to be picked up. Get some rest, Andrea. You look worn out. I'll see you soon.'

She climbs back into her car, and as Andrea watches, she drives away and turns right towards Flynn's friend's house, where everyone has now eaten their fill of pizza and is ready to go home.

Things have gone as well as she could have hoped. Everyone is familiar with the mercurial nature of messaging. If she thinks about it, she's sure she remembers a few times when Flynn sent her a message only for her to get angry at him for not communicating and have him show her the message on his phone. Technology doesn't always work exactly the way it should. Nothing is perfect.

She hopes that she gets the chance to take care of Jack again. She really likes the little boy, when he is not having a meltdown. She took some photographs of him today while he was playing and each one was more beautiful than the next. It's so much easier to use young children to create a social media presence. There are millions of videos all over the internet with toddlers saying hilarious, cute things. Having watched many of them, Gabby knows that if she had started posting when Flynn was little, she would have way, way more followers. Also, people are endlessly supportive of mothers with young children, since taking care of them can be so hard. Once a child gets older and you can reason with them, sympathy falls off a little, especially since that child can do their own posts.

As she drives, she goes over an idea for her next post. She needs to shake things up a bit, to tell some home truths. *My teenage son hates me.* That would be a dramatic title and something that is sure to get a lot of traffic. An argument with Flynn a while back about cutting his hair could be part of the post. She sees his face screwed up with anger as he throws 'I hate you' at her. Even thinking about it makes her heart race. Gabby didn't want him to cut off his lovely curls, but he insisted and eventually Richard took him to get it done, devastating her. Mentioning that her husband took him to get his hair cut will garner sympathy from a lot of women who struggle with spouses who have different ideas on how to parent.

A memory surfaces of her standing in front of her mother with a slightly rusty pair of silver scissors held to her waist-length blonde hair that her mother had forbidden her to cut. Her hair was beautiful and thick but impractical and not in fashion at her local public school, where it was just one more thing that separated her from all the other girls who sported feathered bangs or beachy curls. Every day, at fourteen, she would braid it and curl it around her head to keep it out of the way. If she left it to hang down her back, boys would yank the braid as they ran past, laughing at how old-fashioned it was. Gabby hated her hair.

'You can't tell me what to do with my own hair,' she had screamed as her mother stood watching her in silent fury, and then she had moved the scissors, chopping through her hair and watching in horrified fascination as a whole hank of hair fell to the ground.

'And now you are ugly,' her mother whispered, 'and you are evil for what you have done and no one will ever, ever love or want you.'

'You're wrong about that,' says Gabby aloud, banishing her mother with a shake of her head as she turns right. On Facebook thousands of women follow her and like her and are her friends, and she has Richard and, no matter what she does, he will always love her – won't he? She stops outside a house and puts the car into park, her mother's face swimming before her eyes making her repeat herself. 'You're wrong about that.'

THIRTEEN
ANDREA

For the next few days, Andrea actively avoids Gabby, checking out the front of her house before she gets into the car to take Jack to pre-school to make sure Gabby is not there. It feels ridiculous but she needs some space. Gabby has sent a text apologising for the mix-up but ended her apology with the words *I should have called but then you probably wouldn't have heard the phone anyway*.

'There's something weird about her,' says Terry, and Andrea admits that something feels off, but she has no idea exactly what it is. It's not like she's never had the experience of a text coming through many hours after someone has sent it – but four in a row feels strange.

She finds herself in the nesting phase of her pregnancy and filled with energy in the last couple of weeks before Gemma is due. Every morning she wakes up in the cold house and steels herself to try and be positive about her life and where she is. She remembers to count her blessings and reminds herself that she is healthy, and that Jack and the baby are doing well.

Her sister calls every day, and sometimes she can hear that

the endless rain is beginning to depress her but that Brianna is trying to sound upbeat.

'We're both having a bit of a time of it, aren't we?' says Andrea at the end of one of their calls, and Brianna says with a laugh, 'Yeah, but this will pass and at least we have each other to moan to.' She is grateful every day for her parents and sister. It helps that Terry has begun getting up with Jack in the morning, switching on their old heater and warming the house through, letting her have some extra time in bed. While Jack is at school she cleans and tidies and manages to get the nursery ready, even treating herself to a few bright pink baby outfits, heavily discounted in a sale. It's easy enough for her to spend her days inside the house as the rain continues, heavy on some days but only a drizzle on others. The front garden becomes a patch of churned-up mud and she tries not to look at it, not to compare it with all the other gardens on the street. It's not her garden, after all, and she doesn't let herself think about when she will ever have her own garden again.

Her life settles into a manageable routine, but there is still an edge of anxiety always there. Outwardly, Terry seems to be sticking to their agreement. He goes to work, he comes home and spends the weekends with her and Jack, helping get the house into shape and preparing for the baby. He even does some work on things he can fix, like the hinges on the kitchen cabinets, but Andrea still finds herself listening for the things he isn't saying and watching for the things he isn't doing. She cannot allow herself to miss the signs that he is gambling again. In her dreams, the red car passes in front of her house and the man with the beard and tattoos laughs at her – waking her with a racing heart on some nights.

It is a Tuesday morning, cold but finally clear, when Andrea understands that her husband has been lying to her for some time.

The morning begins easily enough with Jack singing his way through a piece of toast: 'The wheels on the bus go round and round.' The lack of rain allows Andrea a sense of optimism and she finds herself singing along with her son.

'Listen to you two, giving me a morning concert,' says Terry, coming into the kitchen, fresh from his shower, smelling strongly of the aftershave she likes that reminds her of a walk in a forest.

'Today at school, I get to be the bus driver and say, "move on back",' says Jack, taking a final bite of his toast.

'Lucky you,' says his father. Andrea is standing next to the toaster, waiting for her own piece to pop. Terry leans around her to switch on the kettle, planting a kiss on her cheek. The toaster immediately stops working because the plug cannot work both the toaster and kettle at once. 'Sorry,' says Terry sheepishly and he turns the kettle off so she can finish making her toast. 'I'll grab a coffee at work.'

'What was that kiss for?'

'Can't a man kiss his wife?' he laughs. 'What do you think, Jack? Can Dad give Mum a kiss on the cheek for no reason?'

'No reason,' laughs Jack, as though Terry has said something funny.

'I have stocktake tonight, remember,' he says. 'I'll be late.'

'I remember,' replies Andrea because Terry has told her about this, and she's used to the long nights that come with getting everything ready for the end of the financial year. 'Do you want me to make you some eggs?'

'Nah, I'm good. I'll just eat an apple now and get something later.' He grabs an apple from the fridge. 'Have a good day, little man,' he says, ruffling Jack's hair.

Jack immediately smooths his curls down again. 'No, Dad,' he says sternly.

Andrea smiles at how serious her son sounds. She turns to grab the peanut butter from the counter and realises that Terry has left the jumper he was carrying on a chair next to their kitchen table. It will be cold tonight and he'll be working in the warehouse, where there's no heating. She grabs the blue jumper and walks quickly to the front door, opening it as she starts to call for him in case he is already in his car.

But Terry is not in his car. He is across the road speaking to the man with the sleeve of tattoos – the man who she saw watching the house, the man who drives the old red sedan with one unmatched door. Andrea feels her heart catch in her throat. Terry's name dies on her lips.

She stands completely still, the blue jumper clutched in her hand, as she watches the man with the black beard put his mouth close to Terry's ear and say something, too quietly for her to hear the words, but there is no mistaking that the man is angry as he bares his teeth. Terry nods furiously and then the man grabs Terry around the top of his arm, and even from across the road, Andrea can see him squeezing hard.

'T... T...' she begins, her voice a soft squeak until she finds the courage to speak up, to call her husband, needing to stop whatever is going on. 'Terry,' she yells and the man abruptly removes his hand from Terry's arm and then looks across at her. Terry turns. 'You forgot your jumper,' she says, holding it up, her face flushing with fear and embarrassment. She looks up and down the quiet street quickly, hoping that no one is watching what's going on.

'Oh, right, thanks,' says Terry and he walks across the street to grab the jumper from her. The man nods at her and climbs into his car, driving away with a screech of tyres.

'Who was that?' she asks, holding on so that Terry is forced to pull at the jumper.

'No one,' he says quickly.

'That's the man who has been watching the house, Terry,' she hisses. 'Don't tell me no one. I told you about him and you told me I was being ridiculous.'

Terry sighs. 'He's an electrician, working two streets over. I was asking him about fixing the wiring in the kitchen so we can run the kettle and the toaster at the same time. I wanted to see if he could do something quickly and cheaply that was still safe to have around kids.'

'Why did he grab your arm?' Andrea asks, searching her husband's face for the lie.

'He didn't grab me. He was telling me about where he got his first tattoo. Now I really have to go. There's nothing to worry about. You need to relax and trust me, Andrea.' He smiles, his blue eyes widen and he holds her gaze so that she's reassured. At least that's what is supposed to happen, but she can read him the same way she can read his son, who uses the same expression when she asks if he brushed his teeth.

'But there—' Andrea starts to say but Terry yanks the jumper away from her and throws her a kiss, getting into his car and driving away quickly. *He's lying.* How can he not see that it's completely obvious? She wants to call him and demand to know the truth, but he won't pick up. Tears prick at her eyes. She can't go through this again. She drops her head and squeezes her eyes tightly shut. Jack can't see her crying.

'Andrea,' she hears, and she looks up to see Gabby coming across the street. 'Are you okay?' the woman asks kindly. Andrea is so grateful to be asked how she feels, to have someone acknowledge her pain, and she is so scared of the man and of what Terry has done to deserve a visit from such a person that she bursts into noisy tears. Every tiny bit of happiness she has summoned from her unhappy situation over the last few days disappears. How can they possibly be back here after everything Terry put them through?

'Oh, Andrea. Oh, sweetheart, what's wrong?' Gabby's tone is all kindness and concern. She is dressed immaculately as usual, in wide-legged caramel-coloured pants and a soft knitted black top. Her white-blonde hair gleams in the sun and she looks relaxed and in control. Andrea pulls Terry's robe around her, trying to close it more over her large stomach. She hasn't gotten dressed yet.

'Is this something to do with that man Terry was talking to? I've seen his car a few times and always thought it was weird. Does he know him? Does Terry know him?' Her voice is bright with curiosity.

Andrea shakes her head, reminding herself to be quiet, before a full confession emerges into the air. 'No... I don't... It's just been a bad morning, that's all,' she says, a slight twinge inside her at the lie. It had actually been a good morning until she saw the man with Terry. Now everything is wrong and awful – her whole world grey and terrible, as a thousand horrible things run through her mind.

Gabby searches her face, her blue eyes filled with concern, and Andrea feels a touch of irritation at the woman who has nothing in the world to worry about.

'I need to get Jack to school,' she says. 'Sorry, Gabby.'

'That's fine, fine,' says Gabby giving her shoulder a squeeze. 'You can trust me with anything, you know. I'm aware that things went a little pear-shaped when I took Jack out and you were worried, but that was honestly the fault of the phone company and not either of us. I would never have done anything to put Jack in danger. I know what it means to panic as a mother. Believe me, I have some bad days with Flynn, not that I tell many people, but he's become really difficult, so I understand about bad mornings. I'm just across the street if you need me.'

Andrea nods and gives Gabby a small smile. She doesn't

want to be angry with her over what happened anymore. It was all just a mix-up and it's nice to hear that she's not the only one who has bad mornings. Sometimes it can feel like she's completely alone in this new suburb. On one side of her is the elderly man, and she hasn't even seen the neighbours on the other side. Their house is always silent except for someone coming by to collect the mail and gardeners turning up once a week. Andrea assumes they must be away and envies them their long holiday. On days like today it feels like she is the only one struggling to stay positive about her life, but she reminds herself that everyone has their own struggles.

'Maybe we can have coffee after school today if you're free,' Andrea says. The day and the long night alone with her son and her thoughts stretches before her and she would rather have some company. Listening to Gabby talk about her son and about all the people she gives advice to online is easy and distracting. Last night she read through a whole conversation in Gabby's comments where Gabby gave advice to a woman who was worried that her husband was cheating on her. The conversation took place below a post where Gabby had expressed how upset she was about her son cutting his hair and her husband taking the boy to do it. Gabby had been so reassuring, so kind in her comments, telling the woman that the best thing to do was to have an honest conversation with her husband. *Jumping to conclusions never helps and only makes it harder for a rational conversation to take place*, Gabby advised.

Being with Gabby will be soothing. She seems to have an answer for everything.

'That will be fabulous,' says Gabby, her smile wide. 'Flynn is going surfing with friends this afternoon, something only teenage boys are game to do in this weather, but he has a good wetsuit. I'm free, so I'll see you at three thirty? You come to me. I'll make something delicious for tea.'

'Absolutely,' smiles Andrea and she finds that she feels calmer already.

She turns and goes back into her house to find Jack still at the breakfast table, still singing to himself.

He's so innocent, so oblivious to any tension between his mother and father, and that's how he should be allowed to grow up. If Terry is gambling again, she has no idea what they will do, how they will live. She cannot get a job, cannot afford childcare even if she could. Outside, thunder rumbles and she knows that the clear morning is over and the rain will soon return. She sits down at the kitchen table and chews her way through two pieces of toast, her jaw mechanical, the peanut butter she usually loves sticking in her throat.

'Go and brush your teeth, bubs,' she says to Jack, her body tensing slightly because brushing his teeth is something Jack likes to fight over and she's not equipped to deal with that this morning. But he is delightfully agreeable and says, 'Okay, Mum,' getting off his chair and heading for the bathroom. Andrea sighs and glances at her watch. They have to leave in ten minutes and she can't put this off any longer. She has put it off for long enough. She picks up her phone, running her finger over her current favourite picture of Jack, which is her home screen. He is on the swing at a beautifully laid-out park that was only a few minutes' walk away from the house they used to live in. It was taken on a rare sunny day, the sky an eye-watering blue and the air warm on her skin. She had just pushed him a few times to get him started and he was pumping his legs furiously, determined to make the swing work on his own, and, as he achieved his goal and the swing went up, he shouted with joy at the feeling of flying and achievement, and she had her phone out, ready to take a picture and she snapped it at the perfect time. No matter how bad a day she is having, looking at the photo makes her feel better, makes her look forward to better days when maybe there are two children on swings and she is feeling secure enough to only worry about getting the perfect shot. But this morning the photo only makes her want to weep, as the ease she felt on that particular day feels so far away. She unlocks the phone and logs in to her bank account, holding her breath as it comes up. She sees the numbers with minus signs in front of them, so many amounts – small so she wouldn't notice, but there. Minus ten dollars, minus twenty dollars, minus thirty dollars. She starts adding it all up and then stops when she gets to two hundred dollars. She should have checked this three weeks ago when she first saw the car, but she simply didn't want it to be true.

And even as she looks at the numbers, she has a feeling that Terry will explain it all away as 'lunch' or 'coffee' or 'a quick drink because you don't expect me to not buy my round at the pub once in a while, do you?' These amounts are small, but they suggest a pattern. Last time, when she had demanded he let her look at the bank account, she had cursed her own stupidity for not having access to it, for happily leaving everything to her husband. Then, the amounts were huge, in the hundreds and thousands, and she could even see when he had borrowed more money against the house. At the time he had said something about renegotiating their mortgage and she had simply signed the paper he had given her. She had been raised in a home where her parents had traditional roles. Her father earned the money and took care of everything to do with it. Her mother had an account that he kept filled but everything else was up to him. Andrea had been happy enough to hand over the finances to Terry after they got married. He had a degree in business, so she reasoned he was the best person to deal with things. She had been horrified to see the enormous amounts he was taking, and she knows that he will tell her now that what she is seeing is not that at all. But she believes it is. How much does he owe the man with the beard, or the people who the man works for? She shivers, pulling her robe tighter around herself.

'Ready, Mum,' says Jack, a dab of toothpaste on his chin.

Andrea clicks her phone so that she cannot see the bank screen anymore and stands up. 'Then I better get dressed and let's get you to school,' she says, smiling at her son, and he smiles back with Terry's smile, Terry's beautiful smile, without the lies behind it.

FOURTEEN
GABBY

Gabby hums to herself as she makes her way to her kitchen. She'll bake something for this afternoon, something healthy and delicious. She picks up one of the recipe books from the cabinet next to the stove and begins paging through it, when a note falls out.

Dear Mum,

I hope you enjoy cooking and making everything in this book as much as I know we will all enjoy eating it.

Love,

Ben

'That's so sweet,' mutters Gabby, slipping the note back into the book. She wonders if Flynn would ever write her a note like that, would ever express such lovely sentiments. It doesn't seem possible right now, with how difficult he is being. It feels like the distance between them grows every single day, and today, just this morning, he told her he hated her, hissed it at her as he clenched his fists. Not something pleasant to hear, and even now as she sees his face and feels his terrible anger, her skin grows hot. She is ashamed... Yes, that's exactly how she should feel... ashamed that her son no longer seems to love or even like her. It's the same way she felt about her own mother at sixteen, but then she'd felt that way about her for years. As she grew up, she had been determined that one day, when she was a mother, she would do everything differently from how her mother had done it. She would let her child know that they were loved every single day of their life. And that's just what she has done and yet here she is – with a child who hates her the same way she hated her mother. It's hideously unfair.

She puts the recipe book down, open onto a page with a picture of some thick, chunky oatmeal cookies, as the incident this morning returns to her mind. All she had done was ask him to smile for a picture. She shakes her head – yes, that's all she did and she's quite certain that if she posted about it on Facebook, there would be many supporters who understand how mercurial teenagers can be. They are the selfie generation and yet despite how many pictures he posts on his Instagram, Flynn denied her a simple picture over breakfast this morning. 'Come on,' she cajoled, trying to stay light-hearted.

'I hate you,' he hissed instead, his eyes focused on his phone screen. His smiles were only for the new girlfriend now. On Instagram, more and more photos of the two of them have appeared. In some of them, Flynn is gazing at her so adoringly that Gabby has been unable to contain a hot streak of jealousy. How long since someone looked at her like that? According to Richard, the policeman father of Flynn's new girlfriend has not thought to look into the boy his daughter is dating, so at least that's one good thing. But she can't count on no one ever looking into her son. How much time do they have until someone starts asking questions? Gabby takes a deep breath and lets it out slowly, calming herself. She needs to concentrate on the things she can control right now. She needs to focus on her posts and her son, who is leaving her with small steps, walking away slowly, so she will no longer be needed or wanted.

She grabs a pen and a pad from next to the kettle and jots down her idea: *I fear my son actually hates me.* Closing her eyes, she summons all the feelings from the incident so she can accurately portray them to her followers.

Inspired, she moves over to her kitchen table where her sleek black laptop sits and opens it to her Facebook page. Taking a deep breath, she cracks her knuckles and begins to write, knowing that it's time to start telling the truth about some things. She's been posting for nearly four months now and it feels like she has known some of the people who follow her forever. She has researched quite a lot of them, like Monica, who lives in a lovely house by the water and is married to an orthopaedic surgeon. Monica has two sets of twins, turning to IVF to have her children twice, and despite her two nannies, she is constantly overwhelmed and looking for emotional support from her friends. And then there's Becky, who has just inherited some money from her grandfather and is considering giving much of it away. She's very religious and is always thinking about others. Unfortunately, her teenage daughter treats her like a doormat. Gabby always likes exchanging messages with Daniella as well. Daniella is a working mother with some big job in the city that keeps her out of the house all day, meaning that the raising of her three boys is left mostly to her husband and a series of nannies. Daniella often expresses the thought that she has no idea who her sons have become. Gabby makes sure to never judge these women in her comments. Every mother is just doing her best. Her own mother wasn't interested in anything but raising Gabby for long enough to get rid of her, but things are very different with the women who follow Gabby's page. Every mother wants to feel she is getting it right and very few of them do. There are too many women following Gabby's posts to be speaking to all of them, but they are all lovely and kind to each other, and Gabby likes to think that the page is a safe space for everyone. If that's the truth, then she needs to stop glossing over her life and only presenting something shiny for others to view. She needs to bare her soul and accept what comes with that. She won't tell the whole truth, lest her Facebook friends comment that she should not be posting pictures of her son if he doesn't want her to. The whole truth is never entirely necessary.

Today my darling Flynn told me he hates me. I can't even remember what we were arguing about because there are a lot of arguments lately. Arguments about homework and curfew and the way he talks to me. He's never said those words before and the moment they were in the air, I forgot about everything else. I must have looked devastated because he apologised immediately and things seemed fine when I dropped him off at school. I know that the words are not unusual for a child to say. I know from reading your messages to me that a lot of you have heard that phrase, but it's a first for me and it hurt. It really hurt. I counsel myself on the need to love this child through his worst days, but it's getting harder and harder. He even threatened to run away. He used to threaten to run away when he was little as a lot of kids do when you tell them they have to go to bed or eat their vegetables, but it's different when a sixteen-year-old child says it. He could leave if he wanted to, and I don't think the police would be able to force him to come home if they could find him. He will be seventeen soon, nearly a man. A man who hates his mother. I am writing these words because I think it's important to be upfront about this. Motherhood is hard, sometimes impossible. We give and give and give and instead of any reward we get hate and anger, and that can be really difficult to understand. That's when I think it's

important to have a group of friends in the real world or online
that you can call on, and I know I have that. I have all of you
and I can count on you when things feel hard. You can count
on me too. Xx

She puts up the post without a picture of Flynn. There is
nothing on his Instagram that would work and it will have more
impact if she doesn't have the usual photo to go with it anyway.
Sitting back in her chair, she waits for a few minutes until the
likes and comments begin to come in. People are very supportive, offering their own advice. Some are a little smug at her
confession because she always seems so on top of things, but
that's fine. Her earlier post about Flynn cutting his hair got a
little pushback but not too much. Lots of people felt he should
be able to do what he wanted with his body, but there were
plenty who bemoaned teenagers with piercings or tattoos or
strange-coloured hair. Gabby pays attention to the ones who
begin their comments with 'Well I just think...' They are the
self-righteous ones, and the self-righteous ones seem to really
want to help when everything goes wrong as long as you pander
to their superiority. She had easily deflected the negative
comments by indulging in a long discussion with a woman who
suspected her husband of cheating. She could almost feel the
negative comments losing their significance as the discussion
went on and more and more people joined in with their own
advice. It wasn't hard to direct a discussion on Facebook. All
you needed was to keep people engaged and reading – that was
always Gabby's objective.

She has a feeling that things with Flynn are very much
going to go wrong if she can't find a way to get through to her
son. Richard would tell her to just 'leave him alone,' and she
will write about that in another post. It seems to her that fathers
have the ability to stop the metaphorical blows from a teenager
landing, although maybe that's just Richard. But it will be inter-

esting to see how other mothers respond to a post about how easy things seem to be for Richard. She will mention that he travels a lot, so those on the page know that, mostly, she does this alone.

After twenty minutes of thanking people for their comments and adding smile and hug emojis to everything, she sighs and gets up, returning to the recipe book. Oatmeal cookies would be good but maybe cupcakes are better. Jack will be happy with anything, and Andrea will be too, as long as she just gets to sit down for a few minutes. She wants to get this right. She made a mistake by keeping Jack out late and assuming that Andrea would not completely freak out. She had known she would be worried, but what she was trying to gauge was how worried she would be. It's a good thing that she hadn't called the police yet, because that would have been a disaster.

Why would you have done that? What are you playing at? Richard texted her when she explained what had happened.

He's such a lovely little boy. A three-year-old child is such a delight and he loves his mother so much.

Gabby, stop. You need to stop. Finish your project. Concentrate on that and nothing else.

Richard was right about that. She did tend to get close to the end of a project and want to hurry things along. She is supposed to be finding new furniture for the living room. Richard likes to give her these little tasks to keep her occupied. He worries that she will get bored and take up old habits, but she won't do that again – or not so that she gets caught, at least. Concentrating on Jack and Andrea is a much more valuable use of her time.

Deciding on cupcakes, she gets everything together, allowing her mind to churn with the mixing of the batter. She contemplates what she will post about her son next. But she also mulls over the scene she witnessed today. She spends time each morning, after dropping Flynn off at school, watching for Andrea, hoping to find a casual way to speak to her so she can get their friendship back on track.

There was definitely something going on this morning between Terry and the man in the street. Gabby has seen his car far too often for it to be a coincidence. And each time she sees it, her mouth feels dry and her heart pounds in her chest. She hates feeling this way, hates having to wonder if she is being watched. What was the man asking Terry? Was he asking about her? If Andrea hadn't suggested coming over this afternoon, Gabby would have said something about getting together. She needs to know what Andrea knows about the man with the red car, because what if he was saying something about her? He could have been warning Terry – but then surely Andrea wouldn't have agreed to come over later. Richard is still looking into him, still tracing who the car belongs to and how he might be connected with Gabby.

I'm sure it has nothing to do with you, Richard told her over text. He always thought she was too cautious, but then he was safely in the USA, doing his own thing, while she was here dealing with their angry child and trying to figure a way forward.

She had kept out of sight as soon as she saw Terry come out of the house, as she usually did. She had no desire to talk to him, but before he got anywhere, the red car screeched to a halt, the man jumping out and calling, 'Hey, mate, can I get a word?' If it had been her, she would have turned and run for the house, but she watched as Terry hesitated and then walked across the road. She was behind her car so she couldn't hear what was said but she could see Terry's face as he nodded and nodded and then he glanced at her house. She's certain he did.

When Andrea came out of the front, Gabby moved further away, not wanting to be caught snooping. Then, once Terry was gone, she saw her chance to get things back on track with Andrea. The poor woman looked terrified. But what was she scared of?

Gabby stops stirring, realising she's growing cold in the kitchen. The bright morning is over and the sun has disappeared behind a bank of thick grey clouds. The man could be a private detective. It wouldn't be the first time one of them has come looking for her.

She shakes her head. The man probably has nothing to do with her and instead something to do with Terry. She flirts briefly with the idea that Terry is some kind of criminal, but then dismisses it. Terry works in an appliance store and that's not a good cover for someone who's a criminal – although how would Gabby know. The house was obviously bought with family money. But then what was the man doing outside their houses?

She sighs, banishing all her negative thoughts. She'll get the truth from Andrea this afternoon and go from there.

Once the batter is done, she enjoys spooning it into the cupcake cups, choosing different coloured liners for each cupcake. It's amazing how many things this home came with – just amazing.

While she waits for the cupcakes to cook so she can ice them, she looks through her calendar on her phone. Three weeks to go. She needs to move quickly now.

FIFTEEN
ANDREA

At first, things with Gabby are a little awkward. Gabby seems flustered, moving an empty cereal bowl and mug off the kitchen table, muttering, 'I told him to clean up,' as she gestures for Andrea to sit down. The kitchen is still a mess from breakfast, with dishes in the sink and crumbs on the counter – so unlike Gabby. Andrea can feel, as they chat, that they're being overly polite with each other and concentrating on Jack as a way to avoid discussing what happened when Gabby took Jack out.

But eventually Gabby says, 'Look, we can dance around this today and then you can leave, and we can smile at each other as we get into our cars and never really talk again, or we can address it. I should never have taken him out and I'm sorry. I've felt so bad about things, I haven't been able to concentrate on anything. It was entirely wrong of me and I can promise you that I will never do something like that again. That is, if you ever give me the chance to babysit again.' She laughs lightly, her uncertainty at Andrea's reaction obvious.

Gabby has a lot of friends on Facebook and a full life, but there is something in the way she speaks about her husband and son that makes Andrea think she is experiencing some loneliness. Maybe she and Gabby are more alike than she thought.

Gabby seems to need to be friends with Andrea as much as Andrea wants to be friends with her, and she feels her heart go out to her.

The rain is falling softly outside the warm room where Gabby is running the heater. Jack is on the floor with the dinosaurs he loves so much, and the air contains the deep chocolate smell of the cupcakes.

'Oh,' Andrea says, overwhelmed by Gabby's sincerity. 'I really should have kept my phone with me and I should have set an alarm. It was my fault as well.' Her face flushes as she remembers her fear and her shame at losing herself to sleep like that.

'Then shall we just move on?' says Gabby, getting up to pour more tea and arrange the chocolate cupcakes covered in thick white icing on a plate.

'Wow, thank you so very much,' says Jack as Gabby puts one on a blue plastic plate for him, setting it down next to him on the floor. Andrea feels a surge of homesickness for her mother in whose kitchen Jack was just as at home, just as happy. If her mother lived near her, everything would be different.

'You're a very polite young man,' says Gabby. She turns to Andrea. 'What do you think?' she asks, and Andrea realises that she hasn't replied.

'Yes, let's move on.' She smiles, enjoying a moment of contentment as her son picks up the cupcake. 'Let's just move on.' She nods, glad to put the whole thing behind her.

'Oh good,' says Gabby with a smile, putting the whole plate of cupcakes in front of Andrea. 'I was so worried that I would lose you as a friend and, to be honest, I don't have a lot of friends.'

Andrea picks up a cupcake from the plate and takes a bite,

her teeth sinking through the sweet moist cake. 'This is delicious,' she says, placing it on the side plate Gabby put in front of her, 'but you must have lots of friends – look at all those people on Facebook who turn to you for advice.'

Gabby takes a cupcake for herself, swiping her finger through the icing on the top and putting it in her mouth. 'They're not really friends though, are they?' she says, her blue eyes shining with unshed tears, her face falling as she drops her head a little. 'I mean, they're out there somewhere but it's not like I can sit across a table from them and talk to them.' She rubs her hand quickly over her cheek, and Andrea can see she's getting rid of an escaping tear.

'Oh, Gabby,' Andrea murmurs, leaning forward, 'what's wrong?' She reaches out and touches her friend on the arm.

Gabby sighs. 'Have you... I mean you probably haven't, but have you seen my Facebook post from this morning?'

Andrea shakes her head. 'No... I haven't actually looked at Facebook today yet,' she says as she lifts her phone up. 'Do you want me to read it now?'

Gabby nods her head slowly.

Andrea is aware of her watching as she opens her phone, brings up Facebook and reads. 'Oh, Gabby,' she says, looking up when she's done. 'I'm so... I didn't know, but look at all the comments and advice... so many people want to help you.' She tries for a smile as the words she has just read repeat in her mind: 'hard, impossible, anger, hate'. Not words she ever thought Gabby would use when talking about her son.

Gabby sighs and waves a hand, sitting back. 'I'm just being silly. Of course they're friends and I know they would help me if I needed it, but sometimes I think that I've kept so much back from them that they wouldn't believe me if I told them how bad things really are.'

Andrea has no idea what to say, taking refuge in the silence of another bite of the sweet cupcake. The post is raw and honest and not something she ever would have expected Gabby to say. She can't quite believe the woman who seems to have a perfect life, surrounded by a loving husband and son and everything money could buy, is actually struggling. Andrea squashes down a small feeling of relief that she isn't the only one whose life isn't quite going according to plan.

She's shocked by the words Gabby wrote, shocked that she would be so open and shocked at how difficult her son obviously is. It seems impossible that Jack will ever get to the stage when he hates her. Right now, he is happy to be with her every minute of the day.

'You're having a tough time,' she manages, unable to find any advice for someone who has been a mother for a lot longer than she has.

Gabby picks up her cupcake and takes a small bite as she nods her head. 'I am,' she agrees. 'I posted it because everything was just too much, you know. I felt like I'd lost you as a friend and I understood that I probably deserved that, but then Flynn was so angry with me and I wondered what exactly I have done with my life. I mean, I stayed home to raise him and now he can't stand me, and even though all these women on Facebook turn to me for advice, I feel like a fraud. I don't know what I'm doing any more than anyone else. And when I posted, some of them were quite... just rude about my struggle.' She swallows her small bite of cupcake and returns it to her plate as though she cannot bear to eat any more, clapping her hands together to get rid of a few crumbs. 'One woman said, "So you don't have all the answers, do you?" I deleted the comment but it made me feel sick. I know she's right – I don't have all the answers – but all I have ever wanted to do is help other mothers. I never said I knew everything.'

She picks up the cupcake again and breaks it into two and

then into three. Andrea can see that she has no intention of eating it at all and she feels bad about having already finished hers, her hand reaching for another without her even thinking about it.

'No one has all the answers,' she tells Gabby. 'Not even experts with degrees behind them. Every mother is just trying to figure out how to do it right. My mother always says that the minute you figure out how to deal with your child in one stage, they move on to the next, and she's right. As soon as I had worked out how to get Jack down for two naps at exactly the right times, he moved on to one nap. It's frustrating for all of us. I can't imagine how hard it would be to have a teenager. I'm having enough trouble imagining handling two at once.'

'You're so sweet,' Gabby smiles and wipes her hands on a vivid blue paper serviette, 'and I will help you as much as you'll let me. Now eat that other cupcake. When the baby arrives, you'll barely have any time for yourself.'

Andrea obediently takes a bite. 'I wish I could help you... I wish I knew something that would help.'

Gabby stands up from the table and refills her teacup. 'Richard said that I need to leave the boy to grow up without documenting every day of his life, but he can hardly tell me anything about raising him. He's off in San Diego and all he does is text Flynn every couple of days.'

'He's back in San Diego?' asks Andrea.

'Oh, yes... I mean, I think he is. There's so much travel that I never know where he is,' she says with a laugh as she returns to the kitchen table. 'It's easy for men, isn't it? I mean Terry goes to work and leaves you with Jack, and soon there will be a baby and he'll still walk out the door every morning and you'll still have to deal with everything.'

The cupcake is suddenly heavy in Andrea's mouth and she has to take a large sip of tea to make it go down as the thought of the man in the red car and the incident from that morning return.

Andrea nods her head. 'Yes, and sometimes...'

'Sometimes?' says Gabby, leaning closer as though aware that Andrea is about to tell her something.

For a moment, Andrea is ready to confess her worries – but then she pulls back. She has no idea how much she can trust Gabby and she doesn't want to spoil the afternoon by dredging all this up. She's not quite sure what's going on yet and the idea of discussing her marriage and the problems they are having with someone she doesn't know very well doesn't feel right.

'Sometimes I wish you didn't bake so well,' she says feebly instead, and takes a big bite of the cupcake.

'Oh that, anyone can do that,' Gabby says as she sits back, but Andrea can see that Gabby knows there was something else she wanted to say. Her friend doesn't pry and instead they spend the rest of the afternoon discussing Gabby's memories of Flynn when he was the same age as Jack and Andrea's plans to return to work one day when the children are old enough. By the time she and Jack cross the street to go home, she is calm and grateful to have Gabby back in her life. She makes a determined effort not to think about anything else as she spends the evening with Jack, and she is fast asleep when she registers Terry climbing into bed after midnight.

'Get it done?' she asks, her words slightly slurred with sleep.

'Sure, sure, yeah,' he says and her nose twitches at the smell of alcohol on him. In her sleepy state, she's sure Baz wouldn't appreciate staff drinking while doing stocktake, but she cannot rouse herself enough to ask the question, and in the morning he is gone before she manages to get herself out of bed.

That night she prepares a dinner of roast chicken with vegetables, Terry's favourite, and even brings him a beer from the fridge so he can sip it while they eat.

'Special occasion?' Her husband smiles and she smiles back, feeling like a fraud because with every bite she swallows she is rehearsing the confrontation she needs to have with him over the missing money. They talk about stocktake and other staff members, and Andrea counts down until her son leaves the table.

Jack chases the last few peas around his plate, instructing them to stop running away, and then when he is done he looks expectantly at his mother. 'Is it iPad time now?' he asks.

'Yes, your half an hour begins now. Make sure you play with the iPad on the bed in case you drop it.' She stands up from the table and picks up Jack's plate, placing it in the sink.

'I know, I know,' sighs Jack, rolling his eyes and making both his parents laugh. Andrea remains standing next to the sink, shocked to find her heart racing. She is scared to confront her husband, or, more likely, scared about what he's going to say.

When she hears the music that accompanies Jack's favourite game drifting from his bedroom, she pulls out her phone and opens it to their bank account, taking a deep breath and bracing herself for a confrontation. Terry finishes the last of his beer, unaware of what she's doing. 'Can you explain these amounts?' she says, making sure to stay calm, to keep her voice even as she hands the phone to him. She doesn't want him storming off into the night, something he has done before when the conversation gets too difficult.

He stares at the screen and then scrolls down, his head shaking, his cheeks flushing slightly, and for a moment she thinks he's going to tell her that he didn't spend the money. Instead, he throws the phone down onto the table with a clunk and stands up. 'Am I not allowed coffee with a mate anymore, or lunch?' he asks, baring his teeth as he begins picking up dishes from the table.

Andrea sits down, needing to be off her feet, her body heavy with the sad knowledge that Terry has said exactly what she thought he was going to say. 'This is more than just that, Terry; it adds up. Just tell me the truth – are you gambling again?' She doesn't look at him when she asks the question, unable to bear the answer.

Terry slams the dishes down in the sink and then grabs more from the table, rinsing them quickly and shoving them roughly into the dishwasher, making more noise than necessary. 'I am so sick of being watched like this,' he spits as he works with his back to her, knives and forks clinking in the sink. 'I am the one working and earning the money and yet I'm not allowed to spend even a cent as you sit here doing who knows what all day.' He throws the last plate into the dishwasher and slams the door of the machine shut with a clunk, stamping out of the kitchen before she even has time for one more word. 'I'll get Jack into his bath and put him to bed. Why don't you rest,' he calls behind him, the words dripping with bitterness.

Andrea stays at the table, swallowing her tears, sitting in silence, unable to move. Her thoughts whirl and Gemma kicks furiously, she's sure because of all the adrenaline rushing through her body. The longing to just walk out of the door is almost overwhelming, but she cannot leave because she is pregnant and she has a son who needs her.

'Mum, come kiss me,' Jack shouts when Terry has put him to bed, and she raises her body up, sure she must weigh a million kilos, and goes to kiss her son good night.

She and Terry usually watch some television after dinner, but she has her shower and gets into bed, immediately falling into a deep sleep, exhaustion stealing her dreams. At some point in the night, she feels Terry get in and move closer to her.

'I'm sorry, babe,' he whispers. 'I'll cut back on the coffee and lunch. I know we're trying to save.' He kisses her on the cheek and turns away. He has not addressed the issue, not answered her question, but Andrea knows that as far as her husband is concerned the discussion is over.

The next few days have the true Sydney winter feel – rainy and cold with an icy wind that blows through in the afternoon. Andrea finds herself over at Gabby's every afternoon, being pampered with treats while Jack plays.

It is easy to be with Gabby, easy to forget her worries over Terry when she's there.

She is spending more and more time with her, not wanting to be in her ugly house and not wanting to think about her husband and what he may or may not be doing.

Each time they speak, Gabby confesses a little more of the truth about her life. Her husband Richard travels all the time and only suggests she 'leave him alone' whenever they discuss their son.

'I know that single mothers have a hard time raising their children alone,' Gabby has said, 'but sometimes I think that maybe it would be easier than being with someone who has no real interest in discussing their own child. It's like he's checked out until I do something he doesn't agree with, and then he lectures me on all the mistakes I am making. And of course, whenever he flits home for a bit, he and Flynn act like I'm some neurotic mother. I question myself every day.'

Andrea can only offer sympathy and a listening ear as her little boy plays quietly, happy to be with his mother, happy to eat Gabby's treats. It amazes Andrea that Gabby has been concealing so much. But even as Gabby tells her all the problems she is having with Flynn, including his excessive gaming and his dropping grades, Andrea has a feeling that there is more going on.

Gabby seems to spend a lot of time driving her son around wherever he wants to go, and yet from what she tells Andrea, he's ungrateful for everything she does for him. Flynn sounds like a handful and it seems Gabby is struggling to parent her teenage son. Each time she spends an afternoon with Gabby, Andrea looks at her son and is grateful that he's still little and still truly a mummy's boy. She listens carefully to the things Gabby says, filing them away to remember for when Jack gets older. She doesn't want to make the mistakes Gabby seems to have made and she couldn't bear for Jack to grow up so entitled and spoiled.

'Maybe making him stay home would be better, ground him or something?' Andrea suggests tentatively one afternoon and Gabby's face pales.

'Oh no,' she says, 'I couldn't... I mean, sometimes he gets really angry and then...' She stops speaking.

Andrea looks at the woman who is becoming a good friend to her. 'Are you... scared of Flynn?' she asks softly.

Gabby titters nervously. 'Of course not, of course not,' she repeats. But Andrea is not convinced.

Thinking about Gabby's problems stops her thinking about her own worries, but they are still there. She looks for the man in the red car every day, but she doesn't see him. Once or twice, she glimpses the back of a car that might be his but she's never completely sure. Perhaps Terry was right about him working in the neighbourhood and perhaps his work is now finished. Terry is still angry with her about confronting him, despite his apology. He answers her questions and asks about Jack, but they don't talk about much else. Their easy way of being with each other disappeared many months ago, but she felt they had at least reached a kind of peace. Now even that is gone. But – and it's a very big 'but' – the money has stopped leaving the account at such regular intervals. Maybe it *was* just for coffee and lunch and drinks? If money does leave the account, he sends her a snippy text... *Bought myself a new pair of work shoes and they have to be good quality so that I can be on my feet all day. I hope that's okay with you.* What can she say to that? He even texts her when he gets something more than just a sandwich for lunch. *Had a curry today as I was hungry. It cost twelve dollars. I hope that's okay to buy, otherwise I will only get sandwiches from now on.* Part of her wants to tell him that he doesn't need to send the texts but she keeps quiet. She isn't the one who lost the house. Maybe if he feels that she's watching every dollar, it will help him stay away from gambling of any kind.

At the beginning of June, on a bright cold day, she finally understands the true extent of Gabby's problems with her son.

She is still in her nightgown, her hair loosely held back with a clip and her face puffy with sleep, when the doorbell rings. She is only a week away from her due date and she is feeling exhausted all the time.

'Who's that?' asks Jack, clinking his spoon against the cereal bowl instead of eating his Weetabix.

'I don't know. Can you please finish breakfast so I can get you to school?'

'I don't like Weetabix. It's gross,' he says and Andrea suppresses the urge to scream in frustration after he specifically asked for the cereal not ten minutes ago. Slamming her cup of coffee down on the counter, she goes to open the door, her footsteps slowing as she realises that the man she worries about could be standing right there. She wonders if she will ever be able to simply open a door or scan her credit card or walk into a shop without worrying. Shaking off the feeling, she peers through the peephole and feels real relief when she sees its Gabby.

She opens the door. 'Hello – it's a bit early for a—' She stops speaking when she sees Gabby's face. The woman's pale blue eyes are red and her skin is clean of make-up, so Andrea can see all the lines that she usually so artfully conceals. It's obvious she's been crying, even before she sniffs and blows her nose with the tissue she's holding.

'What's wrong? What's wrong?' asks Andrea, panicked, stepping back so the other woman can step inside.

'He's gone... Flynn's gone,' she says.

'Gone where?'

'I don't know,' Gabby cries. 'I thought he was out with friends from his team last night. He told me they were going to dinner and someone would give him a lift home and I... I fell asleep, and when I woke up this morning, I went to get him up and he wasn't there. He hasn't been home. His bed hasn't been slept in.'

Gabby paces around the small sitting room as she talks, taking quick steps as she wipes her eyes. 'He could be anywhere,' she says. 'Anywhere.'

'That's awful... And he hasn't texted you?' Andrea smooths her hair and ties it back more securely, unsure of what to say or do to help.

Gabby shakes her head vigorously.

'But you have one of those apps, don't you?' Andrea asks, because if ever there was a mother who would have an app like that, it would be Gabby.

'I do,' says Gabby, her voice catching in her throat, and she pulls her phone out to show Andrea, opening the app, where Gabby is listed as being on their street but Flynn is listed as 'no network or phone off.'

Andrea feels silly for asking the question. 'Sorry, of course you checked it.'

'What am I going to do? How am I going to find him? I have called all his friends and they all say they haven't seen him, and the worst thing, the very worst thing, is that I called the school and they said he didn't come in yesterday. The receptionist had only just arrived for the day and she said they were going to call me this morning because his absence was unexplained.' Gabby throws the words out quickly and Andrea can see that the woman has been up for hours already, worrying about her only child.

'We need to call the police,' she says.

'The police,' says Gabby. 'Oh God... I... I...'

Andrea studies Gabby's face, registers the naked fear that has appeared. What is she scared of? Surely the police would be the first place she went, but Gabby shakes her head. 'I... I...' she stutters.

SIXTEEN

GABBY

'I... I already called them,' Gabby says and she feels her face flush as she remembers how bored the policeman who answered the phone sounded, as though he didn't care that her precious son was missing.

'What did they say?'

Gabby reels off the questions she had been asked, making her voice sound as robotic as the policeman on the phone had sounded. '"And when did you last see him? And how old did you say he was? Has he ever done this before? Has he contacted you at all? Have you called the school?" I wasn't going to...' She stops speaking.

'Wasn't going to what?' asks Andrea.

'Look, to be honest,' says Gabby, 'I told them everything I knew and I didn't want to lie to them so when he asked me... when he asked me if Flynn had ever run away before, I had to tell the truth, I had to.' She rubs her hands over her face, not wanting to see the look she knows Andrea is giving her.

'He's done this before?' the woman asks.

Gabby nods miserably. 'He has. He usually comes back after a day or two. Richard has given him a credit card for emergencies, and only Richard can see any activity on it and he hasn't returned my call. He always comes back and he's much better after a day or two away, but I have a feeling that this is it, that this time he won't return.'

'Sit down, sit down, come on,' says Andrea as she moves to the sofa, gesturing that Gabby should join her. Gabby understands why Andrea needs to get off her feet: her belly is huge in the last week of pregnancy. But Gabby cannot sit down. She looks around the small sitting room, the creeping smell of mould filling her nose. Andrea has never invited her over here and she can see why.

She could never live in a house like this, she reflects. It's chaotic and she is sure none too clean. Surely if you have enough money to buy a house in this street, you should at least have enough money for a cleaner? And would it have hurt for Andrea to make some temporary renovations? She's never mentioned plans, but they must be renovating – they must be.

Jack comes into the living room.

'I finished my cereal,' he says. 'Hi, Gabby, can I play at your house today?'

'Um,' she says, not quite sure how to answer the little boy who wants nothing more than a treat and some time with the toys at her house. How easy this age is, how simple and straightforward. If they're hungry, you feed them; tired, you put them down for a nap; and whatever happens, they love you with everything they have. Children this age are not capable of the levels of disdain she has been subjected to, and as she looks at the little boy, she is overwhelmed by a wistful desperation to be the mother of a young child and not the mother of a teenager who would rather be anywhere but in her presence. Even in her distracted state, she thinks this would make a good idea for a post one day – one day when all of this is over.

'Not today, bubs. Can you go and brush your teeth while Gabby and I talk?' says Andrea, waving her hand at him to get him to leave the room. Jack hesitates for a moment. 'If you go quickly, then you can have ten minutes on the iPad before we leave for school.' Jack whoops, jumps up and down and leaves the room. 'Thank God for the iPad,' Andrea sighs as Gabby sinks onto the sofa next to her, before adding, 'But even if Flynn has done this before, they still need to try and find him.'

Gabby looks down at the carpet, her eyes moving over the grey flecks, noting a stain, a small patch of orange.

'They said they would look into it,' she says.

'What does that mean?'

'It means that they are going to put him in a database and hope he turns up,' says Gabby, raising her gaze from the carpet.

'That's ridiculous,' snorts Andrea. 'He's a child and he's missing.'

Gabby shrugs her shoulders and then she looks down at her phone, at the text she received from Flynn, and she knows she's going to have to confess everything to Andrea. She doesn't want to, but she needs her help and sometimes, if you tell the truth, the real truth, it makes people trust you more, want to help you more, and she needs all the help she can get. The truth is her greatest weapon now and she has to use it.

'It's not...' She hesitates. 'The truth is...'

'What?' asks Andrea, sitting forward, her hand automatically going to her belly, where Gabby is sure the baby is kicking.

Gabby takes a deep breath. 'He's sixteen and he's run away, but he didn't just run away. I know it's not like the other times because...' She hesitates.

'Gabby, I don't understand,' says Andrea.

Gabby reluctantly opens her phone and shows Andrea the message Flynn has texted her, watches as the woman reads her son's angry words, knowing that they will make Andrea judge her for how she parents. 'I got this text about twenty minutes ago,' she whispers, not wanting to share it but needing to.

I can't take this anymore. Being with you is like suffocating. I have money saved and the credit card from Dad. I'm going to find Dad – wherever he is in the US, I will find him and then I'll stay with him. I would rather be homeless than live with you anymore.

Andrea touches the screen on the phone, and Gabby knows she is reading the messages she sent back to Flynn.

Don't be ridiculous. You're too young.

What about school?

Why would you leave now? What about your hockey team and all your friends?

Please answer me so we can talk. Please answer your phone. Flynn, please.

I'm begging you. Please don't do this. We can work it out. Please don't go.

Don't leave me.

Flynn, I love you and I will do whatever it takes to make this better.

Flynn has not replied to any of her texts.

'But...' Andrea says and Gabby can see that she still doesn't understand, not completely. She hates that she has to tell her friend everything, that she has to confess the horrible truth about her life. But she reasons that she is not the only one with secrets. Andrea is hiding something as well. The man who spoke to Terry may have something to do with what Andrea's hiding. Perhaps Andrea understands about secrets.

Gabby stands up and begins moving around the living room. She cannot help herself from bending down to pick up toys that are scattered everywhere, placing them in a basket that is half-filled with plastic blocks. She needs something to do with her hands.

'Richard and I are divorced,' she says as she leans down and picks up a red toy truck, spinning the black wheels in the silence that follows this statement.

'But you said he was...' Andrea trails off and rests both hands on her belly as Gabby watches. She doesn't want to look her in the face. The enormity of the lie hangs in the air.

Gabby places the truck in the basket and moves to pick up a pile of Matchbox cars.

'Can you stop doing that, please?' says Andrea, the words sharp and irritated.

Gabby closes her eyes briefly and then folds her arms. 'I'm sorry,' she says. 'I just need to keep moving. I can't seem to sit still.' She needs Andrea to be understanding rather than angry because she is going to need her help.

She sinks down onto the sofa next to Andrea and drops her head into her hands. 'I didn't want to tell you. I don't want to tell anyone. I hate that we're divorced because I never asked for the divorce and the worst thing is that what we fought about the most was the way I was with Flynn. He thought I was overprotective, but I knew my baby boy, I knew how sensitive he was. Richard is from a family who believe that boys should be tough, that boys shouldn't cry. It's not the way I raised him, and all Richard did for the whole time we were married was fight with me about it. Eventually he just left. I begged him not to. I told him how bad it would be for Flynn, but he didn't care.'

'When did you get divorced?' asks Andrea, her voice barely above a whisper.

'A year ago,' says Gabby and she meets Andrea's gaze. 'It's been the worst year of my life, but at least I had Flynn. Now I don't even have him.'

'How can he get to the US? I mean, he's a child, isn't he?' says Andrea.

Gabby clenches her fists. There is too much to tell, too much to explain, but she needs to try.

'He took his passport and I know he's been gone for at least a day. I think he's been planning this for a long time.'

'So have you called Richard? Even if you are divorced, he's still Flynn's father, and if Flynn is flying to the US, he needs to meet him and keep him safe.'

'Yes but...' Gabby hesitates, not wanting to share this last piece of information.

'But what, Gabby?' asks Andrea and Gabby sighs. There is no hiding this anymore.

'I don't know where Richard is, neither of us do. When he left for the US, he just disappeared. Flynn won't know how to find him. He will be alone in a foreign country with no way to locate his father. They do speak to each other via text, so maybe Richard will tell him where to go, but what if he doesn't? What if he's moved on with his life and doesn't want his son back in it? I have to save my child,' she says desperately.

'But... but...' stutters Andrea, 'you told me about messages you got from him. You told me...' She stops speaking and Gabby rubs her eyes as her cheeks heat up.

Of course Andrea was going to ask about that. She drops her head onto her legs, as though she cannot bear to look at her friend, blocking out everything as she thinks quickly. She can almost hear Richard warning her, *Never tell so many lies that you have trouble keeping them straight*, and her mother pipes up as well, *Sick, twisted woman. You deserve everything you get.* Gabby takes a deep breath and then she sits up, telling Andrea what the woman needs to hear.

'It was a lie, Andrea. I'm so sorry but I was just so... ashamed. I haven't heard from him in a year, not one single word. I have...' She feels her face scrunch as her shoulders round at the humiliation she is feeling. Will Andrea believe her? She hopes she will. 'I have another phone that I use to send texts to myself, and I kind of pretend they're from him. It's pathetic. I know it's pathetic, but it's helped me function, helped me keep going. I schedule some texts and sometimes I reply to myself with the other phone... I...' She looks at the front door, wondering if she could just get up and leave now, just leave and pretend she never told Andrea any of this. She knows she sounds completely unhinged, as though she needs some serious help, but it is how she's helped herself – that's what she needs to make Andrea understand. 'I prefer the fantasy of him being away and still my husband,' she says, turning to look at Andrea. 'It doesn't harm anyone, and it helps me because sometimes I look through the messages I pretend to get from him and just,' she shrugs, 'believe that we're still together.'

'That's why you kept changing where he was,' says Andrea. 'You don't actually know.' She is leaning away, as though sitting too close may taint her with the same madness Gabby suffers from.

Gabby reaches over and touches her lightly on the arm. 'I know it's not real, Andrea. I'm not crazy. It's a way to help me feel better and I shouldn't have lied to you. I would have told you the truth eventually, when I felt that I could really trust you. I mean... it's not like we don't all have our secrets. Everybody has secrets.' Gabby stands again and goes to look out of the window that lets her see the street. It's quiet and the grey sky is heavy with rain.

'It's shame,' she says, not turning to look back at Andrea, making sure to linger over the word. 'I don't know if you've ever felt ashamed of anything, or if you've ever felt you had to... hide something, but I just didn't want anyone to know. I stopped speaking to all our couple friends after the divorce because I couldn't bear the way they looked at me.' Gabby turns around, folds her arms because it's cold in the living room, and looks at Andrea. 'I don't know if you know what I'm talking about,' she adds, pushing for a reaction.

Andrea meets her gaze, and she knows that the woman understands what she's talking about.

'I know about shame,' says Andrea, her voice a whisper, and Gabby nods quickly.

Andrea is still married and with a child on the way, but she is hiding something from everyone she knows, perhaps even hiding it from herself, and that's the kind of person Gabby knows she can count on for help. Someone who understands that secrets can have teeth, that secrets can bite and that it's even possible for them to swallow you and your life whole. Gabby wants to clap her hands with glee. She has found the perfect person to help her and, even better, she has the perfect little boy as well.

SEVENTEEN
ANDREA

Jack is quiet on the drive to pre-school, as though he can sense Andrea's own emotional turmoil. She feels so sorry for Gabby, but she is struggling to get past the huge lie Gabby has told. She seems to have gone out of her way to tell her that Richard is in San Diego and then in New York, making sure to mention her husband all the time. Why bother with the lie? Perhaps it was needed so that Gabby could feed her own fantasy and somehow still believe that she was married, but whatever the reason, Andrea feels blindsided, and she hates feeling that way.

She drops Jack off with a kiss and a wave to his pre-school teacher. She has no idea what she's going to say to Gabby, if she should encourage her to just let go or if she should try and help her find her son. She would never tell Gabby that she believes the child to be both spoiled and entitled. From what Gabby says, he's rude and used to his mother being at his beck and call. How he thinks he can manage to navigate the US alone she has no idea, but she can remember being sixteen and believing she knew absolutely everything about everything. She cannot say that to Gabby as it would only make her panic more, but perhaps the boy will realise his mistake and come crawling home to his mother.

Suddenly she feels exhausted by it all; she is too pregnant and too tired and too worried about her own life to be involved in any of this, but if she doesn't at least try to help, what does that say about her as a person?

It is tempting to simply not return home, to take herself out for a quiet cup of coffee, even though Gabby is waiting for her. What can she do to help anyway?

Turning a corner, she glances in her rear-view mirror and gasps when she sees the red sedan with the unmatched door. Her heart races as she speeds up, hoping to get away from him, but the car easily keeps up with her. What does he want? Why is he following her? Taking her eyes off the road, she presses Terry's number on her dashboard. 'Please answer,' she mutters.

A sick relief fills her body when he answers. 'Is it the baby?' he asks because she is so close to her due date.

'No,' she yells, 'he's following me, Terry. The man in the red car. He's behind me now. What does he want? Why is he doing this?'

'Calm down, just calm down, okay? You need to concentrate on your driving. He's not following you – you have to understand that. He has nothing to do with us.'

'Not us, *me*,' she yells, feeling her throat scratch.

'Andy, you're going to hurt yourself,' he says, his voice a low whisper. He is obviously in the store. 'Just wait.' She hears him huffing into the phone as he finds a space he can talk.

'How far are you from home?' he asks, his voice at normal volume.

'Nearly there,' she says, a sob catching in her throat.

'Just stay calm,' he says. 'Please just breathe slowly and stay calm. He's not following you. This is your imagination turning a car behind you into something it isn't.'

'I know when someone's following me, Terry,' she spits,

angry that she has to keep trying to convince him of this when he knows exactly what's happening and is just gaslighting her, once again. 'Tell me the truth,' she demands. 'Have you been doing it again?' She doesn't want to use the word, to make it and the consequences of it real. 'Have you? Are you even attending your meetings on a Monday night?

'No,' he growls into the phone, his voice low and furious, 'I told you I wouldn't do it again, and I haven't, but every time you accuse me of it, I think why bother trying to stay away if I'm going to get accused of it anyway. And yes, I am going to the meetings, where they keep talking about how we need to surround ourselves with people who are supportive of us and our recovery, but I don't exactly feel supported when I'm accused of something every second day.'

Andrea glances at her rear-view mirror again and then looks up as the light she is going through turns red. She screeches on the brakes, a terrified yelp filling the air, and braces for impact, but nothing comes.

'Andrea!' yells Terry. 'Andrea,' he repeats, 'are you okay? What happened?'

She takes a deep breath that catches in her throat, turning into a sob. She doesn't want to look behind her as pinpricks of fear dance up and down her sweating body. She could have been killed, could have killed someone else. She needs to get it together. She has to keep herself safe for Jack and for the baby that now pokes and kicks furiously inside her.

'I'm fine,' she gasps, trying to suppress her tears.

'Okay, please, just calm down,' he says, his worry obvious in the way he speaks. 'Please, Andy. I love you and I don't want to lose you. You need to relax and just trust me.'

The light turns green and she pulls away slowly, her eyes drifting up to the mirror. The car behind her is a large black ute, its back filled with scaffolding. Had she seen the red car at all?

'He's gone,' she says.

'Told you,' says Terry, triumphant. 'He's an electrician, and he works nearby. He is not following you, Andy. No one is following you.'

Pulling into her driveway, Andrea shakes her head, even though Terry can't see her. 'I don't believe you,' she says, her voice soft with despair.

'I don't know how to help you with that,' he replies. 'I am not gambling. I am not, and if you choose to believe I am, then that's on you. Now I have to get back to work. I'll have my phone with me in case you go into labour, but I'm asking you to please let this go. You're imagining it, you just are.'

He ends the call without saying goodbye, and Andrea sits in the silence for a moment. Is she making things worse by accusing him? Should she be trying to be more supportive? Right now, she feels like a bad wife and a bad mother and a bad friend as well, who doesn't want to even try and help someone going through the trauma of a child who has run away.

She gets out of the car, wanting nothing more than some time alone to process what she saw. Is it possible that she is imagining the man's pursuit of her, that the conversation between him and Terry was just a friendly one? She doesn't think so, but what can she do about it? The man has not threatened her, and if she goes to the police, they will say he is free to drive around the suburbs; and if she goes to the police and he does have something to do with Terry, then Terry might end up in more trouble.

She hauls her body slowly out of the car and before she has even closed the door, Gabby is there, her eyes red, a tissue crumpled in her hand, her normally neat hair pulled back with strands escaping.

'I have a favour to ask,' says Gabby. 'A really big one.'

EIGHTEEN

GABBY

Andrea looks tired, worn down by the pregnancy. Gabby knows the woman is angry with her for lying about her marriage, but she never thought she would have to tell the truth. Divorce is so shameful. Her mother's face, her mother's disapproval, looms in her mind every time she thinks about her sad state. Maybe she can explain that to Andrea if she is still angry. Surely, she would understand that. She's still lying about what's going on with Richard, but that's a lie she needs to keep telling.

'What?' asks Andrea, her face grim.

Gabby senses a shift in the young woman and that's not good. 'Come and have a cup of tea,' she says. 'Come in out of the cold and I'll explain. Please don't hate me, Andrea. I know that I lied but it was... I can't help myself. I hate the fact that I'm divorced, but none of that matters now. All that matters is that I find Flynn. I have no idea where he's gone except that it's the US and I need to go after him, but I don't...'

'You don't?' asks Andrea as the wind whips up, blowing her dark brown hair across her face and making Gabby shiver in her thin jumper.

'Please, come in. Please,' she begs. Andrea nods her head

reluctantly and follows Gabby into her home, where the heating is going and the smell of cookies fills the air. 'I bake when I'm agitated,' says Gabby. 'I was baking all night as I tried to figure out what to do.'

She can't miss the look of disdain Andrea gives her. 'I thought you fell asleep and only realised he was gone this morning,' she says, her tone flat.

'Well,' says Gabby. 'I got up really early, like at five, so I suppose it feels like I've been... I mean the mornings are so dark and... Look, I'm exhausted, Andrea. I don't know what I'm saying half the time. I'm so scared and so worried about him. He thinks he's an adult and that he's ready for the world but he's not. He's really not.' She busies herself filling the kettle that was already nearly full and plating up a piece of chocolate cake, although it's early in the morning to be eating something so rich.

This was not how this was supposed to go.

Andrea sinks into a kitchen chair and sighs. 'What favour do you need, Gabby?'

Gabby places the cake in front of her, and for the first time since they began spending time together, Andrea doesn't immediately try the treat. Instead, she waits in silence for Gabby to speak, her arms folded and resting on her belly.

There has been a fundamental shift in their relationship. Andrea was in awe of her when they first met, and Gabby knew it. But now she regards her with suspicion. Should she have told the truth about Richard from the start?

'I need to get to the US to find my son,' Gabby says, sitting down and picking up a fork to take a bite of her own piece of cake. The icing is thick and rich and sticks in her throat, so she has to swallow twice.

'I understand,' says Andrea, her voice kinder now that Gabby's lost child is the focus.

'But I don't have the money for it.' Gabby sets her fork down, drops her gaze to the gold tablecloth on the table and notes a small stain of something... coffee maybe. She curls her hands into fists, resisting the urge to get up and grab a damp cloth to clean it off.

When she looks up, Andrea's brown eyes are wide with disbelief. 'I don't...' she begins.

Gabby leans forward, needing Andrea to listen to her. 'Richard left me with nothing. I mean, not nothing, but very little. I had enough for rent for a year and that year is almost up. He told me to get a job. He puts money into an account for Flynn to use and Flynn has his credit card, but he never speaks to either of us... I mean, not on the phone. He and Flynn do text sometimes, I think, but Flynn has stopped telling me anything at all. Only Flynn can access his account. I used to know the password to get into his bank, but he changed it a few months ago. Flynn thinks that because Richard sends money to him, he loves him, but I know that Richard only loves himself. My son is going to...'

Gabby hears her voice catch and she swallows, looking away from Andrea and out to the small garden at the back of her house, at the back of the house she doesn't own.

'Gabby, I don't understand any of this,' says Andrea, shaking her head, looking utterly mystified.

'I was going to...' Gabby begins, feeling herself flush. She is too old to be living a life this precarious. 'I should have gotten a job, but Flynn was so unhappy when he left, and when I had access to the money Richard sent for Flynn, we were okay, but then Flynn got difficult and now I have nothing. I had hoped to turn my advice for other mums into a blog or website and earn money that way, but it's all too late now. I have nothing and I have to get to the US, so the favour I need is money, Andrea. Tickets are expensive and I need money to live and to travel around to find him. I'm going to need to get help to find him, a private detective or something. I don't know. All I know is that I have no money and no way of finding my son, who has run away to find a father who doesn't want to see him.'

Gabby cannot help the tears that fall. Everything is awful, so awful. She leaps up from her chair and grabs a tissue from a box on the kitchen counter, blowing her nose and sitting down again, swallowing the lump in her throat as she tries to stop her tears.

'How much?' asks Andrea, 'How much do you need?'

Gabby meets her gaze. 'I need about ten thousand dollars. But I will pay you back, I promise, as soon as I have found my son, I will get him to release the money and I will pay you back.'

A strange snort-laugh escapes from Andrea's mouth, shocking Gabby. 'What makes you think I have that kind of money?' she asks, obviously incredulous.

'You... the house... I mean, I know it's in bad shape, but I know how much you bought it for – it was millions,' says Gabby, a creeping sense of dread making her skin tingle.

Andrea shakes her head and hauls herself up from her chair. 'It's not my house, Gabby. It belongs to a friend of my father's and he's letting us live in it for nominal rent, which my father is actually paying for a bit so we can get back on our feet. I don't have any money.'

'I don't... don't understand,' says Gabby because though she can't process it, she knows Andrea is telling the truth. Telling someone you're in that kind of a situation is humiliating. Andrea's cheeks are pink with embarrassment, and one thing Gabby does very well is read people. Andrea is definitely telling the truth. She curses herself for being stupid enough not to have found out about this before. She should have put two and two together. 'What do you mean, get back on your feet?'

'Terry gambles... I want to say "gambled", as in past tense, but... I don't know,' says Andrea with a slight shake of her head as she gazes down at the untouched cake on the plate in front of her. Gabby can hear, can see, how much it hurts her to say those words. She remembers the man in the red car and the way he had spoken to Terry. He was after Terry and not her. Relief mingles with frustration. No one is looking for her, but Andrea doesn't have any money to give her at all. That's a pity. Ten thousand dollars was only going to be the start of what she asked her for.

'He says he's stopped,' says Andrea, staring out of the kitchen window, 'but I'm not sure I believe him.'

'What am I going to do?' Gabby says, looking down at the kitchen table, her hand rubbing over the coffee stain. She feels sorry for Andrea, but her own concerns are more important right now.

'I don't know,' says Andrea, 'I really don't know.'

Gabby feels her stomach churn and she slaps a hand over her mouth. 'I'm going to be sick,' she says, and she darts out of the kitchen, running to the bathroom, where she locks the door and tries to breathe deeply.

Silly girl, she hears her mother say. *Silly, stupid girl. You never prepare for the worst and the worst always happens. It always does.*

Where does she go from here? How will she get the money now? Her mind turns over one idea after another. She'll figure it out. She always does.

NINETEEN
ANDREA

Sitting in Gabby's kitchen, watching light rain falling outside the window, Andrea has no idea if she should leave or not. Inside her, Gemma squirms and kicks. She cannot believe she's said the words aloud to anyone except her parents and sister and that Gabby has barely reacted to the truth about her life. She has always imagined that if anyone knew what had happened, she and Terry would be equally shunned and pitied. It has been easy enough to plead exhaustion after moving and because of the pregnancy to avoid seeing the couples that she and Terry usually socialise with. She had allowed them to think that they were moving forward to a better suburb and a bigger house because things were going well for them, instead of telling the truth. Perhaps she should have simply told the truth. Maybe people would have been more accepting of Terry's failing than she thought. Everyone has secrets. Gabby has been hiding so much and now she is suffering because of it. Andrea briefly contemplates calling her parents and asking them for the money for Gabby, but her father would never agree. It's an enormous amount of money, and even if Andrea had it, she wouldn't lend it to someone she has known for such a short time. That amount of money would pay for at least six months' rent on a house, so if she had it, that's what she would be using it for.

Gabby returns from the bathroom, and Andrea can see the slight sheen of perspiration on her face that probably means she threw up. 'Are you okay?' she asks.

'I'll be fine,' says Gabby, going over to the kettle and making herself a cup of peppermint tea. Andrea watches in silence as Gabby sits down and takes a sip and then sighs. 'I'm sorry. I shouldn't have asked you for money. I don't even know where he is. What did I think I was going to do – just fly all over the United States looking for him?'

'You're desperate,' says Andrea. 'It's understandable.'

'You're so lucky with Jack, so lucky to still be in the baby stage. I wish I was still there.'

Andrea nods her head, experiencing a moment of gratefulness that her little boy is safely at pre-school and that he will run to her filled with joy when she goes to pick him up. Gabby has lied to her about a lot of things, but Andrea is lying to those in her life as well. She is no better than Gabby, but Gabby is suffering terrible consequences now and she wants to help. She really does.

'If the police can't be of much help, maybe an appeal on the internet will help you find him,' she says, opening her phone and typing in 'missing child help'. 'Look – there are so many websites where you can post pictures of missing children and missing people. Maybe someone will see it and they can tell you where he is and then at least you'll know where to go.'

'He will hate me if his picture turns up on a site like that,' says Gabby, shaking her head, 'absolutely hate me.' Her shoulders round as she sags under the weight of her son's disdain, her eyes bright with unshed tears.

'But if it means you'll find him? Surely that's—'

'No,' says Gabby. 'No, I need to find another way. You have no idea what this is like. He's my only child and I've done nothing with my life but raise him, and now he's run away from me and that means that I've failed at the one thing I was supposed to be good at. Jack thinks you're perfect, and Flynn used to think the same way, but now everything I do is wrong; I've made nothing but mistakes. I can't make any more mistakes.' Gabby's tears fall without her stopping them, dripping off her chin and breaking Andrea's heart. She silently hands Gabby a fresh tissue from a box on the table and watches as she dabs at her face.

'I wish I could—' she begins, desperate for something comforting to say.

I'm sorry, Andrea,' says Gabby, cutting her off, 'but I think I need some time to just sort this through in my head.' She stands and Andrea knows this is her cue to leave.

Gabby walks her to her front door and just before she heads out, Andrea leans forward and offers Gabby an impulsive hug. 'I'll do anything I can to help. Just let me know. I wish I had the money to give you. I really do.'

Gabby offers her a weak smile. 'I know, and thank you for being my friend. I know that I've held back a lot of stuff, but then... I guess we both have.'

Andrea nods in agreement and leaves Gabby, crossing the road with her mind buzzing.

At home she looks at the posts Gabby has written about Flynn, paying particular attention to the pictures.

If something like this had happened to Andrea, she wouldn't hesitate to use the entire internet to help find her child. She would want the whole world looking for him.

Gabby has been so kind to her and even though her lies have angered Andrea, concealing the truth about how messed up your life really is has almost become a sport these days. Instagram and Facebook are filled with people pretending to be perfect and pretending to live perfect lives.

She walks through to the kitchen and begins stacking dishes

in the dishwasher. If she had the money, would she give it to Gabby? Maybe, maybe not. There would be plenty of people in the world to whom ten thousand dollars meant nothing, but to Andrea it was more than she could imagine ever having again and to Gabby it was a way to find her son. She likes to think she would find a way to at least give some money to Gabby, if she had any.

Andrea stops cleaning and sinks onto a kitchen chair, longing for her bed and the blissful relief of a nap. The house is such a mess despite her recent cleaning. Jack can upend a room in a few minutes and these days she just leaves the mess instead of immediately tidying. She has become a terrible housekeeper. And according to Terry, she's a bad wife and all this stress is bad for the baby, so she ticks the 'bad mother' box as well. She hates that she has to add 'bad friend' to that. There must be something she could do to help Gabby, something that would make a difference. She closes her eyes and has a brief fantasy of Gabby thanking her for helping bring her son home. It would be so good to feel like she's getting something right. It's awful to hear someone say that they have made nothing but mistakes. No mother is perfect and whatever Gabby has done that her son thinks is wrong, she doesn't deserve to lose him forever. There has to be a way to find him, so that they can try and patch up their relationship.

Her phone is on the table in front of her and it flashes with an email from the pre-school about a dress-up day, her screen lighting up with the picture of Jack – and suddenly she has a flash of inspiration, an idea of a way to help.

Gabby says her son will hate her if his picture turns up on the websites to find people, but maybe he can't hate Gabby if it's not Gabby who does it.

If it works, Gabby will be grateful, and even if Flynn doesn't come home but instead calls to berate his mother for putting the picture of him on the website, at least Gabby will know he's safe. And Gabby can always blame her for doing it. She smiles at the brilliance of the idea and then she copies a picture of Flynn from a week ago and sets about putting his picture on as many sites as possible, making sure to state that he is somewhere in the USA and to use her name but encourage people to contact the police.

Maybe someone, somewhere, will know something, and at least, then, she's done something to help.

It is only a few hours until she has to get Jack from school, so she makes herself a toasted cheese filled with sliced tomatoes. She has never really liked tomatoes until this pregnancy but now she loves them.

After eating, she lies down on the sofa for a few minutes, making sure to set two alarms so she doesn't miss pre-school pickup. The red sedan drifts into her dreams, and even asleep she wonders if Terry is telling her the truth.

Waking just before either of the alarms, she is seized by a contraction that takes her breath away. She waits for a few minutes, breathing slowly and paying attention to her body, but the pain is gone and she gratefully gets up. She is not ready for the baby to arrive before she's organised. It will be better if she goes into labour when Terry is home, so he can arrange for his cousin Patricia to come over and babysit Jack. Cousin Patty has always loved Jack and offered to be there for them when the baby arrives when she first heard Andrea was pregnant again.

She feels her aloneness keenly with her own family so remote, and being far away from friends as well. 'You just stay where you are until I have organised cousin Patty to come over,' she tells the baby as she gets herself up and out to the car to fetch Jack. Her drive over is peaceful with no sight of the red sedan.

'I had the best, best day,' shouts Jack when he sees her, running to her and reaching up for her so she can pick him up. She knows she probably shouldn't be lifting him, but she does anyway as he tells her about building a castle in the sandpit and finding his name hidden in three things today, which is something his teacher does as she gets them ready to start learning to read. 'I ate my sandwich and my fruit but then some of my crackers fell on the floor and Miss Lange said I couldn't eat them, so I want some crackers when we get home,' Jack says as they drive.

'That's fine,' she says. 'I have crackers for you.' A contraction grabs at her belly, squeezing hard, and she gasps.

'What's wrong, Mum?' asks Jack.

'Nothing, sweetheart, nothing,' she says as she tries to breathe through the pain. *Not now, not yet. I need more time.*

When she pulls into her driveway, the pain is gone again and she looks down at her phone. How long since the last pain? Getting out of the car, she wonders if she even felt anything at all, but as she picks up Jack's bag another pain grips her, almost sending her to her knees, and she moans.

'Mum?' says Jack, his worried little voice loud in her ear.

'Andrea,' she hears, and Gabby is by her side, helping her stand up straight. 'Are you okay? Is it labour?'

'I don't know.' Andrea breathes slowly as the pain lets go. 'I don't know. It's early but it could be... It could be. I need to text Terry so he can call his cousin.'

'Okay, let me help you, give me your keys so I can unlock your front door. Come on, Jack, let's go inside the house. Come on, it's cold out here.' Andrea hands her the keys she has clutched in her hand. The devastated Gabby from this morning is gone, her voice sure and in command. Andrea lets her open the door to her house and then she sinks onto the sofa as she hears Gabby talking to Jack, telling him to wash his hands and organising a snack for him. Her kitchen is still a mess from this morning but she can't let that bother her now. She calls Terry but his phone goes to voicemail, so she calls again and again and again. Why isn't he answering?

In desperation, she calls the store.

'Wilson Electronics, Baz speaking. How can I help you?' Baz answers.

'Oh,' she says, feeling herself flush. She always finds herself a little flustered when speaking to Baz, as though she might inadvertently let slip Terry's misdeeds and get him fired. 'Hi, Baz, I'm so sorry to bother you. I was just looking for Terry... I wanted to—'

'Terry didn't come in today,' says Baz, his tone going from friendly manager to strident boss in a second. 'He called in sick. Isn't he sick? He said he had a nasty cold.'

'I... I...' Andrea stutters, and then with no idea what to do, she simply hangs up the phone.

Gabby comes into the living room from the kitchen. 'Jack's playing on his iPad. I hope that's okay. I thought you might need a few minutes to call everyone.'

'I can't get hold of Terry,' says Andrea, a thousand thoughts running through her mind. Where is he? What is he doing? How could he do this to her now? He knows how close she is to going into labour.

She checks the app, but Terry has turned his location off. This morning when he spoke to her, he was lying about where he was. Lying and dismissing her concerns over the man in the red sedan. She cannot even begin to think how to deal with this situation. She is suddenly burning up and she pulls at her top, needing to get some air on her skin.

'Tell me what you need me to do,' says Gabby, and Andrea bites down on her lip, trying to get her thoughts straight.

'I need to get to the hospital in case this is labour, but I also need someone to stay with Jack while I try and get hold of Patricia.'

'I can stay with him and I can call you an Uber or I can drive you there – whatever you need,' says Gabby.

Andrea is so grateful for Gabby's presence she wants to cry, but she can't fall apart now.

'I'll call an Uber,' she says, standing up slowly, 'and you stay with Jack and tell Terry what has happened when he comes home.' She thinks for a moment. 'If he comes home,' she adds softly. Everything she has been afraid of is happening, her worst nightmares come true. She has no one around to help her and her husband is off wasting what little money they have instead of here so she can feel like things are under control.

'Oh, Andrea, love, I am so sorry but don't worry. It's going to be fine. You get where you need to go, and I will take care of everything.'

Andrea knows the only way to keep from collapsing into a tearful heap is to keep moving, so she orders her Uber and goes to get her hospital bag from her bedroom, stopping only to kiss Jack on her way out and tell him to be good for Gabby and listen to whatever Gabby tells him to do. She thinks briefly about what Gabby is dealing with right now, with the loss the woman is trying to cope with, but she cannot put her baby in jeopardy. The last time she left Jack with Gabby drifts through her mind, but it won't be like that now. They know each other better and Andrea will have her phone nearby and it's not as if she has any choice at all. Her husband is not answering his phone.

In the Uber, she calls Patricia, who doesn't answer so she sends a text, knowing that Patricia is at work in the retirement home, where she is the activities director. All the way to the hospital she calls Terry's phone over and again.

The journey to the hospital takes twenty minutes and it's only once she's there and inside the building that she realises that she has not had even a hint of a pain. She has been concentrating so hard on making sure to send messages and trying to call Terry that she hasn't noticed the absence of pain. Was she in labour at all? She's heard that sometimes extreme stress can stop labour from progressing. And she is very stressed right now.

She wants to simply turn around and go home, but as she enters the emergency waiting room, a nurse comes towards her. 'Can I help you? What's brought you here today?' the woman asks, eyeing Andrea's belly.

'I'm not sure... It may be labour, but I'm not sure.'

'Best to find out,' says the nurse, and Andrea feels the possibility of returning home disappear.

Emergency departments ebb and flow with the times of day and she can see a whole lot of mothers with school-age children sitting on the grey plastic chairs, but she is still triaged immediately, taken into a small room where there is a chair and a blood pressure machine and the kind nurse with a comforting voice and her hair in a neat bun.

'Let's check your blood pressure first,' says the nurse, and Andrea can imagine how high it will be as her heart races with all the possibilities of where her husband is and what he's doing.

TWENTY
GABBY

She feels better once Andrea is safely in the Uber on her way to the hospital. All thoughts of Flynn and what she's going to do about finding her son disappear for a few minutes. But once Andrea is gone and she is watching Jack giggle with delight every time he manages to guess the first letter of a simple word on the game on his iPad, her missing son consumes her again.

Andrea has no money and cannot help her at all. She misjudged that situation entirely. But her Facebook page is still operating. She's not just someone who goes through life with only a plan A. She has a whole host of other ideas brewing already.

Sitting down on Andrea's musty-smelling sofa, she opens her phone and uploads a message she has ready, having written and rewritten it this morning until she was satisfied that it carried the right tone and that it would get her the help she needed.

This will probably be my last post on this page. I know that I have only recently shared that I was having difficulties with my son, but the truth is, things have been hard for a long time.

Teenagers can be difficult. They are at the mercy of their hormones and their need for independence when they are not quite ready for it. They push against boundaries and fight you on everything, but for most parents it's easy to see that there is a light at the end of the tunnel. They grow out of the difficult stage, as I have read and I am sure you have read again and again. But there is no light for me. There is no end to this situation because my son, my beautiful son, has left me. He has run away to find his father, despite knowing that his father is not interested in him. I concealed our divorce from you because I was so ashamed, but as bad as divorce was, it's nothing compared to this pain, the pain of losing Flynn. He has left Australia for the US and I have no idea where he has gone or how to get him back.

The only thing I am sure of is that if I do manage to get to the US, if I do manage to get on a plane and get myself there, I have a chance to find him and beg him to come home. But I do not have the money for such a journey. Everything I have I have given to my child, and I am without funds for even a simple plane ticket. So, even as I vowed I would never do something like this, I am asking for your help. I have set up a GoFundMe page. I know that everyone is struggling in this economy. I know that we all have our troubles, but even a few dollars will help me – whatever you can give, I will be eternally grateful for.

Gabby hesitates for a moment before adding the link to the page that she reluctantly set up this morning after she had spoken to Andrea. Where else was she supposed to get the money? She has thousands of people who follow her. If everyone gave just ten dollars, she would be able to get a flight and have some money to fund her search. Surely people will be happy to give just a little. Even the price of a cup of coffee will help. She thinks about this and then adds that thought to the post. When you simplify money to the price of a cup of coffee, most people feel embarrassed not to give.

Taking a deep breath, she uploads the post, knowing that judgement will come thick and fast, but also knowing that there will be people willing to help – because there are always people willing to help.

It's taken her hours to convince herself that she should do it. But there are no choices left. She needs the money and she needs to find Flynn. She pictures her son wandering around an airport with no idea of where to go and what to do, tears pricking at his eyes as he tries to disguise his confused state, and her heart breaks for him. If only she had backed off when he asked her to. She will put up another post saying this if she doesn't manage to get enough donations on the GoFundMe page from this first one.

The first comment comes from a woman in Melbourne. *So sorry for what's happened to you. I can only give you ten dollars, but I hope it helps get you there.*

Gabby clicks 'love' so the woman knows how grateful she is, and then another comment comes in, and another and another. The amounts are all small, all just tokens, but she has thousands of followers and every little bit helps. She clicks over to the GoFundMe page and watches as the amount rises, up at three hundred dollars already.

The trolling keyboard warriors appear as well.

You shouldn't ask others for help to clean up your mess.

You always told everyone what to do and how dare you give advice when your own life was such a mess.

You're a fraud of a mother and a person.

The last comment makes her wince but then she looks at

the page again and the figure keeps going up. Some angry words are a small price to pay. She has set the amount she needs at five thousand dollars. That's all she really needs to start with.

'I'm finished my game, now what?' asks Jack, and Gabby smiles at the little boy as an idea of such perfection blossoms inside her that she wants to giggle at the absolute brilliance of her mind. 'Come with me to my house and you can play with the dinosaurs,' she says and Jack happily accompanies her across the road where he is soon distracted by the dinosaurs as he creates a world for them to roam in.

At her kitchen table, she watches him while she does what she needs to do, while her plan takes shape. Half an hour later she is ready. 'Time to pack up,' she tells Jack.

'But what can I do now?' he asks as he reluctantly gathers up the dinosaurs.

'Now you and I are going to have a wonderful adventure together,' she says. Jack's smile is the only sign she needs that this is the right thing to do.

Was this always what she was going to do? Probably. She has been working towards it since she met Andrea, without even knowing that she was.

Richard will be angry with her, in real life this time, but she doesn't care. This is not like anything she has ever done before, but she's feeling the need to do something drastic, something dramatic. *You, you, you, it's always about you – selfish, evil girl.* There is a twinge of pain across her back where the cane came down and actually fractured a rib. She had been brought home by a policewoman.

Her mother had opened the door, her face already set in grim lines, knowing that her daughter had, once more, done something to shame her. She had been trying to steal a car. A silly move, since she only understood the barest concept of driving, but she was looking for a way out. Obviously, she had been caught just as she broke the back passenger window with a brick. She can smile indulgently at the ridiculous teenager she was, but she was also consumed with a terrible, desperate need to escape.

Her mother sent her to her room and conferred with the policewoman, agreed to make sure she got to court for her charges. And then the woman who gave birth to her came into her room and dragged her out, threw her on the ground and unleashed her fury. It was easier for Gabby to just lie there until it was over.

She had been fifteen at the time and she had waited until her mother was asleep and crept out of the small apartment into the, thankfully, warm summer night air. Her whole body ached and breathing in too deeply felt impossible. She had carried only a backpack and the knowledge that she needed to never go home again. Walking to another state would have to do. It hadn't been easy, but Richard had helped her. There is one person she has always been able to rely on and that's Richard. His love for her will never change or die. While he will be angry, will lecture her on the mistake she is determined to make, he will forgive her eventually. He always does.

Flynn has run away, but Flynn is sixteen and almost an adult. Jack is only three and sweet and adorable. He will photograph beautifully.

Two hours later, Andrea is on her way home, her phone clutched in her hand as she continually tries to contact Terry. Everyone at the hospital had been kind, concerned and patient, from the first nurse who took all her details and checked her sky-high blood pressure to the obstetric registrar who came as soon as she could and examined Andrea. Fortunately, as she lay on a narrow bed and practised calming her mind, her blood pressure dropped enough for everyone to feel comfortable sending her home. She had turned to Facebook to try and distract herself and seen Gabby's post about her son and her friend's honest, open pleading for help broke her heart. Despite everything Gabby was going through, she was still helping Andrea by looking after Jack. Even knowing she had little money to spare, Andrea clicked on the link and donated ten dollars so at least she felt like she had contributed.

Thankfully, the baby was fine. The contractions were Braxton Hicks and her blood pressure dropped quickly enough for them to tell her that she could leave but would need to call her doctor in the morning for an appointment.

'You can't admit me. I have no one to take care of my son,'

she told them, and the devastating truth of those words made her want to be sick. Terry was not answering his phone and he was not at work.

'Anything like this with the first one?' the dark-eyed young registrar asked.

'I did have one false alarm but I was still five weeks away, so I was really worried that there might be a problem. I didn't know what to expect. I'm only a week away now, so I thought it had to be the real thing.'

'Yes, I would have thought so too, but you're not dilated at all and the baby is not in position yet. It can happen really quickly, but my guess is that you've a few more days to go yet. It's not an exact science, but if you go home and put your feet up, that's probably for the best. I'm going to run some tests before we send you home, just to make sure everything is okay. Is there anyone you need us to contact for you?'

Lying on the hard, clinical-smelling bed, Andrea had stared up at the ceiling as she shook her head and tried not to cry.

'Okay then, it shouldn't be much longer,' the doctor said, touching her gently on the hand as though she understood some of Andrea's fear and worry, but she had no idea of everything Andrea was dealing with, of just how terrified she was.

Andrea had submitted to the blood and urine tests in silence, her thoughts focused on her missing husband and on controlling her anger so that her blood pressure didn't rise again. She thanked God for Gabby being there, and she texted Patricia to let her know it had been a false alarm. Patricia responded with a thumbs-up and a message: *Looking forward to time with the little man. If I don't respond immediately, here's the number for reception of the home. They can always get hold of me. xx*

The kind message made it harder for Andrea not to cry. She should not have been the one texting Patricia.

It is after six when she is finally on the way home and she texts Gabby to let her know but receives no response. She hopes

Gabby has given Jack some dinner. The thought of having to do anything except slide into bed is overwhelming. Terry has still not answered his phone.

'You all right to get out?' the Uber driver asks her as he pulls up in front of her dark house.

'I'm fine, thanks,' she says, grabbing her bag and walking up the front path as quickly as she can. She wants to be inside, out of the cold and away from his concerned face. Everyone, it seems, is worried about Andrea, except for the man who should be worried about her. Her husband is nowhere to be seen.

She switches on lights as she walks through the house and puts her bag back in her bedroom cupboard, ready to come out again for the real labour. She's had it packed for weeks now just in case. Gabby still hasn't responded.

Andrea would love to take a shower and have something hot to drink but it's not fair to Gabby to leave Jack with her any longer.

Standing still for a moment, she closes her eyes and breathes deeply. *I can handle this. I am fine. I will get Jack and then I will call my parents to come to Sydney tomorrow so that they are here for the birth. I will deal with this and I will be fine.*

In the living room, she switches on the heater to warm up the house and then she opens the front door, switching on the outside light, her phone still clutched in her hand. The autumn wind slaps her in the face and she wants to get her coat but decides against it.

She is standing at her front door, her keys in her hand, when the car, the red sedan with one unmatched door, screeches into the street, squealing to a stop in front of her house, filling the air with noise and the smell of burnt rubber. The streetlight flickers as if disturbed and she squeezes her keys in her hand, her heart racing.

The wind whips around the house, scattering soggy brown leaves as the car idles in front of her house, the engine growling with menace in the dark. Andrea's pulse pounds in her throat, making it hard to swallow.

The back passenger door opens and she squints, trying to see inside, frozen where she is standing, her muscles tense.

Terry emerges from the back seat, his body falling onto the street in a heap. With the door still open, the car roars off into the night, leaving behind the tortured tyre smell and her husband crumpled on the ground.

She cannot move, cannot even think what to do, but inside her the baby kicks frantically.

Terry doesn't move and the words 'he's dead' fill her mind. She starts towards him, holding the keys so tightly in her hand they are cutting into her skin. As she gets to where he is, he groans and uncurls, looking up at her, both eyes swollen and puffy, blue-black bruises visible in the yellow glow from the streetlight.

She looks around her, relieved that no one else is on the street, relieved they are alone as she struggles for something to say, something to do.

Their gazes meet and he stands, slowly, painfully limping towards her. She takes a step back.

'I've messed up,' he says, his throat hoarse. 'I've messed up really badly.'

Everything she has been worrying about, all her fears, are dancing around her with the wind. Here it is now, the very worst-case scenario. Not just a man in a garage, not just a house that needs to be sold, not just a problem she didn't know about, but so much worse. Because here they are with nothing to sell and no way to help themselves, and even though he knew that, he understood it – he did it again. Every morning he kissed his son and left his family in a house that was only theirs because someone else was paying, and he took the money he earned and gambled it away, chasing his own tail in a stupid circle. All these weeks he has been earning commission and probably not telling her about the big sales, and instead of putting the money away for future rent, he has blown it. He has taken small amounts from their account again and again, hoping she wouldn't notice and then yelling at her when she did. And then, when he had nothing left to feed his habit, he has gone to the kind of people who beat you up and break your fingers. He has taken loans that he can't pay back, knowing what they will do to him as he chases the high of a win on a football game. Now his life is in danger – and by extension hers. Hers and Jack's. A hideous split-second thought comes to her mind: *I wish they had killed you.*

He hangs his head, weighed down by shame. She will not comfort him, will not understand.

'Jack is with Gabby,' she says. 'I went... Jack is with Gabby. I need to get him.'

She hurries across the street, leaving her husband standing in the front yard. At Gabby's house every light is on, and when she gets closer she realises that the front door is open.

'Gabby?' she calls as she walks in. 'It's Andrea... Gabby?' The cold blows in through the open door, chilling the air. Gabby's house looks subtly different, although Andrea cannot say why. Everything is still the same and yet it's not.

She keeps walking through the silent house and then catches her breath when she gets to the living room.

Small things jump out at her, like the landscape on the wall hanging askew, the door to the buffet open and a plate smashed on the ground next to it, the armchair moved out of position. All of the silver-framed photographs are gone, every single one of them. She moves through the living room. On the floor near the sofa is a pile of silver frames, the glass fronts cracked or smashed, every one of them empty, bits of glass sprinkled on the blue rug.

Except for the mess, the house looks like a blank canvas, like no one lives here but the furniture.

Andrea's chest tightens, her heart speeds up as she makes her way to the kitchen, where there is chaos everywhere. All the cabinet doors are open as though someone was looking for something. In the sink is a broken mug and the blue plastic cup Gabby always gave Jack to drink from. Andrea peers at it, sure she can see a spot of red blood on the mug. A kitchen chair lies on its side and the gold tablecloth is in a heap on the floor. Her foot angles as she steps on something small, and she looks down to see a dinosaur, and then she spots another and another; they are strewn everywhere. What has happened here?

'Gabby,' she calls as she moves to the stairs, 'Gabby,' frantic now, her heart hammering as she darts up the blue carpeted stairs. 'Gabby... Jack, Jack, Jack!'

The house is empty. The main bedroom has all the cupboards flung open but all the clothes remain. Stepping closer, Andrea tries to see if she recognises any of Gabby's outfits but nothing is familiar. There are also clothes that seem to belong to a man, but that can't be right. Richard has never lived here.

She moves quickly to the second and third bedrooms, one of which obviously belongs to Flynn, but there is no one there. She cannot believe this is happening again. Her stomach churns and she rushes for the bathroom, flinging open doors because she is not sure where it is, finding a linen cupboard first and then an upstairs study before she reaches the bathroom, where she falls to her knees and throws up until there is nothing left in her stomach. Where is her son? Where is he?

Standing slowly, her legs shaking, her face covered in sweat, Andrea moves to the basin and rinses her mouth. In the mirrored cabinet she sees a woman utterly lost, with slicked-down hair and blue-white lips. She is numb with fear and she cannot force herself to move. Without thinking, she pulls open the cabinet. It contains nothing terribly different from her own medicine cabinet, but on the top shelf is a small packet of pills and she reaches for them, picking them up and staring at the label.

BEN JAMESON: TAKE TWO PER DAY UNTIL FINISHED.

In the box there is only one pill left in the packet. Ben, whoever he is, obviously missed the last pill and did not throw out the packet. But who is Ben? If Gabby is renting this house, just like she is renting hers, then why would the owners have left some things behind?

'Andy,' she hears Terry calling from downstairs, and she makes her way out of the bathroom, taking the stairs carefully, everything inside her twisting in turmoil. Her husband looks as bad as she does.

'What happened here?' he says. 'I read, I got... all your messages. I don't understand – where is Jack?'

'We need to call the police,' says Andrea. 'I think Gabby has taken him and I don't...' She starts to cry but bites down on her lip to stop her tears, 'I don't know who she really is or what's happening. Where have you been, Terry? All day – where have you been?' She finally loses her fight with herself and sinks onto the bottom stair, dropping her head into her hand and allowing a guttural cry to emerge from inside her. She is exhausted and weak, and she has no idea how she's going to find her son. Terry touches her on the shoulder, his hand resting there while she cries, as he repeats, 'I'm so sorry, I'm so sorry. I told them I would get the money. They said they would leave you and Jack alone if I got them the money, but I just...'

After a few minutes, Andrea clenches her fists and stands up, sniffing. 'We need to call the police. Either Gabby has taken him or the men you owe money to have him. We've got to find him. We need the police.'

'They'll kill me, Andy. If I tell anyone about them taking me today, they'll kill me.' His blue eyes widen with terror.

A wave of fury roars inside her and she lifts her hands and slaps her husband across his face, and then she slaps his chest and his arm and any other part of him she can get to, her fear and adrenaline driving her to do something she has never imagined doing. 'I don't care, I don't care, I don't care,' she yells. 'My baby, my baby is gone because of you!'

'Please, Andy, please. I'm sorry, I'm sorry,' he says, covering his face with his hands, and she stops to take a breath as the baby inside her pushes furiously as though trying to escape. What kind of child will this little girl be? What kind of a person is born out of all the stress and fear and sadness that Andy has been feeding her?

She steps back, away from Terry, and grits her teeth. Her words emerge in a strangled hiss. 'I don't care,' she says. 'I don't care.' Right now, she wishes him dead. She would trade her own life for Jack's in a second, but she knows that Terry doesn't feel that way. If he did, he would never have done what he's done, would never have put his family in danger like this.

Leaving Terry standing in Gabby's entrance hall, she walks across the road to her house and finds her phone in her bag, her fingers immediately dialling triple zero to contact emergency services.

'My son has been kidnapped,' she says to the man who answers the phone. 'He's only three and he's been kidnapped.' And then she stands in the house, the front door open, watching Terry limp back across the street with his phone pressed to his ear, no doubt trying to find out if those he owes money to have his son. The night air is freezing. Thick clouds cover the stars and only the slight glow of the shrouded streetlights makes it possible to see anything.

Andrea answers one question after another until the man says, 'They'll be there soon,' and she can hang up and drop onto the sofa to wait. She is nauseous and exhausted, defeated by everything that has happened in her life, not just today but over the last nine months, and she would like to close her eyes and never wake up again.

What will she do if Jack never comes home? If her blue-eyed baby boy is never sitting at the breakfast table again, singing a song he made up that morning about dinosaurs? What then?

TWENTY-TWO

GABBY

In her pocket is the email she printed out, filled with all the information she asked for on the red sedan. When the email came in, just as she made her decision about Jack, just as she knew exactly what she was going to do, she took it as a sign from the universe that she was doing the right thing.

She printed it out and read through it a few times as Jack played with the dinosaurs one last time, and she sat at the kitchen table one last time, not that she told him that.

Once he agreed to an adventure, clapping his hands with glee, they had gone back across the road together to Andrea's house. Together, she and Jack had chosen enough clothes to fill his Hot Wheels backpack, and he had also taken his stuffed tiger from his bed because Gabby said, 'Tigers love adventures.' Back at her house, she had fed him a healthy snack so that he would not be hungry. She had no idea how long Andrea would be at the hospital. If she was having the baby, it would be ages, but if it was a false alarm, she could return any minute.

Just waiting to see the doctor – may be a false alarm, Andrea had texted. *Thanks so much for staying with him. Terry should be home soon and I probably won't be here much longer.*

Please don't stress. He's with me at my house and everything is fine. I won't let you down. Just make sure the baby is okay, she had replied, knowing then that she would have to move quickly. Terry could return at any moment as the day moved from late afternoon to early evening. That's when Gabby called the cab and packed up the small suitcase she carried with her whenever she moved.

The red sedan is owned by a career criminal who works for some very nasty people as a debt collector. If she had known this information this morning, she would never have asked Andrea for money, but she wasn't sure exactly who the man in the red car was – that's why she asked Richard for help. Regardless, she is happy enough with how things have turned out. Lying to Andrea about not being in touch with Richard had been necessary. It made her seem more pathetic, more in need of help, but in a few hours no more lies to Andrea will be needed.

In the taxi, Jack is happily digging through the small bag of dinosaurs she allowed him to choose to pack, promising him, 'We'll come back for the rest later.'

It had been good of the taxi driver to stay with Jack while she went back into the house 'to get a few things', but, in reality, to make sure that she left everything in a mess. Let them wonder what happened. Let them believe it had to do with the money Terry owed. It was perfect, so perfect she found herself smiling, unable to contain her joy. The universe wanted her to have Jack. Otherwise, why would everything have fallen so beautifully into place? It's the only explanation. She smiled as she smashed the picture frames, quickly dragging out pictures of Flynn.

It's always satisfying to leave a mess. Anyone who rents out their house on Airbnb should know that there are going to be people who leave the place in a state. She's never left a mess like that before, but she needed to sell the nefarious-people angle.

That will be the first place the police look when they are called, because they will definitely be called.

'Where are we going?' asks Jack, his little brow furrowed.

'The airport,' says Gabby. 'We're going to Queensland where there is sun and it's warm. We'll fly to the Gold Coast where there are lots of hotels and so many beaches.' She likes the idea of the Gold Coast, a place where she can easily disappear amongst all the tourists. They will be hard to find there. Rows of hotels and apartment blocks line the beach and there are people in and out all the time. She can imagine how hard it would be for police to find a woman with a young child since the place is crawling with young families on holiday all the time. She's been there just once for a few days when she first arrived in Australia, but it was too crowded, too noisy, and every restaurant she went into had a child throwing a screaming tantrum or a table full of slightly drunk teenagers. It is the perfect place to get lost.

'But what about Mum?' he asks, walking a dinosaur up and down on the door handle. Outside, the sky grows darker as the wind whips through the trees they pass. Gabby risks a glance at the taxi driver, who is staring at her in the rear-view mirror. She would really like Jack to just keep quiet, but he deserves an answer to the question. She speaks loudly and clearly, making sure the silent man driving the car hears her answer.

'Well, you know how Mum is going to have a new baby sister for you?'

'Mm-hmm,' nods Jack as he makes two dinosaurs fight each other.

'The exciting thing is that the baby is coming now, and Mum has gone to the hospital and Dad is with her, and I told them I would take care of you for a few days until they could come home. I thought that you and the dinosaurs would like to have a lovely little trip to see the beaches in Queensland.'

'But Mum said that when she had the baby cousin Patty

was coming and she is going to do drawing with me and she is going to stay with me. Patty can draw the best in the whole family,' he says with certainty.

'Cousin Patty had to work,' Gabby says quickly. She hadn't factored in Jack knowing about arrangements for when the baby arrived.

She risks another glance in the mirror and feels her skin prickle at the way the man is staring at her. The cab has a strong pine smell from the air freshener hanging from the rear-view mirror and Gabby wrinkles her nose. She hates the smell. It reminds her of the bathroom she had to use every day growing up with her mother. Pine-scented disinfectant was sprayed liberally everywhere all the time and all she can think of when she smells the horribly familiar smell are the nights she spent on the street after she had run away, as she tried to figure a way forward. She had to use some filthy bathrooms then, until Richard caught up with her. She doesn't think she would have survived without Richard, but she's capable of surviving without him now. She doesn't want to, but she will if she has to. *I'm not that girl anymore. I'm the adult now and I'm in charge and I've got this all under control*, she reminds herself. She wishes the cab would drive faster, wanting to get to the airport and onto a plane before Andrea or Terry even return home.

'Can I get a milkshake?' says Jack. 'Like last time.' And she wants to celebrate because the man takes his eyes off her and returns them to the road, obviously having decided that she is a legitimate caregiver.

'Of course you can, love,' she says indulgently.

She allows herself a moment of thought about Andrea, but the woman is pregnant and in a matter of days or maybe even hours she will have another child. Jack will be better off with her. She needs some time alone with him so she can figure out how this is going to work. Once they get to Queensland, she can dye his hair so he looks different. She smiles, feeling bold and brave. This is a big step forward. A missing child gets some sympathy, but not enough. An unwell child, however, is sure to lead to many, many donations. She wouldn't hurt Jack, of course she wouldn't, but people on the internet are so stupid, all with their hearts on their sleeves as they search for ways to help others. Gabby has never wanted to help anyone except herself.

You are selfish and nasty, she hears her mother spit, but her mother was the nasty one. Her mother was the one who made Gabby feel like an unworthy human being. It's so sad that she has received more love from people on the internet than she ever did from her own mother. She will not be a mother like that to Jack. She will make him feel worthy and loved, and even if she stretches the truth a little on her Facebook posts about his needs, he will still feel loved every single day.

'Virgin terminal?' the taxi driver asks. Gabby has already booked tickets for her and Jack. She's glad she brought a suitcase and Jack's backpack. Travelling with a small child without those things would have looked suspicious.

'Yes, thanks,' she tells the taxi driver as he slides to a stop at the right terminal at the airport. She and Jack climb out of the taxi and then she waits patiently for the driver to take her suitcase out of his boot. She pays him in cash, making sure to tip him only a small amount. Taxi drivers remember those who leave big tips, and she doesn't want this man to remember her at all. She used a fake name when she booked, one she has a driver's licence for. Janet Jones is flying with her son Jack because she would never change the child's name. Janet Jones and Jack Jones – they could not be more ordinary. She is wearing her big coat with the collar up, so she feels like she's done as much as she can to avoid detection.

'Come on, young man,' she says, extending a hand for Jack to hold. 'Let's start our adventure.'

'Yay,' says Jack, clutching his bag of dinosaurs, his backpack on his back. He's so easy, so sweet, so different from a moody sixteen-year-old that Gabby cannot help the streak of pure happiness that runs through her. Flynn can stay with his father. Gabby is starting again and this time she's going to get it right.

In the airport, after checking in and securing their boarding passes, she treats Jack to a hamburger and chips, making sure he eats enough so he doesn't get hungry. She buys him a chocolate bar as well, but tells him he is only allowed to eat it on the plane because she doesn't need him having a sugar meltdown before they get on their flight. As she walks towards the departure gate, her phone buzzes in her pocket.

Hey, I haven't heard from you – everything okay? The text makes her heart race because she hasn't shared her plans and she doesn't want to just yet, but Richard hates it when she doesn't keep him in the loop, as he likes to say. It takes only a minute to type up a text and send it. Once he reads it, he is sure to understand that this is a good move for both of them. It's a fresh start and a new life. He will be happy for her, for both of them, she's sure.

She doesn't have to wait long for Richard's return text but when it arrives, it's not what she wanted at all – not at all.

OH MY GOD, WHAT HAVE YOU DONE?

Gabby clicks her tongue and deletes the text. She doesn't need him to scold her. She's the mother, not him, and she knows what she's doing.

Through the windows in the food court at the airport, she can see that it's already dark, even though it's still only early evening. She is sure the light will be different in Queensland. The air will be warmer, the sky will be bluer and she will be a mother of a young child.

Over the loudspeaker, their flight is called, and Gabby clutches their boarding passes, giddy with excitement like a schoolgirl on her first trip away. Her whole life is about to change in the most wonderful way.

'Come on, Jack, aeroplane time,' she says, holding out her hand, and he stands and puts his small hand in hers. 'Here we go.'

'Here we go,' he shouts happily.

TWENTY-THREE
ANDREA

Unable to sit still, Andrea stands and begins pacing back and forth across the living room, as Terry stands by the sofa, his hands jammed into his pockets. 'I can't believe this,' she mutters over and over again, unable to process what has happened. It's only been a few minutes since she called the police, but it feels like hours already. Andrea can feel her son getting further and further away from her with every passing second.

'Please don't tell them about what happened to me today,' Terry suddenly begs, and Andrea stops her pacing, shakes her head.

'What if both Gabby and Jack have been taken by whoever you owe money to?' she says, trying to contain her surging anger.

'That's not what happened,' Terry says, folding his arms. 'I just blurted those words out, but they told me they would give me two more days... before they...' He stops speaking.

'Before they *what*?' she shouts, shaking a fist at him. 'Took your child? Killed your wife? Before they bloody what, Terry? How could you do this? What kind of a person puts their family in danger like this? Who are you to do this to me, to us?' She wants to put her hands around his neck and squeeze until the life leaves his eyes. The hatred she feels for him is dark and twisting and she can feel it taking over her body.

'They wouldn't do that. They wouldn't take a child. They told me and I think I can—'

'DON'T YOU DARE TELL ME YOU CAN TRUST THEM!' she roars and Terry steps back against a wall as though blown into a corner by the force of her fury.

There isn't time for any more conversation as the police arrive in their driveway, no siren but flashing lights casting blue and red eerily over the dark yard and through the window. With one more furious grimace at Terry, Andrea opens the front door.

She watches as a woman and two uniformed constables climb out of the car and walk towards her.

'Detective Sergeant Abigail Eddison,' says the woman, holding her hand out to Andrea as Terry shrinks back into the living room. The detective is a tall thin woman with deep-set blue eyes and a roman nose, her grey hair tied back in a severe bun. 'Why don't you tell me what happened,' she says to Andrea after a quick glance at Terry once they are all inside the house.

'I thought...' begins Andrea and then she explains about her false labour and her dash to the hospital as the detective nods and makes notes on a small pad of paper she is carrying.

'And you were where, sir?' asks the detective once Andrea has stopped speaking.

'Not here,' says Andrea bitterly, 'not answering his phone.' The detective looks from her to Terry and then makes another note.

'Right, if you could both just stay here while we take a quick look across the road,' the detective instructs. 'Liv, can you just look through this house while we do that, please,' she commands the female constable.

'He's not in our house,' says Terry.

'Just procedure,' says the constable named Liv. 'If you could just sit down, I won't be long.' She smiles; the gesture, just a quick movement of her mouth, contains nothing genuine. There is nothing to smile about.

As the police are searching their house and Gabby's house, Andrea finds herself watching the time on her mobile phone. *One minute, two minutes, three minutes, how far away could they get in three minutes?*

Finally, the detective and the constables are back in the living room and Andrea takes a deep breath as the detective starts asking questions.

'How long have you known your neighbour?' she asks.

'Only for a few weeks,' Andrea says, a sickly creeping guilt dousing the flames of her fury at Terry. How could she have left Jack with Gabby? 'She's not a bad person. I think... I think that she's been taken with Jack.'

'Taken by who?' asks the detective. Andrea turns to Terry and says, 'Why don't you explain, Terry, and maybe show the detective the other bruises I'm sure you have.' The detective has obviously already registered his black eyes, so she probably knew something was coming.

Terry's face turns a green shade of pale as he clenches his fists and takes a deep breath, and then Andrea listens as he confesses everything, holding nothing back, she hopes. The detective's face remains impassive as she occasionally nods while she writes things down.

Andrea wants to feel some sympathy for Terry as he stumbles through his explanation, but all she's concentrating on is that he is telling the truth.

The detective does not react to Terry explaining about betting on football games with anything more than a slightly raised eyebrow, and as Andrea watches she is slightly comforted by the detective's calm demeanour. It seems as though the woman has seen all of this before and that must mean that she knows what to do, knows how to find Andrea's son. All that matters now is finding Jack and getting him home safe.

'But I told my wife,' Terry says. 'I told her that these people, they aren't the kind who take children. I've been with them all day... They stopped me before I even got to work and made me call Baz. They kept me...' He sighs. 'They... they let me know I had two days to get the money to them and I said I would borrow it from my father-in-law. He has the money and I promised I would get it.' In her mind, Andrea sees Terry sitting in some abandoned building, his captors hitting him as he promises to get the money. She wants to feel sorry for him, for what he's been through today, but she cannot find an ounce of empathy inside herself for her reckless husband.

'What if they didn't believe you?' she asks dully. She is sitting on the rocking chair she has left in the living room until they finish building the cot in the room that would be used for Gemma. She loves the chair, made from honey-coloured timber with a soft blue and yellow padded cushion her mother stitched for her and sent up for her to use. It is the place she fed Jack, watching the night move to dawn when he was a baby, and she had imagined many sleepy but happy hours in the chair with Gemma. Even as she sits, she can feel the beginnings of contractions passing through her body, but they are not overwhelming and she cannot have this baby until her son is home. It's not something she can contemplate. They are probably still Braxton Hicks contractions anyway, her body's way of telling her to get ready. In a way, she embraces the pain as it ripples through her, needing to feel something other than fear and guilt and even shame as the detective talks to Terry. Perhaps the woman is wondering how she could have married someone like him, or how she could have stayed married to him. She rubs her hands over her belly, the words to the song 'Hush Little Baby' running through her head, wanting to calm herself and her unborn child as she remembers Terry standing next to her as she laboured with Jack. He had held her hand as the contractions took hold and smoothed her hair back, speaking quietly and continuously, 'I love you... You can do this... You're amazing... You're incredible.' She had held on to those words, drawing strength from his belief in her as the time came to push.

Terry looks at her, and in his blue eyes she can see a depth of pain she wishes she could respond to, wishes she could feel something for him aside from this vicious, hateful anger – but her son is gone, her little boy, and she doesn't know how she will live without him.

'And you don't think that Gabby, your neighbour, could have taken your son as your husband is suggesting?' the detective asks her now.

Andrea shakes her head. 'You've seen the house,' she says. 'Why would Gabby do that to her own... I mean, it's not her house, but it's where she lives, so why would she have made such a mess?'

The detective nods. 'Yes... that is something we have to think about. I have an Amber Alert out for Jack, so the whole country is now looking for him.'

Andrea nods, tears spilling and falling onto her chest. She cannot believe she is living this surreal nightmare.

There is a knock at the door and one of the constables says, 'That's probably forensics. I'll take them across the road to begin,' as he walks towards the door to open it. But it is not another policeman at the door. Instead, it is a man with grey-brown hair and hazel eyes, tall and well built. He is dressed in an expensive dark grey suit and a light grey shirt, a yellow tie a pop of colour in the gloomy evening. He looks like a lawyer or a banker, someone who works in the city.

'Excuse me,' he says. 'I'm looking for Andrea Gately.'

'Yes,' says the detective, standing from the kitchen chair she has been sitting on, 'and you are?'

'My name is Richard Burrell,' says the man.

'What can I do for you, Mr Burrell?' asks the detective. Andrea feels her body tense, and for a moment she has no idea why, but then she remembers the one picture Gabby showed her, the picture on her phone of a man. 'That's my husband,' she had said before quickly scrolling past to get to another picture of her son. Andrea had only seen the picture briefly but she recognises him now. She slowly stands and walks towards him. 'Richard, you're Richard,' she says.

'Yes,' he agrees, 'and you're—'

'You're Gabby's ex-husband,' she interrupts him, 'but I thought you were in the USA?'

'I'm not,' says the man, running his hands through his hair, messing his neat hairstyle. 'I mean, I'm not in the USA, but I'm not her ex-husband either.' He has a strong American accent and he looks tired.

The words settle in the air, and Andrea hears them but she's not sure she has heard them correctly. How can that be possible? She covers both ears with her hands and presses down for a moment, certain that the problem is with her hearing. 'What?' she says.

'I'm not her ex-husband,' Richard says slowly, as though he thinks she is having trouble understanding him, and she feels like she must be, because how can this be the case?

'But she said you were divorced. She said Flynn had run away to try and find you,' she says, her voice shrill and desperate. How can another lie be possible?

'It's... it's complicated,' says the man, and he runs his hands through his hair again, his discomfort obvious. He shakes his head and then straightens his already straight tie. 'Can I come in and explain? There's so much to explain.'

'Yeah, mate, come in, come in, sit down,' says Terry, gesturing towards the sofa, his brow creased with confusion, looking so much like his son it breaks Andrea's heart anew.

The man steps inside and one of the constables closes the door behind him. He sits down on the sofa, resting his hands on his knees, a deep flush spreading across his face. Andrea tries to breathe slowly as dread takes over her body. She stands up as another pain moves through her, clenching her fists so she doesn't make a sound. Moving to stand behind the rocking chair, she grips the back tightly, centring herself as she rides out the pain.

'Perhaps you'd like to explain what's so complicated, Mr Burrell,' says the detective, her tone sceptical and low.

'I'm her brother,' says the man, his voice slightly breathless over the words. 'I'm her brother, and Flynn doesn't exist. He doesn't exist.'

TWENTY-FOUR

GABBY

She feels better once they are on the plane, once they are seated and Jack has been fussed over by the flight attendant, who brings him a colouring book filled with pictures of Australian animals and some crayons and promises him a treat once the plane takes off.

Gabby thinks about the first time she saw Sydney from the window of an aeroplane. It was only eight months ago. She had looked down on the Opera House as the plane came in to land and felt like she was finally in a place she could stay in forever. She had moved about a bit before she found a house where she was able to stay for six months, and then she had moved in and brought Flynn with her, lovely Flynn with his hockey trophies and his wide smile. She really loved Flynn. She had known as soon as she saw his Instagram profile that he was perfect. She had imagined that the Australian accent would be hard work, but she quickly adapted and now she can't imagine not speaking this way.

She has turned off her phone, not wanting to hear from anyone at all. She just needs to get to Queensland and then she can make a plan and call Richard. He will understand once they speak, and she can actually explain it all to him. With Jack, she can have an international Facebook page. It won't matter where the posts go because Jack will be hers. She won't have to be so careful coming and going from where she lives either. The constant checking to make sure no one was in the street every time she left and retuned with an empty car when she was supposed to have Flynn with her has been very stressful. She never really wanted a baby when she was younger, needing to take care of herself first, to learn how to live in a world that her mother told her would reject and dislike her. But as she has grown older, she has felt that something is missing. Richard wants her to fly under the radar, to behave and do what he tells her to, but she wants something different now. Flynn was a mistake and she doesn't want to do that again. If Richard can't get on board, then perhaps it may be time to branch out on her own, to run her own show. She loves him deeply but something inside her has changed. She reaches towards Jack and strokes his cheek and he smiles at her. 'I'm going to colour a kangaroo,' he says.

'You do that, love,' she replies, and he returns to his picture as she stares out of the window. Over the speakers, the safety briefing plays and the plane begins to pick up speed. They will be in the air soon, on their way to a new start, and she couldn't be happier.

You have taken something that doesn't belong to you. Again, you have done it again, she hears her mother say and her cheeks flush as a memory of being dragged back to a store by her hair for the very first time returns. She was only eight years old and all she wanted was a small chocolate. It had been so easy to take it, simply slipping it up her sleeve, the thrill making her giggle as she left the store. But her mother caught her before she had even managed a single bite, forced her to return the chocolate, and she told the man who owned the store that she was ashamed of her child. Her mother believed that dragging her back to the store would teach her to never take something again, but all it taught Gabby was that she needed to plan better, to be more aware and to hide everything she took from the woman who raised her.

Gabby shakes away the memory. No one is going to make her return this treat. This child is hers to keep forever and she will be the kind of mother she always wanted, always needed, but was not lucky enough to have.

'Mum will like my colouring,' says Jack.

'Yes,' murmurs Gabby, as the plane lifts off the ground and soars into the dark sky. 'Yes, I will.'

TWENTY-FIVE
ANDREA

Her thoughts are nothing more than a jumble of confusion. She cannot believe the words Richard is saying. *Flynn doesn't exist. Flynn doesn't exist. I'm her brother.* Nothing makes sense. How can such a thing be possible? She's seen Flynn's room, seen so many pictures of him, and Gabby has posted about him every day. Obviously the boy exists. How can this be possible? Is Richard lying to protect Gabby? Is he crazy – or worse?

'Can you explain that again, please,' says the detective.

'I can, but before I do I think you should know that she's just used a credit card to buy two tickets to Queensland. To the Gold Coast. She's bought tickets for a Virgin flight, but I'm not sure what time. I imagine it would be soon. Please be gentle with her. She's really not well and she has no idea what she's doing.' Andrea looks at him in disbelief. He sounds so sad, so upset for Gabby.

'I'll call and alert the airport,' says one of the constables, and he moves away from them, speaking urgently on his phone.

'I don't understand,' Andrea says, and she feels her stomach tighten and at the same time her knees feel too weak to hold her up.

Terry is instantly by her side. 'Sit down,' he says, moving her back to the rocking chair. 'Sit down.' She drops into the chair, her hands automatically going to her child, to the child that is here and needs to be protected from stress so she can be born safely.

'She posts about him every day,' says Andrea to Richard, who is watching her, his face pale with worry. 'I've...' She begins to say that she's met him, but then realises that she actually hasn't. She has never seen the boy. He is always at school or with friends or at hockey practice. He is always somewhere else, but it feels like she's met him because Gabby talks about him so much, because Gabby has confessed the problems she is having with her son, because his pictures are everywhere in the house. *Were* everywhere. Gabby received texts from him all the time. Andrea feels like she must have met him at some point... but she hasn't. 'Oh God,' she says, swallowing so that she doesn't need to run to the bathroom and throw up.

Her phone is lying next to her on a small round table and it rings. She grabs for it but doesn't recognise the number. 'What do I do?' she asks, but before the detective can even reply the call is gone. Andrea stifles a sob. *What if that was Gabby wanting to give Jack back, or someone who has seen them? Who lies about having a son?* Andrea cannot stop the questions circling in her mind, the questions and the guilt and the blame.

She looks at her husband, who says, 'I told you this wasn't about me.' He says the words quietly, as though even he doesn't want to hear himself justifying his actions.

'If you had been here,' she whispers, her voice strangled by her anger. 'If you had answered your phone...' She stops speaking and he drops his gaze to the cheap grey carpet that feels nothing like the soft pale green carpet in their old house. When he looks at her again, she can see he is going to apologise, but she cannot hear another 'sorry', so she shakes her head.

A double beep indicates a message and she grabs her phone.

'Listen to it on speaker,' says the detective, and Andrea opens her phone and plays the message.

'Hello, hello... Look, I am assuming that this is the Andrea Gately who is listed as a contact on the Missing Children of the World website. I know your post said to only contact the police with information, but I found you on Facebook – where you have your phone number. I have no idea why you would have your phone number on your Facebook page, but that's not what this call is about. I know you're in Australia and I am in the USA, so I'm not sure about the time difference, but I really don't care. I'm calling to let you know I've given your number and contact details to the police over here and they have assured me they are going to look into this immediately.

'Why are you using a picture of my son on a missing children's website, Andrea Gately? Why are you using it and where did you get it?'

The room is stunned into silence. Richard shakes his head sadly. 'I...' he begins and then he seems to falter and he drops his head into his hands. 'I'm so sorry, so sorry, so sorry,' he repeats, the words sounding more and more desperate with each repetition.

'Can I get you a water?' Terry asks and Andrea looks at her husband, who she has screamed and shouted at. Jack has not been taken by the men he owes money to, but the truth remains that if she had managed to get hold of him, Jack would be here safe right now. If Terry cared about everything she had lost because of his gambling, everything Jack had lost and everything their little family had the potential to lose, he would have been at work and he would never have even contemplated betting on anything at all. But he didn't because Terry only cared about himself. When Jack is returned to her – she tells herself to think *when* not *if*, though every part of her is wracked with fear that he has been taken forever by the crazy woman Andrea was forced to trust – she has no idea how they will stay married, stay together and raise their children.

'Yes, thanks,' says Richard, and Terry turns to look at her. She drops her eyes, not wanting to meet his gaze, not wanting to see him at all.

'It's not that she's a bad person,' Richard says to her. 'It's not. She's just... She's suffered all her life with delusions and she really believed that Flynn existed. She saw a picture of him on an Instagram account and it was like she fell in love with him, not like an attraction, but a deep maternal love, and nothing I could do could make her give him up.'

'But she has given him up,' says Andrea. 'She's given him up because she has found another son to take his place.'

Her whole being is numb, overloaded with emotion. What has she done? What has she allowed to happen? No stranger in a white van needed to snatch her child off the street. She simply handed him over and left. 'She's found another son,' she murmurs, heavy horror settling over her.

'That's what I'm afraid of,' says Richard as Terry hands him the glass of water and Richard gulps it down like a man dying of thirst.

TWENTY-SIX
GABBY

Once they are above the clouds, she feels her breathing slow. 'Isn't this fun?' she asks Jack.

'Uh-huh,' he says, his small hands busy with a big blue crayon as he colours in a patch of sky. 'Where is Mum having the baby?' he asks. 'I wented with her to the hospital to see her doctor and he said that I am very big now. But we didn't go on an aeroplane. Mum said she is having the baby in the hospital.'

A woman sitting on the other side of Jack looks up from the book she's reading and looks from Jack to Gabby and then back at Gabby again. She shifts a little in her seat and then takes out her phone and Gabby can see her texting something.

'Good book?' Gabby asks.

'Oh, very,' says the woman with a flustered smile. She is older, probably a grandmother already, her grey hair a soft bob and her face settled into lines and wrinkles. Gabby has never pictured herself as a grandmother, but maybe now she can begin to see that in her future. She would be a wonderful grand-mother, always baking with her grandchildren, always willing to babysit.

'What is it about?' she asks, wanting to keep the woman

talking, keep her interested and not have her thinking about what Gabby is doing on an aeroplane with Jack.

'It's um... It's about interfering when you see something you feel is wrong,' says the woman and she meets Gabby's gaze with faded green eyes.

'Hmm,' she says. 'I've always found that poking my nose in where it doesn't belong gets me into a lot of trouble.' Gabby's voice is soft but contains just a trace of menace. The woman may or may not pick up on the warning, but Gabby is in no mood to have her plans thwarted this close to getting what she wants.

The woman sniffs. 'Aren't you lucky to be on an aeroplane with your granny, young man,' she says to Jack.

'She's not my—' begins Jack.

'You forgot about your chocolate bar,' says Gabby, a touch loudly, pulling the treat out of her bag and handing it to Jack, who eagerly takes it and begins ripping off the wrapper, biting into it with gusto.

'Slowly now, darling,' says Gabby, trying for patience. He is getting chocolate everywhere.

'Here you go,' says the woman. 'A grandmother can never be too prepared.' She takes out a packet of wipes from her bag and hands one to Gabby, who flushes and nods. 'Thank you,' she says.

'Where did you say his mother is?' asks the woman, leaning slightly closer to Gabby.

'I didn't,' says Gabby shortly as she concentrates on wiping Jack's hands.

'Mum is having my baby sister and I am going on a holiday with—'

'With Gammy,' she says loudly. 'Away with Gammy for a few days. That's what he calls me,' she says to the woman, desperate for this conversation to be over. She is far too young to be a grandmother, but Jack has already mentioned his mother.

And she's hoping that Gabby and Gammy sound close enough to the woman's ears.

'My one granny lives in Queensland and the other one lives in Perth,' says Jack with confidence, and Gabby clenches her fists so she doesn't lash out at him.

'Oh really,' says the woman, her interest piqued.

'I think we need to visit the bathroom,' says Gabby, abruptly, standing up. It takes a few minutes for Gabby to get out as the woman, who is sitting on the aisle seat, moves her things and then slowly stands up, but finally she and Jack are walking down the aisle to the bathroom. After he's used the bathroom and she is helping him wash his hands she says, 'Jack, please stop talking to that lady. She is a stranger and some strangers are not nice.'

'You're talking to her,' says Jack, logical and certain.

'That's different,' she snaps. 'Now, no more talking or there won't be any treats on our holiday.'

Back in their seats, they go through the whole rigmarole again until everyone is seated, and the woman says to Jack, 'That's better, isn't it?'

Jack looks at Gabby and then looks at the woman and mimes zipping his mouth shut. Then he drops his gaze to his paper and goes back to colouring.

'He's a bit tired, as am I,' says Gabby stiffly, and the woman finally takes the hint and returns to her book.

Gabby looks out of the window at the dark cloudless sky. It's nice to be above the rain, to know that, even though they came from grey skies, they are heading to blue ones and sun-filled days in the future.

They have only another forty minutes of flying time, and then as soon as they are out of the airport they will be home free. Richard is sure to shut down her bank account if he's not happy with what she's done. It wouldn't be the first time, but he's not aware of the credit card she applied for and got without him knowing. She should have used that one to book the tickets, but she just grabbed the first one in her purse, needing to get on the first plane out of Sydney. She folds her arms and sighs at herself. Now Richard and the police will be able to find them. The police trace credit card transactions when they are looking for someone. Trapped in her seat, she wants to punch something as anger at her own stupidity rises inside her. Why did she not use the credit card Richard doesn't know about? 'Stupid,' she whispers into the air, earning herself a glance from the old woman.

Tilting her head back, she closes her eyes and breathes deeply to calm herself. By the time the police know that she's made it to the Gold Coast, she and Jack will have disappeared into the labyrinth of hotels along the beach. And, in a couple of days, she will find a place for them to stay for a while, somewhere in Brisbane, perhaps. She can hire a car and drive there. No one will find them. Not ever.

The card she applied for has a fairly high limit, so she can set herself and Jack up and then... She turns to look out of the window again, where everything is black. She's not sure what will happen then. Hopefully, Richard will come around to her way of thinking and join her and Jack in Queensland. His job is portable, so he can work anywhere. He will be a big help in raising Jack. A boy needs a male influence in his life. But there is a chance that he will not come around to her way of thinking. He may force her to give Jack back. This thought sends a little shiver through her body. Surely not? He only ever wants her to be happy and calm, so surely he will let her keep the boy if that's what she wants?

You can't just have everything you want, Gabrielle, she hears her mother say. Perhaps this will be more difficult than she thought. It's true that she didn't really think this through, but then she knows for sure that she wants to keep Jack, to raise

Jack, and that's all she needs right now. She's not giving this child back.

'Ladies and gentlemen, we are about to begin our descent into Gold Coast Airport,' says the flight attendant, and Gabby grabs Jack's hand.

'We can go to the beach tomorrow,' she says.

'Wow, I can't wait,' he exclaims.

'Neither can I,' says Gabby.

TWENTY-SEVEN
ANDREA

Richard gulps down another glass of water, making Andrea feel like he is buying time. She wants to feel pity for him, but her little boy is with Gabby, who is not well; with Gabby, who is delusional; with Gabby, who has been allowed to continue being out in the world, where she can harm others.

'I don't understand,' she says. 'How can you just let her do things like this? How can you let her pretend to be a mother to a child who belongs to someone else? She should be somewhere she can get help, somewhere she is not a danger to the people around her.'

She can feel herself getting angry again and the angrier she gets, the more the contractions that are passing through her hurt. She should be in a hospital right now, but she cannot go anywhere until she has her son back with her. She curses the house she is sitting in, the suburb they had to move to and the husband who got her here in a situation where she will likely lose the most important thing in her life. Everything bad that has happened traces back to the first time he bet on a football game and won, and didn't just stop there. Everything is his fault. She glances at him and wonders how hard it would be to raise two children alone. Her parents would help, but it would still be her doing everything and she would have to get a job. Heavy exhaustion flows through her body, even as another contraction hits. She just needs her son back and then she will make a decision, after she's had the baby and can think straight.

Richard shakes his head. 'She's been like this our whole life. My mother, our mother was... She wasn't a very good mother and I think that some children are just born more sensitive. Gabby was born needing kindness and she never got that from our mother. We never knew our father and we were both raised with a great deal of shame at our own existence. He left soon after Gabby was born, and my mother seemed to blame her more than she blamed me. She thought he left because he didn't want a daughter. I think he just didn't want to be married with children, but there's no doubt that my mother took it out on Gabby, both emotionally and physically.' He shakes his head as he speaks about his mother, and Andrea knows that memories are crowding into his mind, because they must be. 'Gabby knows what it is to be hurt by an adult in her life and I know she won't hurt your little boy,' he says urgently to Andrea. 'You have to know that she won't hurt him at all.'

'How do you know? How can you know?' asks Andrea, unable to hold back some tears.

'Well,' he says, sitting forward and reaching into his back pocket, 'I'm not just her brother. I'm also a qualified psychiatrist. I qualified in the US, but I decided to move out here after my divorce. I brought Gabby with me because I knew that she couldn't manage without me.' He takes his wallet out and then pulls out two business cards, handing one to the detective and one to Andrea, his hand shaking slightly.

She holds the thick cream-coloured card in her hand, reading the black raised letters: RICHARD BURRELL, MD

(HONS), RANZCP, CERT. PSYCHOTHERAPY PSYCH. She runs her fingers over the many letters, hoping they mean that what Richard has said is the truth, that Gabby won't hurt her son.

'Why did she take him?' she asks, still trying to understand, because maybe if she understands she can believe that the woman will not hurt her son, that at least while he is with her he will be safe.

'Well,' he says lacing his fingers together, 'I think what she wants most in the world is to be a mother, but she never found anyone to realise that dream with. She struggles to cope with everyday life, and so she invents a fantasy family life. She moves around a lot, but she always stays in contact with me so I know what she's up to. I knew that she had rented the house across the street from you and I also knew she was posting images of a boy she called Flynn. At first, I kept encouraging her to stop, kept trying to point her in the right direction so that she would understand that what she was doing was wrong. But posting about Flynn made her so happy and kept her calm and engaged with people without...' He stops speaking because he can't say that she hasn't hurt anyone, and Andrea knows that's what he was going to say. 'I let her keep doing it when I shouldn't have. It has been difficult for me to convince her that I love her and want to help her when she has so many people she talks to on Facebook who believe her fantasy. It becomes completely real for her – you have to understand that. If she posts that something happened with Flynn, it's because she has actually felt it happen, has seen it in her mind. When she was younger, it was her way of escaping our mother, of finding a way to survive the way we were treated. She is happier in the fantasy, and though I tried to convince her this one needed to stop, as I do every time, the truth is that she wasn't really harming anyone, and I hoped she would move on in time. She's never, ever done anything like this.'

'How long has she been doing this for?' asks the detective.

Andrea can see the woman has no patience for Gabby's issues. She has been standing listening to Richard and now begins pacing around the small living room. 'I mean, you do realise that this is fraud, don't you?'

Richard rubs at his head. 'Flynn is not the first "child" she's claimed to have,' he says, gesturing in the air. 'She's had a daughter she called Amelia and a son named Michael. They're always different ages. She moves somewhere new and invents a life around the child. She finds their pictures on Instagram and then she joins mother's groups and opens a new Facebook page. It's mostly harmless. It's always been harmless, and eventually something happens, and someone catches her in a lie, and she immediately shuts everything down and moves and starts again.'

'How can you allow that?' asks Andrea, her voice high. 'It's monstrous.'

Richard stands up and comes closer to where she is sitting. 'There are so many people lying on Facebook and Instagram, Andrea. The whole social media world is a façade. Nothing is real, and as long as she was posting about some mythical child, she was fine – calm and happy and not stealing or getting into trouble. She has never done anything like this before. You have to believe me,' he says, wringing his hands now. 'I would never have let it continue if I knew she had anything like this planned. She told me about you and your little boy, but I thought she was just spending a few hours with you here and there or I would have stepped in immediately. Usually what happens is that someone on a Facebook group asks a question she can't answer or calls her out about something, and she shuts everything down and comes to stay with me for a bit. She's never spoken to her neighbours before. Last time when she left, I was helping her move and the woman who lived next door said, "I never knew anyone was living there." She never usually interacts with anyone, except on Facebook.' His voice is desperate with his need for her to believe him.

'I don't believe psychiatrists encourage their patients to remain in a fantasy world,' says the detective, writing in her notebook as she speaks.

'Yes, well,' says Richard, his face neutral but his voice laced with an edge of anger, 'my degree means I am the one to decide appropriate treatment for my patients, whether I am related to them or not.'

'She should be locked up,' says Terry, coming to stand behind Andrea. He rests his hands on her shoulders and she shrugs him off.

What is it about her that made Gabby decide to talk to her, to take advantage of her? Was it the same thing that made Terry gamble away all their money and think he could get away with it? Did she have some sort of sign on her head that she couldn't see that invited people to treat her like someone who was stupid and powerless?

'Perhaps,' says Richard, sighing and nodding, 'but if we locked up everyone pretending to be something they are not on social media, the jails would be overflowing. As soon as she texted me that she was going to Queensland, to the Gold Coast, with your son, and sent me a picture of her with your little boy, I knew it was real, and I had to get here and talk to you to find out if it was true. I kept hoping it was just something she was saying she was going to do, but as soon as I saw the police cars, I knew it was happening.' He drops his head into his hands. 'I am so sorry,' he says.

'Show me,' yells Andrea.

'Could I just—' begins the detective, but Andrea reaches forward and holds out her hand. 'Show me,' she demands, and Richard unlocks his phone and shows Andrea a picture of Gabby and Jack. Jack is holding his Hot Wheels backpack and has a wide smile on his face. Andrea's heart races and her hands feel clammy as she peers at the picture and recognises Gabby's white sofa in the background.

'Let me see,' says the detective and Richard hands her the phone. 'It was taken at 5:30 this evening, so it was only a few hours ago. It looks like the house across the street but there's no evidence of the mess that's there now. Would she have deliberately trashed the place?' she asks Richard.

Richard opens his hands wide. 'She's never done anything like that before,' he says, and Andrea would like to smack the stupid repeated phrase out of his mouth.

'Why would she have done that?' asks the detective.

'I think something has changed. She's formed an attachment to this little boy and something has changed. I'm not sure why she trashed the place. Maybe she wanted you to think someone else had taken him or taken them both.'

Andrea glances back at Terry, who is standing behind her, and then turns away.

'And have you had any other contact with her?' asks the detective, still holding on to Richard's phone.

'I have, yes,' says Richard, hanging his head.

'The screen has locked. Can you open it for me and show me any conversations between you two?'

Richard looks at the detective, his face blank of emotion. 'I would prefer it if that didn't happen. I'm not just her brother; I'm her doctor as well. It's privileged information.'

'Not right now it's not,' spits the detective, her eyes narrowing. 'A little boy has been kidnapped and you have a duty to help us any way you can. I am familiar with the rules around psychiatrists and their patients, Dr Burrell. If someone is in danger, you need to help the police.' She stands up and moves over to Richard, holding the phone out to him. 'Unlock it,' she says.

Richard reaches up and takes the phone, his hands trembling a little as he punches in the passcode. 'Here,' he says, his voice just above a whisper, 'you can see when she tells me what she's done – I'm appalled and I'm trying to get her to come back. But now she's stopped responding.'

The detective takes the phone and steps away from Richard, her head down as she swipes through screens. 'This only goes back a couple of days,' she says, 'I would like to see conversations over the last week or so.'

Richard shrugs. 'I dropped my phone and this is new. I haven't switched over all the data yet because I need someone to help me do it.'

Alarm ripples through Andrea's body. *Is that the truth? What could Richard be hiding? Has he known of his sister's plan all along? Could he even have encouraged her to take Jack?*

'It's the truth,' says Richard as though he has read her thoughts, and then he holds her gaze until she looks away. Is she going mad? It feels like it.

The detective opens her mouth to say something and then closes it again as she stares hard at Richard. 'Fine,' she says tightly and hands him back his phone.

She takes her place on the kitchen chair again, reading through everything she has written. 'Just to be clear, Dr Burrell, you say she has never formed an attachment with another child before?'

'Never, never,' he says, shaking his head, sliding his phone into his jacket pocket. 'She's sad and she wants to feel that people look up to her, but it's only on social media. She uses Airbnb to rent somewhere in a different suburb, and then she lives this fantasy for a few weeks or a few months and then she moves on.'

'Obviously things have drastically changed,' says the detective.

'Obviously,' he agrees. 'I am so sorry,' he repeats, his gaze beseeching Andrea to understand, but she cannot find anything to say to him. All her interactions with Gabby are running through her mind as she tries to figure out exactly when she should have realised that everything was a lie.

'She asked me for money to go to the US and find Flynn,' she says, and Richard's face pales.

'That's unusual as well,' he says. 'I give her money to live, enough money just to keep her from having to work. I have no idea what would have happened if you had given her money.'

'Yes, well,' says Andrea bitterly, opening her arms to indicate the shabby living room. 'We have no money. My husband is fond of placing a bet.'

Richard looks at Terry, who has the grace to hang his own head. 'I may just...' he says and he leaves the room.

'She set up a GoFundMe page as well,' says Andrea, grabbing her phone. 'Let me show you. I even...' She hesitates, humiliated at her own stupidity. 'I even donated.' She shrugs, and opens the phone to show Richard.

'Oh God,' says Richard as he stares at the page, 'there's obviously been some kind of escalation. Don't worry, once this is over and your little boy is home, I'll sort that out and refund any money she's been given. I've made a huge mistake by not stopping her sooner. I am sorrier than I can tell you. This is my fault. It's all my fault.'

His face, and the way he wipes at his eyes to prevent any tears escaping, knocks a tiny piece out of Andrea's wall of anger. Relationships with siblings can be complicated. She knows that she has absolute support from Brianna and that they would do anything to help each other, but they also have wonderful parents who have raised them kindly. She cannot imagine what it would be like to have a terrible, unkind mother and have to cling to a sibling for support. People forgive the ones they love their eccentricities, and perhaps Richard felt Gabby wasn't doing any harm. She lets the logic of her thoughts wash over her for only a moment before her fear and panic and anger return. She would like to be the kind of person who can think of others before she thinks of her own pain, but her baby is missing, her little boy, and no one else matters. She has to get him home and in her arms. She should call her mother and sister but she cannot think how to begin the conversation that would explain why she had to leave her child with a stranger when her parents would have been on the first plane to Sydney if she had asked them. They already have tickets to be here the week after her due date, to stay and help for at least a month, but they would have come earlier if she'd asked. She knows they would have, and her son would be here now, playing with his grandma and grandpa while she allowed her body to do what it needed to do to bring another child into the world. She meant to text them from the hospital to tell them to come earlier, but she got involved in all the tests and talking to the doctors.

'I may just use the bathroom and call my parents,' says Andrea, heaving herself out of the chair.

The detective's phone rings, and Andrea stands still as she answers quickly. 'Yes,' she says, nodding. 'Yes, yes. Okay, let me know.' She stands up and looks down at her phone. 'There's a Virgin flight landing at the Gold Coast soon. We have people there now,' she says.

'And what if she's not on that flight?' asks Andrea.

'Then we wait for the next one,' says the detective.

Andrea feels a strong contraction ripple across her stomach. She clenches her fists, not wanting to alert anyone to it. She cannot have this baby now. She cannot have this baby until she knows Jack is safe. She makes her way to the bathroom quickly, wanting to be back and standing right next to the detective if they tell her they've found her son. Her heart is racing and her head is pounding as she breathes through another contraction in the bathroom. They are too close together for her to just wait. She will have to go to the hospital soon.

Returning to the living room, she lowers herself into the rocking chair, her hands across her belly.

The detective's phone rings again, and Terry comes to sit near to her. He takes her hand and she lets him, squeezes hard. 'You have no idea—' he begins, but she shakes her head. Now is not the time for sorry. Now he just needs to let her squeeze his hand as she tries to breathe slowly, picturing her little boy's face, willing him home.

TWENTY-EIGHT

GABBY

Jack holds her hand as they touch down, fascinated by the sounds of the wheels lowering.

'I love it when they make a *grrr* noise,' he says.

She has her phone on flight mode, but she snaps endless pictures of him as, in her mind, she begins writing the posts she will use. She may just use Instagram this time, since there seem to be a lot of younger mothers on there. *First flight with my son. Holiday time with my boy. Mother and son fun*, she tries out in her head. She is a single mother, raising her child alone after a nasty divorce. She'll let people know just how difficult things got. Everyone loves to hear about someone else's messed-up life and she will keep them all entertained and they will love her and listen to her advice for raising a child alone, and there will be so many new friends.

She doesn't want to take her phone off flight mode, but she does, knowing that Richard will have tried to contact her many times. She could have just kept this all a secret from him, but she loves Richard more than anyone in the whole world and she needs him to get on board with her idea.

'You'll have fun with your gammy, won't you,' the woman

says to Jack, and Gabby grimaces. She is too young to be his grandmother – anyone can see that. She will paint a picture of a pregnancy at thirty-nine, something that's not completely uncommon these days, of a second chance she has been given to live a truly worthwhile life. *Liar, liar, pants on fire. You'll burn in hell for your deceiving ways,* she hears her mother say, and she mentally bats her voice away. She will be the mother now, a real mother, and she will never think of the mean old woman again.

Her phone beeps continuously as the messages from Richard load up.

Are you mad?

Please don't do this.

Call me. Call me now. Please call me.

Gabby, this is a mistake. What are you doing? You will ruin your life. You will ruin our lives. You have abducted a child. I will go to the police. Call me now. I don't care about what you are trying to do. This is a mistake and I am telling the parents. I am going there now.

Gabby gasps at his last message.

'Bad news?' asks the woman sitting next to Jack, obviously curious.

'No,' she says, shaking her head and starting to stand as the flight attendant opens the doors. She feels like she can't breathe properly. If he goes to Andrea and the police, they will come and find her and they will know all about her, everything she works so hard to conceal. She needs to hurry, needs to get Jack out of the airport and far away. Richard will tell them where she is going. They won't even have to trace the credit card. She should have used a different credit card. She should have. She should never have told Richard what she was doing. Panic blooms in her chest, tightening the muscles around her racing heart.

'We have to go,' she says, grabbing Jack's hand.

'Hang on a minute. I'll just get up,' says the woman, who is blocking her escape. 'I'm here to see my grandkids. I haven't seen them in a whole year.' She leans down and starts rooting around under her seat. Gabby wants to scream in frustration.

'Please, I need to get out,' she says, her voice high with desperation.

'I'll only be a moment,' says the woman, her grey-haired head moving as she searches for something. 'I think I dropped my glasses case.'

Gabby leans down and lifts Jack up and over the woman, placing him in the aisle as a whole lot of other passengers watch her, and then she stands on the seat and steps over the bent-over woman, grateful she's wearing pants. 'We're late,' she says to a giggling teenage girl who has nothing more to worry about than the small backpack she is carrying. She moves down the aisle, pulling Jack and saying, 'Excuse me, we're late,' again and again. People move aside but there are sighs and grunts of disparagement. 'Rude,' she hears someone say, and 'Hey,' she hears from a man as she elbows him aside.

'I dropped my yellow crayon,' says Jack.

'I'll buy you a new one,' she snaps and finally they are at the door. The pretty flight attendant nods and smiles as she ushers them out and down the steps onto the tarmac, where the night air still holds just a touch of warmth from the day, a lingering smell of sunscreen in the air. She pulls Jack towards the terminal, but he is slow and eventually she picks him up and walks quickly inside, only putting him down when she gets there.

'I want my mum,' he says, cross at being rushed, and Gabby clenches her teeth together. She cannot have him throwing a tantrum now, not now. Her phone beeps continuously as Richard obviously keeps trying to contact her and she resists the urge to throw it in the nearest garbage bin. He won't like that and she doesn't want him to get even more angry with her, and it will be a nightmare to purchase a new phone and get it set up and, most importantly, Richard controls the purse strings. Her credit card can only last so long before she maxes it out. Children are expensive.

'I'll take you to her right now,' she says to Jack. 'We're going there now.'

Mercifully, this works, and he moves faster, happy that he will soon be with his mother. A slight twinge catches at her heart. Is she doing the right thing by taking this child from Andrea? She shakes her head as they hurry past slow-moving travellers who drag large suitcases and stop every few minutes to shift the bags they are carrying. Andrea will have a new child soon and Jack will become one of those children on a website, gone but not forgotten, and she will have a lovely boy and a new life, and Richard will be happy about it. He will be. As she gets closer to the doors, she realises that she needs to pick up her own suitcase but decides to leave it. All her important stuff is in the bag she is carrying. Richard will be happy to let her buy a new wardrobe.

She hurries Jack through the airport, her head moving left and right. They can't get caught, can't get stopped.

Finally, she can see the glass doors that will lead them outside, where taxis wait to take them anywhere they want. She smiles as she quickens her pace.

'Come on, Jack. Mum's waiting,' she says merrily, as though this is all great fun and her heart is not racing, sweat not forming all over her body.

She is nearly free, nearly free to be the mother she has always wanted to be. It's going to be glorious. She can't wait.

TWENTY-NINE
ANDREA

'I need you to keep messaging her, Dr Burrell,' says the detective, and Richard nods, takes his phone out and immediately begins texting Gabby.

'What will happen if they can't find her?' asks Andrea, hating herself for allowing the words to pollute the air.

'Let's not think about that,' says Terry as he stands up from the sofa before the detective can reply. 'Can I get anyone some tea or coffee or anything?' he asks, as though this is some kind of friendly gathering.

'Yes, let's not,' she says, bitterness thick in her throat. 'You're really good at that, aren't you, Terry? At not thinking about your family, because if you thought of us even once a day, even for a moment, you would never do what you have done. You have cost this family everything we own and now you may have cost me my son.' She stands as well, fury making her hot as she speaks. Another contraction grabs her body and she clenches her fists, driving her short nails into her palms so that she doesn't cry out.

'Andrea, please,' says Terry, holding up his hands to calm her, to make her cease her tirade.

But she cannot be stopped as adrenaline and fear mix with her anger. 'You did this to us, marooned me away from my friends, so I had to trust her, and now we are...' The pain that grips her belly is so strong that she can no longer speak. 'Ooh,' she moans as she sinks down, her knees bending and her hands holding where she can feel the tightening muscles. She can't pretend this isn't happening anymore.

'Hey, hey, Andy, are you okay? What's going on?' asks Terry, coming to her and kneeling down in front of her.

'Is it labour?' asks the detective, her phone already at her ear to call for an ambulance, but Andrea cannot go anywhere until she knows her son is safe. She will not have her baby until Jack is here to greet his sister.

She shakes her head, panting as the contraction loosens its hold on her body. 'Just Braxton Hicks,' she gasps, but she knows she's lying, and from the look the detective gives her, she can see the woman knows she's lying as well. Does the detective have children? Probably. She is older, so they could be grown up now, grown up and living their lives because their mother knew not to hand them over to a stranger.

'I'm calling an ambulance anyway,' says the detective.

'I'm not going anywhere until I know he's safe,' shrieks Andrea. 'You can't make me. You can't force me. I'm fine, I'm fine and I need to know he's safe!'

'Okay, okay, please calm down, please, I'm just going to get them here in case. I'm not going to force you to go anywhere.'

Andrea swallows a sob of relief, knowing that if she leaves this house, she will be a mother of only one child. She has to stay here. It's not logical but she has no room in her heart for logic now.

Her labour with Jack lasted for twelve hours but she knows that second babies sometimes come faster. She should be in a hospital, where there are doctors and nurses in case anything goes wrong, but she cannot shake the feeling that if she leaves her home without knowing that her son is safe, she will never see him again. 'I have to stay here... I have to wait,' she murmurs.

Terry touches her arm, so she looks at him as he tilts his head to the side a little. He also knows she is lying about being okay because she is not okay, but she needs him to keep quiet for now.

'As soon as we know he's okay, we're going to the hospital,' he says, his tone firm, and for a moment she has a glimpse of the man she married, the assured pragmatic man who told her, 'We can handle anything as long as we are together.' He pulls his phone out of his pocket and looks at the screen. 'I'm going to start timing them,' he says, and she doesn't argue, grateful to have him do something for her.

She returns to the rocking chair, where some movement is physically comforting, and she leans back, dropping her head and staring up at the ceiling, riddled with cracks. How did the two of them get here? How did two people who never wanted more than each other and their own small family get here?

'Okay,' she says, her eyes counting the cracks so she has something else to focus on. 'Okay.'

Her feet move the rocking chair and her hands cradle her stomach as the detective speaks into her phone, and Terry leaves the room to make tea, his phone in his hand. Andrea gets to fifty cracks and keeps going, concentrating on her breathing, concentrating on being in this room right now until she knows where her son is.

THIRTY

GABBY

Ahead of her, the automatic glass doors slide open and closed, a beacon she is moving towards. The airport is packed with people, all moving in the same direction, some dragging huge suitcases, some with just a single small bag. A woman in a business suit walks purposefully towards the doors, her voice carrying as she speaks to someone on her phone: 'I'm just getting a cab. I'll be there in twenty. Start the dinner without me.' Gabby wonders what it's like to have such confidence, such meaning in your life, and then she realises that she will know soon enough. She will be a mother and there is no job more important than that.

The doors open and close, and she speeds up, but Jack lags behind, looking at the people, the shops, stopping every time there is an announcement calling a flight. The smell of fried food from the food stalls drifts over them and reminds her that she's hungry, but she will wait to eat until they get to the hotel. She wants something healthy for her and Jack. She needs to start as she means to go on, and giving her child healthy food is the best way.

'Come on, Jack,' she says, pulling a little.

'But look, that boy is crying. Why is he crying?' he asks.

'I don't know,' she says, struggling to keep from sounding irritated. They are so close to the end. She pulls harder on his hand and he speeds up as ahead of her the doors open and close. They are close enough to smell the petrol fumes that waft in on warm air.

She's done it, actually done it. No one will find them now. She can take a taxi to a hotel for the night and then leave the Gold Coast for somewhere else tomorrow. The tourist destination has far too many hotels for anyone to find them and, anyway, she'll use her new credit card, which matches her fake driver's licence. Janet Jones is an ordinary name and surname for an average woman who no one needs to remember.

The doors slide open as she steps towards them.

THIRTY-ONE
ANDREA

'I'm waiting for confirmation that they were on the flight that's just landed,' says the detective. 'Someone has reported seeing a woman with a young boy, but they described her as having dark hair and I'm assuming Gabby wouldn't have changed her hair in such a short time.'

'She could be wearing a wig,' says Andrea, because right now anything is possible.

Richard stands and begins his pacing again. 'That's right, she could be. She has some wigs. I know she does. God, this is such a mess, such a complete mess. What was she thinking, what was she thinking?' he mutters, more to himself than to them.

Andrea grips the arms of the rocking chair, breathing quietly through another contraction, wondering if one day she will be able to tell this story to Gemma and Jack, or will it only be Gemma she tells?

Terry stands next to her, his eyes on the phone. 'We need to get to the hospital,' he says. 'This is dangerous, Andy.'

'No,' she whispers, 'no.'

'The ambulance is waiting outside. Can I get a paramedic to come in and check you over please?' begs the detective.

'Not yet,' Andrea yells. 'Not yet.' They will take her away from here, away from the last place she saw her child and she will not let them. Andrea feels her eyes spill tears, hot on her cheeks and salty in her mouth. Her baby is not home, and if she leaves, she will never see him again.

THIRTY-TWO
GABBY

It's after 8 p.m. and probably past Jack's bedtime. She knows that she has only minutes until he gets hungry and tired all at once and she has to deal with another meltdown. She steps through the glass door and then looks around for the start of the line for taxis.

'This way, Jack,' she says, striding forward, her eyes searching for an available taxi. Someone hoots and a man behind her laughs and Gabby looks right in front of her.

Her feet freeze in place when she sees the woman walking towards her. A policewoman. The woman's red hair is wound in a bun – a beacon of contrast to her blue uniform under the bright white lights that illuminate the area. Gabby's mouth is dry. The policewoman is looking at her mobile phone. Gabby takes a step, and the woman looks up as Gabby moves. She blinks in recognition. Her mouth opening. Clutching Jack's hand tighter, Gabby looks down at him but he is oblivious to anything, his attention on everything he sees, his head moving back and forth.

Gabby sees another one, a man, broad shoulders straining his blue shirt. 'Hey,' the policewoman calls. Gabby stops walking and turns to look behind her and then back again. She can run back into the airport and try to disappear, hide somewhere. She sees herself crouching in a bathroom stall with Jack, but that won't work. It won't work. He won't stay quiet. They've seen her, they know, they all know. For a moment she is unsure what to do, her feet unable to move as they walk towards her.

And then another policeman appears from inside the building on her right, slipping through the glass doors, and she can see he is on his phone. He looks up and sees her and she looks to her left, but there is another one, an older man. She turns around and there is another woman, her hand at her side, resting on her gun, her other hand holding her phone to her ear. 'Yes, yes,' she says.

Suddenly they are everywhere – at least ten or more.

They are all looking at her, all staring at her, and she holds her breath. How have they found her?

And now there is a blue swarm coming towards her, coming for her – here to sting. Her knees grow liquid and she sags before righting herself.

There is nowhere to go, nowhere to hide.

'What's wrong?' asks Jack. 'Aren't we going to see Mum?'

'No,' she says softly, her shoulders rounding with defeat. 'No.'

'Excuse me, ma'am,' a policeman says, 'may we have a word with you?'

Gabby nods sadly and in her mind the pictures of Jack fade, the posts she was going to write, the stories she was going to tell, the life she was finally going to live.

It all fades and disappears until there is just nothing left.

'Hello, Jack,' says someone else, a man who looks very young, like he could be about sixteen if not for his uniform. He crouches down and Gabby catches the slight scent of his sandalwood aftershave. 'My name is Constable Blake, and I've come to take you back to your mum.'

'Mum's having the baby. We're going to visit her. I flew on a plane with Gabby,' says Jack to the policeman, unaware of what is happening, his innocence intact. 'She's taking me to see Mum and the new baby in hospital. Last time we didn't go on the plane when we wented to the hospital.'

'Mum hasn't had the baby yet, Jack,' says the man, and Gabby looks down at him. He has chestnut brown hair like Flynn does and a beautiful smile like Flynn does. But this young man is not Flynn and the little boy next to her is not her son Jack. For a moment, just a moment, she hoped it could be so.

She has lost everything. She has lost her past because it will be revealed that Flynn never was, and now they are taking this boy away from her and she has lost her future. Everything is gone. Her reasons for being are gone. Richard was right. She should never have indulged this moment of madness. She should have stuck to doing what she has always done. But she wanted for just a moment to feel like a real mother, to know what it was to have a child in your life who depends on you. She wanted her posts to be true for once, with only a little alteration for sympathy and interest. At night when she turned off the computer, she didn't want to be alone with just her thoughts and texts from Richard. She wanted someone there – a child who would love her no matter what, a child who would appreciate how good a mother she was and how different she was from her own mother.

She wanted that, but she is not the kind of person who can have that, and Richard is going to have to work very hard to save her from this situation. She hopes he is prepared.

Behind her, someone places a hand on her shoulder. 'Gabby Burrell...' a voice begins, and Gabby lets the words drift over her. Her head drops and she cannot help her tears.

THIRTY-THREE
ANDREA

The paramedic, a young woman with her dark hair in a plait, crouches beside her, her hand on Andrea's wrist. Andrea will not look at her, cannot make eye contact, because she will be dragged away then. The paramedic has a stethoscope she is using to listen to Gemma's heartbeat every few minutes. Andrea is counting cracks.

One hundred and twelve, one hundred and thirteen... If she keeps counting, keeps her eyes moving across the ceiling, then her body stays calm and still, and she needs it to stay calm and still until her son is safe. Terry is sitting next to her, his hand opening and closing the clasp on his watch, the *click-clack* noise comforting more than irritating. She remembers him doing it at their wedding before he stood up to make his speech. He does it when he's nervous, unsure. He keeps checking his phone, logging her contractions with strict attention.

The constables are hovering by the door as though Jack might walk in at any minute, and the detective is walking up and down the small passage between the living room and the bedrooms, her eyes glued to her phone.

No one is speaking.

The ringing of the detective's phone pierces the air, and Andrea turns to look at her as she swipes her finger across the screen once and puts it to her ear.

'Yes,' she barks and then she listens, nodding her head. 'Are you sure? Where was this?' she asks, and Andrea's heart suspends her between one beat and two.

Looking up, the detective meets her gaze and nods her head, holding up her thumb to let them know – *they have him*. They've found him. A smile spreads across the woman's face as she relaxes in the knowledge that the little boy is safe.

A cry comes from deep inside Andrea, loud and raw as she hunches forward, moaning, 'Oh God, thank you, thank you, thank you.' Sobs wrack her body, relief flows through her veins and the baby who wants to be born takes her breath away with another strong contraction.

'These are too close now,' says the paramedic.

'Shh, shh,' says Terry, his arms around her, and she glances at him to see his own tears. She feels a dam break inside her, everything spilling out, and for a few minutes she cries with her husband over what has happened to their lives and over the luck that has allowed their little boy to be found.

The detective comes to stand over her. 'If you can, you need to speak to him. Tell him to go with the police so that he isn't scared.' Andrea nods and sniffs, takes a deep breath that shudders through her body. The detective hands her the phone and she tries to control her voice and the tears that threaten to overwhelm her as she says, 'Hey, Jack. Hey, bubs. It's me. It's Mum.'

The female paramedic stands and gestures at her partner standing in the doorway, and he pushes the stretcher into the room.

'Can you climb on?' asks the woman.

'I can do anything,' says Andrea through her tears as she listens to her son's voice, 'anything.'

She feels another policeman come to stand next to her. There are so many of them they seem to have appeared from the ground, sprouting right in front of her. Where have they all come from? People coming out of the airport openly stare, simply stopping in their tracks at the spectacle. Ahead of her, taxi cabs leave the line, roaring off with tourists or business-people or those returning home. Those inside are safe from the cold wind that has suddenly blown up, from the dark sky above and from their dreams being erased right here, right now, as the night grows later.

The constable hands Jack a phone. 'Mum wants to speak to you, Jack,' he says, and Gabby hears Andrea's voice, can hear the tears behind her words. She has really messed up this time.

'Hi, Mum,' says Jack, his voice filled with excitement at his adventure. 'Me and Gabby flew on the aeroplane high in the sky,' he says, raising his arm to indicate how high they were, 'and I ate some chips and a chocolate and it had caramel in it like you like and we're coming to see you.' The words spill over themselves as he tries to tell her everything but then she speaks again and he grows quiet as he listens to his mother – his mother and not Gabby, who will never be a mother.

'Um yeah... okay, but why can't I stay with Gabby?' Andrea has obviously told him to go with the police. 'Grandma? Really?' he asks, and Gabby remembers that Andrea told her that her parents live in Queensland. 'Okay, and will Grandpa take me to the beach and buy me a chocolate ice cream? Yay!' he says happily.

He hands the phone back to the constable and looks up at Gabby. 'Guess what! Guess what!' he says. 'My grandma is coming to get me and she's going to take me to the beach at her house tomorrow and we are going surfing on the boogie board that my grandpa bought me and I get to have a holiday just with me and Grandma and Grandpa and chocolate ice cream.'

His blue eyes sparkle with delight at the unexpected turn of events. Jack has no idea what has just happened, no idea. He is uninjured by her decision. She would never have hurt him, but as she listens to him tell the policewoman standing next to her about all the things he is going to do, she realises that this is the best-case scenario. She's not meant to be a mother, not a real one anyway.

She feels her arms pulled behind her, but the hands placing cuffs on her wrists are gentle. She is not resisting, not fighting. She has been fighting forever, for the whole of her life, and she is done now.

Consequences, you evil child. You terrible liar, you awful girl. Her mother's voice returns, spitting her fury at Gabby, and she cannot help some tears. She wanted to banish the woman for good and instead she is back with a vengeance.

Her fight is over. Whoever has placed the handcuffs on her wrists says, 'This way please,' and pulls slightly. Gabby sniffs and some more tears fall. It will be better to adopt an attitude of someone who has made a tragic mistake. That's what she needs to do now. She will shed tears and apologise over and over. She will say she doesn't understand what she has done. She will act confused when they explain it and she will maintain that Flynn has run away. All this needs to be done now so that Richard will be able to save her from prison. That's what matters. She will have to reassure him that she will behave from now on, and she will.

Look at what you have done to your life, at what you have done to others. You're pathetic, she hears her mother say and she allows herself a small sad smile at the woman's persistence. She will never leave Gabby's mind. But this will be over soon, and Gabby can begin again, somewhere new, as someone else. It will all be over soon.

EPILOGUE

ANDREA

Andrea shifts in the hospital bed, sitting up and leaning forward to pull Gemma's clear bassinet over to her. She should be asleep because the baby is asleep, but she just needs to look at her one more time. Gemma looks more like her than Jack did when he was born. He had been a mini Terry from the moment he breathed his first gulp of air. Gemma has dark grey eyes that she believes will turn brown like hers. Blonde whorls of hair cover her head, and Andrea knows they will darken to a similar burnished brown like Jack's hair. Her lips and chin come from her mother. Andrea cannot help but marvel at her daughter's perfection.

One day her daughter will tell her that her curls need to be cut or coloured or changed, but right now she is perfect, her rosebud lips moving in her sleep as she seeks milk.

Andrea can't remember the ride to the hospital in the ambulance because her body had been taken over by the pain. She does know that once the paramedics had her on a stretcher and in the ambulance and she knew that Jack was safe, her labour became a speeding train, and there had been no time for pain relief, no time for anything but the pushing sensation that was threatening to pull her apart when they arrived at the hospital. Only when the startled-looking registrar had placed Gemma on her chest saying, 'That was so fast,' did it dawn on her that she could have put her baby in real danger by waiting so long. As Gemma howled, she thanked God for the outcome as she had already thanked God for her son's safety.

She had been edgy until she knew her mother had her son in her arms, edgy and waiting for something to go wrong.

'They gave us a police escort,' her mother said on the first wonderful phone call to let Andrea know that Jack was with her parents, that he was in a place where she knew he was as safe as he was with her. 'You rest now, darling. Dad and I have everything under control.' Her mother's calm voice travelled through the air, comforting her and making her cry with relief again.

Jack will be here this afternoon with her parents, who kept him with them for two days in Queensland and then flew to Sydney to stay in the house while she recovers a little. Jack is looking forward to holding his little sister, and Andrea is glad that he's embraced the idea of his new sibling. It's a big change for a three-year-old but it's just the first of many. He is still blissfully oblivious about what really happened to him. She and Terry have agreed to tell him that Gabby took him to visit his grandparents and that's it. When he's old enough to understand they will tell him the rest of the story.

He was waiting at the police station for only an hour on the Gold Coast until her parents arrived to fetch him, and his biggest thrill from the whole experience had been that he got to ride in a police car and he was allowed to switch on the lights and the siren. A dream for a three-year-old boy.

The whole labour feels surreal now, as it did for Jack. Andrea loves looking at her new daughter, but she is also a little afraid to sleep. She fears Gabby coming to find her child or the men Terry owed money coming to make him pay. But Gabby is safely locked up and will have to return to the US, where she and her brother come from. Terry no longer owes any money to anyone. Her father took care of that.

She is looking forward to leaving Sydney – and everything that has happened – behind her.

Three weeks from today, when she's had more time to recover physically, she and Jack and Gemma will board a plane with her mother to Brisbane, where her parents live. Terry will drive there with her father in their family van, and she and Terry and her children will move in with her parents.

That was part of the deal that Terry and her father made when he paid off Terry's debt of over twenty thousand dollars. Her father is a gentle giant of a man, not one for a lot of conversation, but Terry said that he had accompanied him to make sure the money was transferred and Terry's debt wiped clean, and he had said to the burly man taking the payment, 'You should be ashamed of yourselves, letting this boy lose everything and then letting him do it again.'

'I wanted to tell him that I wasn't a boy, that I got myself into it and as a man I would get myself out of it, but I just kept quiet,' Terry told her.

'As you should have done,' she said, cradling her newborn daughter in her arms.

'I will spend my life making this up to you and your folks, Andy, I promise you that,' he said, and this time she knew that he was telling the truth, that something inside him had shifted on the day Gabby took their son. He hit rock bottom hard and fast. Losing a house was one thing, but nearly losing a child because your wife had to trust someone when you weren't there was entirely different. She wanted to stay angry at him, but his despair is so plain for anyone to see that it was a struggle to hold on to her fury. She gave him a second chance and he messed things up spectacularly, but it feels like the reality of what happened, of what could have happened, has shocked him into clarity on how he was living his life. There is a shift in him, something in the way he speaks to her and looks at her makes her believe that he understands how close he came to losing his family, to living life alone. The man she married has not returned, but in his place is a more mature man, someone who finally seems to understand the value of his wife and children, and that is the man Andrea cannot help forgiving, cannot help loving.

In Queensland, Terry will go to Gamblers Anonymous every day, and he will work for her father for the next two years to pay off his debt and take care of his family. He will be trained to lay carpet and he will start from the bottom, which Andrea knows will be a humbling experience for her salesman husband, used to dazzling with big sales and coming home every day with smooth soft hands. But her father paid off his gambling debt, and therefore her father has the right to demand whatever he wants. She likes the idea of her father watching Terry every day for the next two years. He will not accept any unexplained absences the way Baz did. 'I will do whatever I need to do,' Terry said, and Andrea could see he meant it.

Andrea doesn't want to stay in Sydney anyway. She couldn't bear to see Gabby's house every day and know that her own naivety almost cost her Jack.

It will be better to start again in Queensland. Her mother will help with the baby and her father will supervise Terry – and even though she has a feeling that eventually she and her husband will chafe at the arrangement, it's what's best for now. Terry may even end up enjoying the work and making his way up to salesman in the carpet showroom.

He has agreed to everything she asked of him. Not that he had a choice. It was that or lose his family. Despite her exhaustion from giving birth, Andrea feels stronger today than she has ever felt. She will not allow anyone to get between her and her children again, not Terry and not a stranger who comes disguised as a friend.

Gemma opens her mouth and squawks a little, and Andrea gently pats the rainbow-striped hospital blanket she is wrapped in. 'Shh,' she whispers and Gemma is quiet again.

On a small chest of drawers that stands against one wall of the hospital room is a large bouquet of pink chrysanthemums. The bouquet is from Richard, Gabby's brother.

Congratulations on the birth of your beautiful daughter. Wishing you a life filled with joy and peace, the card reads.

Andrea feels sorry for the man, who has been dealing with his unwell sister his whole life. She knows he could never have anticipated that Gabby would do what she did. She had never attempted anything like that before, content to live in her fantasy lives online.

Flynn's real name is Aaron Philips and he's a seventeen-year-old boy who lives in Michigan. His mother is threatening to sue Richard over his knowledge of what Gabby was doing, and though she feels for the man, Andrea thinks he does need to be held accountable. He knew she was using another child's picture and he just let her keep doing it, because it meant he didn't have to deal with his sister. It may have seemed harmless, but it wasn't. A screen gives everything a feeling of distance, but real and great harm is being caused every day behind those screens. Andrea has always believed that she would never fall prey to a scammer on the internet, but she fell prey to one in real life. In the future she will regard everyone she meets with a degree of suspicion. Terry took her ability to trust her own husband and Gabby took her ability to trust a new friend. There is a wall around her now against those who would betray her trust, but it needs to stay there so she can protect her children. She is not entirely sure her marriage will survive what has happened, but she is willing to give Terry the chance to prove himself the man she married, rather than the addict he became. This is his very, very last chance.

There is a soft knock at the door and then it swings open to reveal her parents and son. 'Hello, bubs,' she whispers and holds out her arms for Jack, whose smile lights up the room.

'Mum,' he shouts as he runs towards her, leaping onto the bed, already in the middle of a conversation with her about everything he has seen and everything he has done.

'Thank you, God,' Andrea whispers as she holds her son and gazes down at her daughter.

'Family picture,' says Terry coming into the room from getting a coffee, and as they gather together for the photo, Andrea's smile is so wide it hurts her cheeks.

EPILOGUE

GABBY

The nurse watches as Gabby gathers up her things. She has very little, only one change of clothing and some spare underwear, along with a toothbrush and toothpaste. She's been wearing a hospital gown for a week and the clothing she has been given to change into was bought for her by Richard, who has no idea about such things. The grey pants are a little too big because eating has been difficult. She never could abide tasteless food, preferring to exist on fruit instead. The top is a lovely shade of blue, but the material is cheap and Richard obviously grabbed the first thing he could.

She is looking forward to getting out of her clothes and into a long hot shower and then throwing away everything she is wearing. The stiff material scratches at her skin and smells horribly of chemicals. She left a couple of outfits at the house she was living in and she's sure that when the owners return, they will be discarded without a second thought. It was unusual to find a house in the suburbs available for such a long period of time. When she saw it, it felt like the universe was talking to her. The owner had an overseas posting for six months and hoped to find someone to move in, and Gabby was there right when they needed someone willing to watch the house and pay for the privilege.

'Your brother will be here soon,' the nurse says softly.

Gabby likes this nurse, she is kind and gentle and seems to really want to help her patients recover, but this is a state-run hospital and they are not equipped for long stays, and from what the therapist Gabby has spoken to told her, she is going to be in a hospital for a long, long time. Deported from Australia and sent back to the US, she will be allowed to go only because Richard is a psychiatrist and has received permission to take her away from this country, where she very nearly destroyed a family. The Australians have no desire to house and treat her. They were going to send her to a detention centre to await deportation, but Richard managed to get her released to his custody so he can take her home and get her treated there. He's always had a way with words and the impressive letters after his name give him gravitas and authority. He convinced everyone that her mental health would not stand for time in a detention centre, and he's right about that. Being locked up in this hospital has nearly driven her mad. She has been unable to go anywhere or do anything without being watched and has found herself surrounded by crazy people. She is not one of them, will never be one of them.

Jack is safely home with his family, so no real harm has been done. The little boy was confused about having to ride in a police car but happy enough about the experience when lights and sirens were promised. He turned back once to look at her at the airport before walking away. 'Bye-bye, Gabby,' he called and then he went off with the policeman to ride in his car with the lights, chatting away about being on an aeroplane. Her heart was a stone of sadness in her chest, but as she watched him go, she understood that it was for the best. She hadn't really understood what it would take to look after a child, and she doubts she ever will. It is easy enough to steal something from a store, to enjoy the secret rush of having it and then put it away in a drawer when you have no interest in it anymore. But Jack would have been her responsibility forever, and she can admit now that the dream didn't entirely live up to the reality. She would like to find a way to apologise to Andrea, but it's best she doesn't contact her. Taking Jack was an impulse born of a desire to have a different life, but she needs to find a way to simply be content with this one.

She can imagine the kind of place that Andrea and the police believe she belongs. They want to see her in a prison masquerading as a hospital, where doctors will pick her brain and no doubt find her mother there, sneering and cold. She hates discussing her mother. Her mother is dead to her, and may very well be physically dead as well – Gabby hasn't seen her for decades. Sometimes she likes to imagine her alone and in pain, stewing in her own bitterness as she curses her evil daughter for abandoning her. Bad parents deserve to die alone. Getting old and frail does not exempt you from being an awful human being while you were young and strong.

'Thank you,' Gabby says to the nurse as she is guided to the entrance, where they will wait for Richard.

She has not been allowed to hold on to her phone in here or to read newspapers or watch the news. It's considered problematic for some of the patients. She hates being out of touch, hates being away from social media, but she is sure that Andrea had the baby, and she hopes everything is okay. She wishes only the best for Andrea and her little family, though she knows that once she leaves here she will not give them much thought. Richard has shut down her page and removed all the pictures of Flynn. The name Flynn suits the boy she chose better than the one his parents gave him. That's how she chooses the children she chooses, searching through Instagram and Facebook until she sees a child wearing the wrong name entirely. Aaron is boring and safe, but Flynn is a boy who will change the world. He looked like he could change the world.

At the front, Richard is standing at a counter, talking to another nurse. He is holding a thick file and has his glasses perched on top of his head. He needs bifocals but won't buy them because he hates the idea that he's old enough to need them. Her spirit lifts at the sight of him, as it always does. People are all around, but as he looks up and their gazes meet, for just a few seconds it's only the two of them and he is here to rescue her once again.

She waits quietly until he is done with the myriad of forms he has to fill in.

He doesn't hug her when the nurse hands her over to him, but rather, he takes her elbow and guides her to his car, slowly and carefully, as though she might be elderly or infirm. She makes sure to hang her head, to appear slightly confused by everything, to be ashamed of who she is and how she got here.

They are silent in the car for the first few minutes of the drive as her mind fills up with everything she wants to say to him.

'I'm sorry,' she finally whispers.

'I know you are,' he says.

The trees they pass are bare or holding on to the last of their brown leaves as the full force of winter hits Sydney. She closes her eyes and pictures somewhere warm, somewhere new.

'I've booked us on a five fifteen flight to New York. I had to show that I had tickets so that they would allow me to take you.'

'I love New York,' says Gabby. 'Not all of it, but parts of it.' She stares out the window at the buildings they pass, at the cars filled with people all going somewhere and doing something on a Tuesday afternoon. Lots of the cars have children in the back seats. Little ones with their heads barely above booster seats and older ones in school uniforms, their heads bent over phones.

'I don't understand,' says Richard, 'why on earth you made

such a choice. It could only have led to you being caught. This is Australia and they don't allow children to just disappear. Why would you have done something so reckless – and how could you not think that I would have to step in to stop you?' He doesn't sound angry, just confused. He knows she has these lapses, little lapses when she makes impulsive decisions. But this was bigger than anything she'd ever done before.

Gabby looks ahead as the car merges onto the highway. 'I can't explain it,' she says. 'I guess Mother was making an appearance more than usual and I just needed something to be different. I thought having a child, a real child, would help. And he was so lovely and he behaved so well. When I bought the toys, it was because I originally wanted a younger child, a really young child, but then Flynn was there and I had to go with that, but I wished for a little boy, one who would hold my hand.' She bites down on her lip, not wanting to confess, but she knows it's best to tell him everything. 'I get so lonely sometimes and you seem so far away and I just...' She stops speaking and blinks a few tears away.

He takes a hand from the steering wheel and grabs her hand. 'You don't need to be lonely. Even if I am not with you, I am always here for you, and you know that. You always have me, for ever and ever.'

Up ahead of them, there is a small bay for cars to pull over if they need to stop, and Richard does this, turning off the car and facing her. 'I was worried about you, darling,' he says, and she leans towards him and kisses him. As the kiss deepens, she runs her hands across his chest, loving the feel of him after so many months apart. He's right, she does have him, and she has had him for a long, long time. She looks at him, seeing not his grey hair and weathered skin but instead the nine-year-old boy she met one freezing day outside the flat in Brooklyn where she lived with her mother. It was snowing and she was outside in only a T-shirt and a pair of jeans. She was a filthy, evil child who had angered her mother so intently by asking for something to eat that she had been pushed outside to see just what it was like to be cold and starving so she would be grateful for everything she had. Her name wasn't Gabby then, it was Gabrielle, a big name for a little girl who was a perpetual disappointment. Her mother hated it when anyone called her Gabby, which is why she now uses Gabby whenever she can. She remembers she was standing by a wall, shivering and crying, her head hanging down with shame and despair, when he came up to her and asked her if she was okay. She had tried to nod but her tears gave her away. Richard, who had been Michael then, took off his jacket and gave it to her, draping it over her shoulders and standing with her until her mother shrieked her name. 'Parents suck, but I live just over there,' he said, as he pointed to another building that looked similar to her own, 'and you can always come to me for help.'

They built a strong friendship that turned into love without either of them noticing, and when they were old enough, they left everything else behind them and they have been together ever since. It wasn't like they planned for this way of life; they drifted into it because people are so gullible. The first time Gabrielle and Michael lied to a man at a gas station about needing to get home for their father's funeral, and he handed them a fifty-dollar note with tears in his eyes, they knew what they had. Michael had a way with words and Gabrielle's fragile appearance always elicited sympathy.

'I'll be Richard, like the king,' he said when they chose who they would be as they left the state.

'I'll be Gabby, because then every time someone says my name, I'll know it's making her unhappy, even if she can't hear it.'

Now, when the kiss ends and they reluctantly part, she can't resist a smile. 'I wish we could have just one night in a hotel before we leave,' she says.

'Now, Gabby, you know the drill,' he says.

'Oh, don't call me that,' she huffs, suddenly aware of a change in herself. 'I'm done with that name now. It doesn't suit me anymore. Maybe if I let go of Gabby, the old witch will finally disappear.'

'Well, you let me know what you want me to call you. Anyway, it won't be that for long,' he says as he checks the traffic and pulls into the stream of cars heading to the airport. 'Gabby and Richard Burrell are flying to Dubai on their way to New York, but they will disappear after that, and Steven and Roberta Peterson will go on to wherever they want to go.'

'And you don't think that will be a problem for the Australian authorities?'

'I imagine that once we are off their pretty shores, they won't care too much. They just want you out of their country. Someone may follow up, but you will have completely disappeared. Now we're a nice normal couple of tourists from Kansas who have just had the most amazing time here in Australia.'

She laughs. 'That sure is true. Everyone has just been so kind. How kind have they been?' The Australian accent she has been holding onto disappears and a Midwest drawl effortlessly appears.

'The GoFundMe page raised a whole six hundred dollars to help you get the USA to find your long-lost son before it was shut down, after the police and I alerted the site. But the credit card details yielded a lot more. You had some friends with quite high limits, and everyone will be finding out soon just how much they lost. I cleared about three hundred thousand from twenty people.'

'Hmm,' says Roberta, wrinkling her nose. 'That's not a lot. We'll have to try again in the States. Maybe we need to try California?'

'Well,' he says, 'I guess I can be the psychiatrist brother of an unhinged sister in California just the way I was in London and Ireland and Washington. No one has ever thought to question my impressive business card, at least. We need only a couple more of these and the nest egg will be enough for us to buy that smallholding on Maui and finally relax.'

'I can't wait,' she says as they pull into the airport, where someone named Simon James will return his rental car and Richard Burrell will escort his sad sister Gabby to Dubai and then Steven Peterson will get on a different plane back to the USA with his wife.

By the time the police figure out what has happened, they will be untraceable. They have been doing this for decades now, going everywhere that there are people who are kind and willing to help a distressed woman whose son has gone missing or whose daughter has been taken by her father or whose child is unwell and needs an operation. The Facebook page leads to the GoFundMe page, and while those donations are never very big, the man who will be known as Steven for a while is very good at extracting credit card details. His IT skills are invaluable when it comes to making fake identity documents as well. Getting to know the neighbours is never part of the plan for a very good reason. Richard knows that it's best to stay away from them, and that's why he was so upset when she started speaking to Andrea. She won't do something like that again.

Just before they board the plane, Roberta visits the bathroom to comb her hair out. Steven has picked a tacky oversized red bag for her to use, but it's perfect for Roberta really, as are the clothes she's wearing. In California she will become another woman, a woman who dresses a lot better than Roberta. She wishes they were flying business class, but economy makes you less subject to attention. The hot shower and new clothes will have to wait for a few days because the plane is leaving soon. She can't wait to wave this country goodbye forever.

A woman about her age comes to stand next to her, also giving her hair a quick brush, and Roberta pulls her silent phone out of her pocket and pretends to contact someone, speaking into it, wanting to give her new personality a try as she begins to form a history for Roberta so she is convincing until she settles on a new identity. Roberta has three children and she has really enjoyed her holiday. 'Oh, hey, honey, it's Roberta,' she says into the phone, leaving a message for her oldest daughter. 'We're about to leave but we have had the very best time. I can't wait to get back home and tell y'all about it. Bye now.'

The woman next to her smiles warmly. 'Good holiday?' she asks.

'It was just the best,' sighs Roberta. 'The best.'

A LETTER FROM NICOLE

Hello,

I would like to thank you for taking the time to read *The Stay-at-Home Mother*. If you did enjoy it and want to keep up to date with all my latest releases, just sign up at the following link. Your email address will never be shared and you can unsubscribe at any time.

www.bookouture.com/nicole-trope

The unreliable narrator is a commonly used trope in psychological fiction. Gabby is the most unreliable narrator I have ever written. The truth of who she is and what she's doing appeared only as I was writing her epilogue in the first draft. That changed the whole story for me, but when I began editing I could see that she had been dropping hints all along. Some characters are funny like that. I hope that readers will find a little sympathy for her because growing up with a mother like hers can't have been easy and she is a product of her environment.

Scams on social media are pervasive, and every time I think I've seen them all, another one pops up. It's difficult to know who or what to believe in an era of fake news and filters.

I know that you will have felt moved by Andrea's plight and perhaps found a small amount of sympathy for Terry. Addiction is an illness and Terry desperately wants to get better. I see him succeeding and becoming the best possible husband and father.

I know that some people may not like Gabby and Richard going off to scam some other unsuspecting people, but not everyone who commits a crime is caught. I'm just glad that Andrea and her family are safe and well and can move on with their lives.

If you have enjoyed this novel, it would be lovely if you could take the time to leave a review. I read them all and experience true joy when readers connect with characters and stories.

I would also love to hear from you. You can find me on Facebook and Twitter, and I'm always happy to connect with readers and I try to reply to each message I receive.

Thanks again for reading,

Nicole x

facebook.com/NicoleTrope

twitter.com/nicoletrope

instagram.com/nicoletropeauthor

ACKNOWLEDGEMENTS

My first thank you always goes to Christina Demosthenous for her faith in me and my work. I love sharing ideas with her and wait for her reaction with each new novel.

Thanks to Victoria Blunden for the first edit. As usual, her skills have made this a better novel. She makes a fabulous first reader and I so enjoy reading her comments.

I would also like to thank Jess Readett for all her work and enthusiasm as she tells the world about my novels.

Thanks to Ian Hodder for the copyedit and Liz Hatherell for the meticulous proofread.

Thanks to the whole team at Bookouture, including Jenny Geras, Peta Nightingale, Richard King, Alba Proko, Ruth Tross, Mandy Kullar and everyone else involved in producing my audio books and selling rights.

Thanks to my mother, Hilary, who is always ready for a new novel.

Thanks also to David, Mikhayla, Isabella, and Jacob and Jax.

And once again thank you to those who read, review, blog about my work and contact me on Facebook or Twitter to let me know you loved the book. Every review is appreciated and I do read them all.